my summer of love

my summer of love

HELEN CROSS

BLOOMSBURY

First published in Great Britain 2001
This paperback edition published 2002

Copyright © 2001 by Helen Cross

The moral right of the author has been asserted
Bloomsbury Publishing Plc, 38 Soho Square, London W1D 3HB

A CIP catalogue record is available from the British Library

ISBN 0 7475 5782 9

10 9 8 7 6 5 4 3 2 1

Typeset by Palimpsest Book Production Limited,
Polmont, Stirlingshire
Printed in Great Britain by Clays Ltd, St Ives plc

For my family

trifle

Today, the weather has the exact same temperature it had the day two people died. I've never seen the same numbers displayed before. Though perhaps because of what happened then, I'm now obsessive and peculiar about weather; I could probably name as many weathermen as jockeys and brands of vodka.

It all started with a wedding, if you believe – as I've come to realise most psychiatrists do – that behavioural extremes of any kind are often reactions to loss.

It was 23 May 1984, the day of my sister's wedding.

'I'll bet not many bookies are taking money on your sister making a success of her second marriage,' PorkChop said when the racing came on. A clip showed two horses being whipped to a frenzy for the finish; a throng of gamblers clinging to the rails delirious with hope.

'She's your sister too,' I goes.

'No she's not,' he said.

'Yes she is.'

It went on like this for a while.

Then Lindy began to scream at her daughter.

'Calm down, love, you'll only make her worse,' Cleo said, hooking up Lindy's basque from the back, with quick, deft jerks. Lindy was pregnant, four months gone, but she'd still chosen a dress that gave her a Miss World figure.

I was, of course, most disappointed she looked so good. She still had all her punk make-up on and because it was a special day had plucked her eyebrows out entirely and drawn thick black wedges in their place. She wore black lipstick.

'Where's me hair thingy?' she yelled.

'With yer veil.'

'Clee, please don't let Dad be drunk. We've got to get Siouxsie's dress on. Clee, where's Siouxsie's dress?'

Siouxsie, Lindy's daughter, was three. She'd still only got her knickers on and was moulding lengths of plastic wrapping over her chest then smothering what was left round Jaws, our Alsatian. Lindy tried to grab her – lurching over in one shoe 'til she noticed PorkChop, in his grubby dressing gown, curled in an armchair in the shady end of the room with me. He was sitting on Siouxsie's dress.

Despite the noise, which drummed throughout our house, I felt very tired, like my family exuded a powerful anaesthetic.

'PorkChop, yer great oaf, get off the fuckin' dress,' Lindy shouted, flinging an almost empty can of Kestrel Lager towards his head.

'Cheers, nice one, Lindy,' PorkChop said, catching it and draining the last warm dregs out of the can. Barking drowned out the TV.

A fight broke out.

Cleo got her Instamatic from the sideboard and, putting one hand firmly on her hip, she raised the camera to eye level and pointed it at her son. 'Mam, don't, no, leave me. I've got 'angover. Stop, I'm going.' Cleo took a picture anyway, just as he was getting up, with his dressing gown gaping open.

Lindy shouted above the sound of the barking and the TV: 'Ha! This is the 'appiest day of my life. Serves you right, yer lazy BASTARD.'

It went on like this for some time.

PorkChop changed his mind, turned back to the racing papers and said: 'A colt will always beat a filly.'

I remember this: *A colt will always beat a filly*. A filly has to be really exceptional to beat a colt. Of course, you can get a filly who can beat one or two colts, but she has to be good enough to beat all the colts. It does happen but not often.

It's what happened when two people died.

Eventually, Cleo went and closed the window so people on the street wouldn't remark it was Lindy's wedding day again. She fanned herself with the slimy picture of PorkChop. I went to look over her shoulder and she tutted and dug a stray grip tight into my scalp. PorkChop sneered, said we'd all got too much make-up on, that we looked like we were in a pantomime. I gave him my special look of scornful sorrow, shaking my head very slowly.

There were two policemen in short-sleeved shirts on the opposite side of the road, one speaking into a walkie-talkie. So badly did I want to commit crimes I was fascinated by the police before I'd even done anything.

'D'you like your outfit?' Cleo said. I nodded dreamily. I knew people who'd been on probation and romantically I imagined it as a state-owned dating agency to put teenage girls in touch with blond, hunky policemen.

Cleo asked me again. It wasn't the dress that bothered me, Cleo'd made it to my exact instructions ensuring it made the most of my bottom half while minimising the horror of my chest, on which were still two freaky peaks, like salt collected in the egg-timer. The problem was my hair. It was coiled in a ridiculous flute on the back of my head and PorkChop was right, I looked like a bustless pantomime dame after a humour lobotomy.

And the make-up. I wore loads then regretted it. I knew the blue eyeliner was trembly and the blusher made me look like I'd been slapped hard round the face.

I turned away from the window. I wanted a spellbinding sexual allure, and instead I was about to get, at best, encouraging smiles, and at worst, whistling ridicule. Still, I wanted to play

3

the fruity so bad I'd have gone downstairs knickerless if I had to.

Lindy marched out of the room and Siouxsie trailed after her gurgling wet clotted cries. Cleo scooped up the crumpled dress and followed. 'I want you dressed by the time I get back,' she shouted stabbing a pink-nailed finger at PorkChop, like he was a toddler too. It worked because he snorted, turned off the TV and lumbered out after them.

I went back and opened the window. The heat pushed in. The stink of blood too, the scraped gut juice and gristle that hung like crimson phlegm from the peeled-off skin of an animal. The smell from Hoggins, the factory where they turned skins into leather, was at its strongest. The rawhides were carried through the streets from the skinning part of the factory to the warehouse part on chugging three-wheeled mini-lorries. The stinking bloody skins, dripping red gunge and sinewy slime, were piled on pallets on the back of the little lorries like coats, wet on a bed at a party.

I'd need the Ventolin all day; definitely no fags, definitely not. Vodka, Malibu, lager and lime, but no fags.

I leant out the window and scoured the street, looking for police.

Whitehorse, where I lived, is a small Yorkshire market town where nothing happens and lads think a good night out is lying on a bale of straw in a barn injecting each other with pig tranquillisers.

Viewed from this side our street was decent; messy glass-porched semis, a short terrace, caravans, bikes, kids, a postbox on a crescent of yellowing grass.

Round the back was certainly the sort of place you'd dump someone you'd killed: shattered windows, splintered wood, dead factories, abandoned warehouses, old men shuffling with small arthritic dogs on canvas leads, or cycling bow-legged to the far end to fish.

Cleo thought they might dredge the canal; they'd already sent divers down. Pallets were in there, still mucky with cowskins and pig-stomach chew. They'd been in the factories and sent dogs over the fields. Yesterday they found a girl's shoes in a Presto bag on the canal (some accounts said floating, some said sunk; the newspaper didn't report it). They could've been thrown down from the flyover, out the window of a passing car perhaps.

No police anywhere.

Someone had bought Lindy a bottle of Babycham as a present. It had a tag round the neck with her name and kisses on. I wondered if one of her punk friends had sent it for irony. Then I wondered if our mam had sent it from beyond the grave. It was her style. How she would've liked us to be; popular and sweet.

Then, I needed a drink desperately and cracked this little bottle against the windowsill. I hit harder than I thought and a chomp of wood splintered from the sill. It was open now and tepid but still sour enough to make me shiver.

Cleo came in, holding Siouxsie in her arms. 'You OK?' she asked. Since she started supporting Arthur Scargill and campaigning for the miners she'd adopted a calm and serious tone. 'I know, Mona. I know how much . . .'

Cleo began to make a soft speech. She used to sing in a band, knew exactly how to pitch things. PorkChop said Cleo had once screwed Jimi Hendrix. She touched my back, on the skin where the dress scooped down, with her cool, pink-nailed fingertips.

'It's a shame for Lindy,' I said, but really thought how my sister was now more concerned with bragging about her new stone cladding than missing me mam.

Cleo touched me again. I liked fingers and hands the best of any part of the human body. The uniqueness of fingerprints seemed to me then, though hardly later, the most romantic of things.

I needed another drink. Once you started you always needed another drink. Thoughts could sometimes make you feel your head was going to explode, like your life was nothing but a pan of milk always on the tip of boiling over. And drink turned the heat down, kept you cooking on a low simmer.

And I needed to play the fruity. That first touch of a morning, when you were the one to set the flickering thing in motion.

So I went down to where me dad and Bob, who'd brought the pony and cart, and Ted and Ken were having a drink. I paused and my embarrassment stiffened before I entered the bar, but no one said anything about my hair or my titlessness. Usually I hated the bar when it was chock-full of men-stink, and had to be well drunkish to cope.

I could never be relaxed with these men around, because when they didn't make crude remarks about me I thought it was because of my foul ugliness, and when they did it was because they were slobbering perverts.

And now perhaps there was a murderer among them.

All the windows had been pushed open but it was still too hot. Beer overrode blood though, and down in the bar the rawhide stench was weaker. No one pounced when I entered, too doped with the heat.

An oily smell was coming from the kitchen. At Lindy's last wedding they'd passed round trays of cold, salty roast potatoes too.

The tatty paper chains and frayed fronds of tinsel piled up on the stools were from Lindy's party last night. Ted and Ken looked like they'd been left over as well.

'You look good enough to eat,' said Bob, hooking a meaty arm around my waist and tensing up against my chest.

'You smell like you've been rotting here all night,' I said, imitating his gruff accent.

Though I'd recently realised that to be cocky with men was more flirty than to be coy, it really wasn't my style, and I often got it wrong and seemed not cocky but aggressive and strange. If Lindy caught me at it she'd roll her eyes and apologise for me: *Please forgive my strange little sister.*

The fruity was switched on and unplayed, fresh as a flower first thing in the morning.

'Henough of that!' Bob said, breathing on me with revolting emphasis.

'Did you know it's illegal to be drunk in charge of a pony 'n' trap?' I said, looking out the open door where the pony was tied to the railings along the side of Black Beck. Two policemen were crossing the road, looking over into the slime: I knew what they'd see, because I was watching from the railings earlier that morning before anyone else was up. In winter the pub was in danger of flooding but now the water had receded so far that a spongy tractor tyre and a rusty supermarket trolley were revealed.

Around the junk floated a shoal of beer bottles.

No bodies.

But that morning, for once, no one was talking about the level of the water, or picketing, or revision, or the possible death of a girl, because it was a fine day for a wedding.

'Those coppers'll get yer, Bob,' I goes.

'And the RSPCA,' said Ted.

'And dole,' said Dad.

'Oi! Watch it, and I'm not drunk,' said Bob slapping his forehead. 'And it's a carriage not a cart, young lady.'

Then began some chirpy farmyard bantering.

I wondered sometimes how men came to rule the world.

'Will she be all right with all of us in – I don't mind going in the taxi if you think it would be better. Shall we just let Lindy and Siouxsie go in the trap?' I said sulkily. I liked to think I preferred ponies to people, and I wanted them to know it.

'It'll be able to do you all as long as you don't want our Cleo in there,' said Dad, not looking up from the bar on which was spread the *Sporting Life*; he was jabbing a pen at the afternoon's runners. 'Or PorkChop.'

'Oi! Clee's a good woman,' said Ken. 'A good, big woman.'

We were safe, it was sunny and Ken was a builder with muscles and a tattoo. He drank too much and told good jokes and made blokeness look easy and great fun. My hormones fancied him but I didn't.

Everything was fine.

I wandered around the bar, waiting. I was trying to breathe in a regular, happy way, despite not having a drink or playing the fruity. I knew I should try not to have Ventolin because the doctor said you must have it no more than three times a day. Even if you were desperate.

On the tables over in the far corner of the room Cleo'd laid out the buffet. The cling film was puckering in the heat. There were stacked triangles of sandwiches with the crusts off, honey-coated sausages flecked with herbs, waxy cheese with pineapple spiked on sticks, crisps, pale dips pitted with parsley, a mountain of bread cakes, cold gold nuggets of butter and a trifle over which someone had already dragged a finger.

'It's hot in here,' I said, closing my eyes and exhaling. I could hear the dry boom of tyres over dusty tarmac and a policeman shouting far away.

'When'll it be your turn, Mona?' said Ken, twisting round, looking me up and down, then stretching out a paw to pat me on the back. He was bald, big and square, like a polar bear on that bar stool.

This heat would kill someone soon. It was probably more dangerous than the monster who'd taken Julie Flowerdew.

'Mona don't want to get hitched, which is fine by me. I've already given t'other one two goes,' Dad said, eyes down, elbows anchored to the paper. 'Daughters are expensive, believe me. I'd need to win t'pools to keep these two in the style they're accustomed to.'

They discussed daughters in jokey terms for some time.

If I closed me eyes their voices reminded me of lads calling out from stalls at the fair.

Dad was all prinked up in a bad suit and he was prickly. I tried to focus on him though I was sickly with the heat.

'Can I have some money, Dad?' I said.

'Oh! Oh, yes, I see. I see now,' he said. But pleased because I was proving him right, showing I still needed him.

'Please,' I whined obligingly. Then Bob gave me some money. A whole tinkling palmful of cash which he poured into my cupped and trembling hand. I kissed him and smiled like a simpleton. Everything was OK.

And as my lips met his hot cheek I remembered that any of the men in the bar could be the one who'd taken Julie.

I went over and touched her; flashing, and full of money as a pregnant bank vault, and played, played, played. Ken, Bob and Ted had more pints and watched me sleepily until PorkChop came flumping down the stairs and they discussed whether heat affected two-year-olds more notably. That day PorkChop was most appropriately named (by Lindy when he first arrived), because his suit jacket wouldn't fasten and the top button of his shirt was undone, but I didn't want anything to do with making him look right.

Ken, who was feeling generous because he'd been awarded the honour of playing landlord while we were all at the wedding, passed me a vodka and I pulled up a bar stool, put an ashtray on top of the machine and played another two fifties.

It was nice, that morning of Lindy's wedding; everything was jolly, soft, like we were all in a comedy film.

Nothing had happened yet.

'See, you're not as clever as you think you are, young lady,' Dad shouted from the bar when I lost the money. The previous evening, in the middle of the party, I'd got the jackpot. You have to be very smart to do this, because it's really not luck, it's about responding to a set of choices quickly, with accuracy and precision. Good training for crime.

I didn't know then whether I would ever really dare to commit a crime. Though I could not envisage my future without it.

Yes, I would! Yes! Yes!

No, no, I never could, never!

'I don't know why you waste all your money on that thing,' Dad said.

'Can't think of anything better to waste my money on,' I said, not looking round, and the men laughed. Making men laugh seemed an enormous achievement.

'There's many folk better at it than you, and they're still all losers.'

'Impossible,' I said quietly, with my face close to the lights and the numbers and the noise.

There was a sudden burst of applause and the photographer came in groaning. He was Philip Rush, people called him Phil the Flash, he was a regular in the pub, but that day he was wearing a brown shiny suit and an ironed blue shirt. This was the first time I'd ever really noticed him. It was that dizzy time of life when you started to notice men, rather than boys. He looked good, in a seedy way. I even noticed him deep in my bones, so I had to squirm on the seat.

'Where's the lovely lady?' he said, unloading his equipment on to the bar.

There was then some cartoonish teasing of Phil which made the men wobble on their stools.

Lindy and Cleo came down. Lately, feelings had been appearing on Cleo like bruises. Lindy had such a foul face on her you'd think she was coming in to start a fight. The word *bitch* bubbled up in me throat and to stop it getting out I played another fifty pence sloppily and lost it. The nudge on the machine was a bit loose and if you didn't hit it real firm you missed it. Around that time, where Lindy was concerned, I could go from loving to loathing in seconds. She looked funnily orange from the sunbed and this combined with the black make-up made her look tigerish. She was holding the half-naked picture of blubbery PorkChop that Cleo had taken, which she sellotaped above the bar next to a photo taken last night of Cleo dancing with her new friend from the Labour Party. I looked at the picture very closely. You could see a little pink shrivel that was PorkChop's penis.

On the white shiny border Lindy had written in purple felt-tip pen, MY GORGEOUS STEPBROTHER ON MY WEDDING DAY, MAY 1984.

'Leave 'er, Steve,' Dad said, pointing at PorkChop.

'What did I do?' Damp patches of powerlessness were seeping out round the armpits of PorkChop's suit.

'It's 'er wedding day, you can duff 'er up tomorrow.'

'You'll 'ave to reckon with my 'usband tomorrow,' Lindy said, and everyone laughed, thinking of Shred, who was five feet seven inches and a born-again Christian, and PorkChop, who had the physique, if not the wit and intelligence, of an obese wrestler. I remembered how when me mam was around we used to have a game where we'd bet on the number of times Shred'd say church or God or Lord in one hour.

This was before I started my own feverish praying.

Dad sprang out from behind the bar and drew the curtains across all the bay windows. I liked the way Dad was alert, no matter how much he'd drunk, never slow or slouched; prepared, guarded, and I wished I was like that; usually when I was pissed, I cried.

The sun streaming behind brown curtains gave the room a scorched, dusty glow. Lindy, puffed up in stiff cream lace, spread herself across the seat the photographer had arranged. It was a registry office job this time but she was pushing the boat out all the same. Cleo said to me, confidentially, that in her opinion it was Lindy's optimism that'd got her into trouble too many times before. So there.

Cleo went round zizzing with an air-freshener so there was no animal blood gut whiff in the air for the photos. PorkChop exposed a wet armpit and reached high up to turn on the TV, and then Dad reached over and turned it off and gave PorkChop a slap round the head. PorkChop was Cleo's son;

Dad'd got problems with him. We'd all got problems with him. We'd all got problems with each other, my ex-friend Anne-Marie said.

Poor old Anne-Marie.

Cleo put a bouquet of gormless lilies at Lindy's side, moving the vase left and right an inch or two either way until Phil said, 'Right.' Bob, Ken, Ted and PorkChop turned round from the bar and watched, arms folded, heads on one side as Lindy made a series of sour pouts.

Phil the Flash took the photos of the last wedding, though I didn't notice him because I was too young. I liked ponies and pop stars then.

Everything was still and quiet. Phil looked at me and smiled. He looked me up and down and smiled again. I tutted and turned away, me hormones were rioting, setting light to cars and uprooting trees.

That song with the lovely story and the deep croon, *My darlingg you lurk wundurfool toniiiite*, made my nose run every time.

'You've the right idea, Phil, haven't you? Ogling beautiful young women all day, without having to apologise,' said Bob loudly.

''Ollywood should make a movie of your career: *The Life and Times of Phil the Flash*,' said Ken.

'It won't be family viewing,' said Dad softly, his ferocity melted by the ovenish heat.

This went on for some time.

Lindy wasn't smiling. She was looking grim at various angles. Her bodice was cut in a small tight V, like the nip at the top of a cartoon heart, and for the last few shots she inhaled, leant forward and stiffened so a wave of white breast flesh curled slowly over the top of the dress. 'Try one with the veil down,' shouted PorkChop. 'Looks better that way.'

'Shut the fuck up, arsehole,' she shouted and I was happily reminded that in many ways, despite the new baby, husband, house and tan, Lindy was still the cider-swigging social delinquent me mam had once tried to get social-workered.

A slanging match began and Cleo had to intervene.

They took one with Siouxsie, and one with Cleo and Dad, and then one of just me and Lindy. Shapeless next to my pneumatic sister, I generously told her I felt like the 'before' picture in a cosmetic surgery ad. She kissed me on the cheek and cooed pityingly. She loved it when I made jokes about myself.

PorkChop refused to be photographed and Lindy called him a miserable bastard. Phil said he could do something posed later. Lindy roared that she wanted one with him NOW.

It turned out to be all three of us girls in the trap. Cleo, PorkChop and Dad were going in a taxi. Shred and his five-year-old son David were meeting us at the registry office. Bob had put on an old suit jacket with gold braiding round the collar and cuffs, and a dusty top hat. Already his fat neck was aubergine from the sun. Ken, Ted and Phil came out with their drinks to watch from the pavement. They started singing: *Stand and deliver your money or your life*. Cleo'd fetched her camera and PorkChop'd got Jaws on a lead. We got in, all squashed up together, Siouxsie on my knee still clinging to her plastic sheeting, Lindy's dress pushed up and over the edge of the cart which only had a low door on each side and a board for a roof. The pony edged round with dozy steps. I could feel Lindy's arm cool against my side.

She loves me, she loves me not, she loves me . . .

Though she was often trying to injure me when I was young – pushing me off my bike, feeding me dandelions and sour berries and encouraging the dog to bite me – I felt, as a child, that she adored me. In a pathological way.

Psychiatrists and counsellors often bring her up.

'Do you remember when we used to play princesses?' I said, because perhaps this was what we looked like, though there were no crowds lining the route. Slowly Lindy reached into her

Little Bo Peep bag and put on black sunglasses so she resembled a Mafia bride.

'We were princesses, Mona; the pub was our palace, Black Beck was the moat, the car park the magic forest,' she said wearily, applying more black lipstick and looking at her dark self in a little mirror. She smiled in a sinister way.

Like she thought herself magnificently interesting.

I knew Lindy believed the murderer had his eye on her especially.

She made a great fuss about going out alone. She asked men in the bar to walk her across the road if Shred wasn't able to collect her. She carried a pot of mustard powder and a penknife in her handbag.

To be Lindy was to feel you were always on the brink of a great dark fame.

Perhaps it was the princess game that had given Lindy funny ideas about love, and me the feeling of perpetual imprisonment.

'It's like a fortress,' she said, reading my mind.

It was black and white, mock Tudor with leaded bay windows and wide, studded doors: the Adam and Eve. In the five years we'd been there four cars had nutted the outer walls and not made a dent. Our bedroom windows, angled over the main road, had pointed wooden canopies and frail iron balconies. There was a plump brick turret on the roof, cold and full of me mam's forgotten junk.

It was totally fairy tale, and later that summer when I hung weeping and wailing from the balcony, ranting about love and longing, it only added to the Rapunzel effect in my addled mind.

'We're off!' called Bob and we moved out of the shade on to the main road which was by then steaming heat.

scotch

I have a memory that it was on the afternoon of the wedding that I encountered her for the second time.

But I cannot be sure. I remember something that goes like this: she was standing on the high outer wall in a short beige dress. Like a stone angel. On the plinth opposite was a mossy lion or dog, crumbling round the jaw and tail. She was missing only wings. She was crying, no, she *had been* crying, her face was damp and sore. I looked up, terrified, and she said: 'Do you remember that my sister died?'

But now, in a steelier midday recollection of that wedding-day trip to the Fakenhams', she does not figure at all.

After the wedding buffet, and before the evening do, at around 5.30 p.m., I cycled at goose-pimpling speed down the narrow country lanes to the Fakenhams' house at Goldwell.

Goldwell is a small village three miles from our pub. Pretty and posh, with a village hall, riding stables, a church with a steeple, and a little shop that sells olives and wine to doctors, dentists, violinists and accountants.

I was drunkish.

'*Get thee to a nunnery*,' I shouted (raising my fist in the air); this was my favourite, and only remembered, exam quote.

I breathed deeply and because the rawhide factory only worked mornings on Saturdays, the throat-clogging stink of fresh blood was fading. Breathing increased the intoxicated, drunkish feeling.

Lindy was gone. I was desperate and I was free.

Get thee to a nunnery – hell, I could truly think of nothing worse: securing the adoration of men; sex, alcohol and crime were my only desires.

I touched me face and the skin felt magazine soft. I'd done a lot of face work already that day: two face masks, a peel-off and a wash-off, a blackhead-loosening steam bath and the application of my own cucumber juice toner. Later, I would moisturise with a home-made raw-egg-and-honey-enriching preparation before slapping on another thick, creamy layer of Nivea. I might even go to a shop and lift more expensive creams.

I'd also shaved myself in all necessary, and some unnecessary, areas, and then oiled mesen, so I was raw and meaty, like something about to be slid into the oven.

I'd been home to get changed and to open the till. I'd tugged from under the till's steel trap a soft ten-pound note and tucked it down the waistband of the pedal pushers.

At home I had a box where I'd been saving stolen money. A white shoebox. I ironed the notes so they were crease-free before stroking them, still warm, against the grey bottom of the box. I liked to imagine the box's brickish weight when, one day, full to the lid, it was packed tight, like puff pastry, with heavy layers of money. It was a fantasy of an almost sexual dimension.

I'd had two shots of voddy and a Scotch, on top of the champers and brandy and wine.

I didn't eat any buffet, though I looked at it for a long time.

Lindy had said loudly, in front of all the pastel guests, that she hoped I wasn't going *Cambodian* again.

I whizzed past the allotments, which extended back through boundaries of dock leaves and blackberry briars to parched fields and the limit of the town. Over the past three and a half years that I had been going to the Fakenhams I'd devised a speedy route from Whitehorse to Goldwell, and could do the three-mile journey in less than fifteen minutes.

Things felt good, the edge was off the day, my skin was pale and soft and I was made-up and happyish. It was light and sunny and there was surely no danger of bumping into a murderer.

After two miles I stopped at my regular café to play away all my change, but when I got inside the woman shook her head and said *stolen*. Someone had *stolen* the fruity, which was something I'd never heard of before and I wobbled the bike with laughing, almost wet the seat with excitement. Imagine, I thought, to do that. Where'd you hide it, where'd you secrete it away?

Then I felt angry that I couldn't play and had to have a couple of blasts on the Ventolin. It was a selfish thing to do, steal a fruity. It was a good one, *Bounty Hunter*, with a picture of a tropical island, palm trees and a busty girl on the front. And they probably won't play it. They won't have it polished up, gleaming in their bedroom or in a den, even in a shed somewhere, where they could play alone whenever they liked. Which would have been a very understandable reason to steal a fruity. A noble thing. No, they'd hack it apart with hammers and saws, finger its insides, rip the leads out like guts, and just take the money, leave the lovely carcass to rot and rust somewhere.

Where would you hide a girl's dead body, or the carcass of a fruity? In Black Beck, in the deep dark cellars of a warehouse, in the grain store of an animal feed factory?

So I went on without a win and when I arrived I saw Mrs Fakenham, in her red smart dressing gown, putting cereal boxes on the pine kitchen table. My digital watch said 5.58 p.m., but such things happened at the Fakenhams'. Right from the beginning there was an air of loon about the place.

There were clues that should've warned me about the Fakenhams.

Mrs Fakenham was an actress, apparently – though I'd never seen her on TV, and me dad had declared: *If that bloody woman's an actor I'm the fucking Princess of Wales!* But then Cleo had told him to shut it and said she believed Mrs Fakenham had once been an actress but her life had since been hijacked by children and caring for men.

Who knew what was true.

Once, soon after me mam's death, when I was on a moonlit wander, I saw Mrs Fakenham outside washing the dog at midnight, another time she was stirring herbs into a black rubber bucket of oil. On a bad day you could hear her shouting for miles. She always was witchy in a way. It seemed no surprise that a girl had died in that house, though no one talked about it. I did not think this strange because no one talked of me mam either. Except Cleo, and then we pretended not to listen.

Cleo spoke of me mam softly, almost hymning her words, like a far-off solo singer in church.

I passed the living room which was cool-looking even in that wilting heat. The enormous fireplace, a mottled black marble like a headstone.

At the beginning I was most inconsequential in the Fakenham family's life. They rarely spoke to me even though I had been coming to the field regularly since I was twelve.

All the time that I had been looking after Willow, Tamsin Fakenham had been away at school. A few times over the last three years I had seen her watching me out of the window, though the only time she had come to speak to me was seven months ago, to tell me about the death of her sister.

It was thrilling to me the way rich kids went 'away' to school. It reminded me of African boys marching into the jungle, or alcoholic actresses residing in Californian clinics, or petty thieves going in borstal and learning arson and armed robbery. I felt I too had been away for the past three years since me mam had left. Over the hills and far. My family were too busy dying and loving to notice I had drifted.

That day of Lindy's wedding I wheeled my bike carefully down the long drive, moving it lightly over the gravel and twisting it between their cars. I didn't wave in the direction of the house as I sometimes did, an embarrassed and servile gesture, instead I just leant the bike against the garage and walked down to the field past the shed that was sinking under the black weight of soil and leaves.

Willow was at the gate. Dirt and sweat on her back had formed tiny pellets of grime. I wobbled while I walked, drunker than I'd thought. Then into the stable. It was always so quiet and cool in there it made me think of home which was the opposite.

I had to leave home; commit crimes and be free.

I hadn't mucked out properly for weeks. Over the stone floor was a slick of rancid slime like boiled spinach. The whole place needed swilling down with a hose. The thought of it made my drunkish limbs ache. I needed a drink of water.

I did what I could of the cleaning then sat out on the gate and rested, rubbing me fingertips into the back of me neck.

I'd only been out there ten minutes when Mr Fakenham came down the path towards the gate. I'd not seen him for several months. I had never seen him coming purposefully towards me before.

It did not bode well.

Most fathers never said a word when you went round; miserable deaf mutes. Mr Fakenham was different; though he had only spoken to me two or three times in the past three years, he was always animated and keen.

I was glad I had on a full mask of make-up. Mr Fakenham was a very manly man.

It was teatime, the sun low in the sky, and he approached with a rim of light like the angelic Ready Brek glow around his sporty dad body. He was walking weirdly fast, like he was on a moving walkway, or skating a couple of inches above the ground. *Superadvert Man*, Anne-Marie had called him.

Oh, poor lost Anne-Marie. There was a time when people at junior school sent us joint Christmas cards and we'd share them, two days at a time each.

Anyway, Mr Fakenham was not a man people usually liked. Dad met him once and said: *That bloke'd be out of his depth in a towpath puddle*, despite the fact that reputedly he had letters after his name, and a staff of 350. Each day Mr Fakenham cruised into Whitehorse in a silver car and stopped in a private car-parking space with his initials painted on the tarmac.

I carried on firmly with the drunken brushing as he came up to me, keeping my eyes fixed on Willow, watching the muscles on her flanks ripple when I struck with the brush. In summer she was plumped over with pleasing pads of pony fat, but in winter she was almost skeletonised no matter how much you fed her. Like me mam when she was in the hospital.

Get thee to a nunnery!

I didn't want to talk to Fakenham. I didn't think I could form sentences. In my experience you only realise how drunk you've gotten when you start trying to talk.

Behind me there was a faint strumming of guitar music coming from an upstairs bedroom. It was 'Wild Thing' played very quietly and hesitantly by someone just learning the chords. It reminded me of Lindy bouncing on the bed, her white hair piled up and sticky as candyfloss.

Then he was there in his white workday shirt, tie, belted slacks and moustache. The day, still and clear, seemed glassy and across it slid a sparkling of minty toothpaste, a mist of piney aftershave. He'd got bright red pimples of blood dried on his chin like tiny berries. It was 6.12 p.m. on Saturday but he was acting like it was eight o'clock on a Monday morning.

'Mona?'

''ello,' I said nervously, surprised he knew my name.

'How are you? My wife tells me it's your sister's wedding today. I wasn't sure if you'd be coming along to see Willow.'

'I won't be staying long,' I said.

The 'Wild Thing' had paused, like someone was frozen, listening.

I wouldn't turn round. I didn't want him to see me.

'You all right?'

'Yep. Just the asthma.' Sometimes with the asthma when you

were just trying to breathe it sounded jagged and hard, like silent sobbing.

We enthused about the wedding for a while, like this was a normal conversation, then he asked me about disco.

'Disco? Oh, no. Lindy is very anti-disco. She hates disco.'

'Oh.'

'She's got a badge that says, "Death to Disco".'

'Oh.'

'Yeh, really 'ates it.'

'And do you like disco, Mona?'

I looked up at him and shrugged. I didn't like this way he had of getting right under your skin, of knowing just the right questions to ask. I figured this was a management technique. He was talking to me like a staff member. I feared I would be thinking about the answers I'd given for ages afterwards.

As it turned out, Mr Fakenham's management techniques, his influence and his money, would be very necessary later that summer, when, as my dear father delicately put it: *The fucking chickens came 'ome to roost.*

But that was later; in the beginning it was just disco and ponies.

'I'm sure Tamsin likes disco. She listens to a lot of funky records that's for certain. I'm a bit of a mover myself actually. Dance: the body's purest expression of its innate beauty,' he said, making a few tiptoeing steps on the mud. 'And are all your family well?'

No, actually, they are not, I thought. Not at all. But none of us knew why. And if he could smell a complete off-licence on me lips he didn't say nothing, which was kind.

'Fine,' I said with a big grin like I was on the front page of the evening paper.

'Good, good.' He sucked on his teeth, grimaced and looked over my head and out to the far end of the field. 'Mona, there is something I, or rather my wife and I, would like to ask for your help with.'

'Oh,' I said and the 'oh' went right though me like vodka. There was a spotlight, a million TV viewers.

'I think we can trust you. We're rather concerned about our daughter Tamsin. She's been having a few, er, problems at the, er, school. Nothing that won't pass, of course, but problems.'

'Problems.'

'Yes, yes, problems. But she's home now. She came home yesterday.'

'Oh.'

'Yes, I wasn't . . .' He paused and seemed to swallow down a too-feverish word. 'Er, happy about it actually. The way it was all handled. She's a very, er, sensitive girl, person.'

I realised he was confiding about the 'girl person' and I felt both excited and deeply embarrassed. The idea of a father begging for friends for his loon daughter was seriously appalling. The 'Wild Thing' had still not started up again, and there was no wind or traffic or aeroplanes. Even I, the most friendless person I knew, had not stooped to the level of asking me dad to accost strangers begging for companionship.

I could picture her away in the candlelit land of cruel girls.

'Anyway if you could find time to show her some kindness. Perhaps . . .'

He stopped. Neither of us could envisage what kindness I could show her. He rubbed his face. I continued brushing. Kindness, I couldn't really remember what it was: it made me think of old people and animals.

Back at the house I could see Mrs Fakenham, the actress, standing at the window with a bowl of cereal in one hand and a fag in the other. She had a large nose and visible cheekbones and perhaps before motherhood got to her she could've been throwing herself about on a stage and having her photo in magazines.

The high stone house with its ivy and wide solid doors seemed to swell around her. Something about the womanly way she stood, bunched up with secrets, was thrilling. I liked this crazed repression older women often displayed. I would've liked to speak to her, have her as my friend. A mummy. I would've liked to have spoken to her about the plays she starred in, about death and dying. About her dead daughter and how she sleeps at night. I'd tell her about me mam and Julie Flowerdew who'd gone missing and all my sorrow.

But husbands were like fences to wives, and mostly you couldn't cross.

It was probably better to deal with deaths and disappointments alone.

Poor lost Anne-Marie. Poor sad Tamsin Fakenham.

I knew my old friend Anne-Marie had many boyfriends now, not just Barry, a whole new pack of them I didn't know. Boys who almost seemed like men. They held their sour cigarettes close to their knuckles and had bullet-like three-letter names: Lod, Fig, Sug, Ned. They had money, motorbikes, torn leather jackets. Lod, the eldest, had a car; a black Mini with a tiny padded steering wheel, crimson bucket seats and an extra set of headlamps. He took her *driving*.

She was not interested in me any more. She'd been through the death of me mam, a year ago next month, and was perhaps exhausted by our misery.

'If she wants to come out with me, well, she could,' I said doubtfully and went back to fierce brushing. I didn't go anywhere Tamsin could come. Hell, I didn't *go* anywhere. I imagined us sitting at our bar waiting for the menopause.

'Yes, if you and your pals could include Tamsin in your plans.'

'Sure,' I said and cooed at Willow to show Fakenham how much I loved her: how inferior men were to ponies.

'If you would . . . er, basically I suppose what we're asking is, if you, er, could be a *friend* to Tamsin.' He was speaking very seriously now. 'Because, actually, in fact, well, things are a little difficult round here at the moment. To be honest.' He sniffed and fiddled with his cufflink.

A Friend To Tamsin. It sounded like the title of a hardback story about boarding school.

'Yes, things are a bit sticky round here right now.' There was a pause, then he said: 'I don't know if the two of you have met. Tamsin said she couldn't remember. She took a look at you yesterday out of the window but told me you had one of those faces you feel you've seen before, but she couldn't be sure.'

This was the first of many insults I was to receive from Miss Tamsin Fakenham.

'Yes, we have definitely met, sometime last year.'

Had Tamsin forgotten me, or was she just lying to her father?

'Jolly good, jolly good. As I say, things have been sticky round here lately, so your help would be most appreciated.'

I hoped he wasn't going to confess his domestic horrors to me. In the pub I'd met many oldish men who liked to confide their miseries in teenage girls. It was appalling.

But instead he discussed revision for a while and I answered his questions.

'Jolly good. Tamsin has to revise too, of course. Exams, phew, hard work, eh?'

Tamsin. It was sinking in. This new person, this name. The daughter I'd spoken to only once, the daughter whose older sister, Sadie, died of starvation in hospital while Tamsin was 'away' at school.

Tamsin was the only person who had bothered to mention Sadie's death to me, such was the lowly position I held within the family. One day, early morning, about seven months ago I had been to muck out Willow before school and had seen Mrs Fakenham weeping out on the step. She was wearing a silky black dressing gown and a pair of heeled slippers. She was splendidly thin. She was drinking and smoking. She looked most womanly. It was winter, very cold, the lane to the field sogged with mud. My feet were numb in my black rubber boots. My fingertips ached with cold. I watched Mrs Fakenham as her face grew grey with grief, but didn't ask what was wrong. I walked by her several times in case she wanted to call out to me, to confess anything, or ask for my wise help, but she ignored me like she didn't even notice me.

Tamsin had trusted me with her secrets. And now I was to help her. There was a justice in it, though the world had never asked anything of me before.

On that day seven months ago, just before I was leaving, when Mrs Fakenham had collected her fags and her bottle of booze and gone back inside, Tamsin came out and watched me grooming. She came slowly towards me, her eyes on the ground, her feet kicking through the mud, and told me Sadie, her older sister, had died a couple of months earlier in hospital, and that was why her mother was drinking and crying.

And now Tamsin was back and she needed my help.

Mr Fakenham was continuing to discuss. 'Ivy said you might be looking for a job in a stables after your exams.'

'Maybe,' I said.

I wondered why Ivy, one of their servants, seemed to be acting as my agent. Perhaps me and my glittering future had become a major topic of dinner-table conversation in the Fakenhams' wood-panelled dining room. As it turned out this did happen, later that summer, though not for any reasons I could've predicted then.

'Well, if you need any advice about courses or good jobs, come and ask me.' I thought of my lost friend Anne-Marie: *What crap! A good job like an insurance executive!* and then she'd put her hands together, press them against her ear and start snoring. We didn't know then if this was what he did for a job, but we thought he looked like that type. There was not one man we had ever come into contact with about whom we had not formed an immediate and powerful opinion.

I don't remember Anne-Marie and me ever talking about the dead daughter. Right from the start I probably knew the information was radioactive and kept it sealed.

'Yeh, OK, I will if I need anything.'

'Are you not quite sure what area you want to work in?'

'I'd just like to make money,' I said, truthfully, though it exhausted me just thinking of how I would make my way in the world; make money, make friends, make love, make, make, make.

Get me to a nunnery, please!

'She's an old girl now,' Fakenham said, stretching over the gate and patting Willow's neck roughly so she flinched.

'Yeh.' I smiled at her in a deliberately adoring way.

And I knew at the same time that soon I wouldn't give a damn about Willow any more. Soon, I would have left all this childish tenderness behind.

'I don't know what she'd do without you. Tam isn't interested but we couldn't bear to get rid of her, and with Sadie not being here . . .'

This was because Willow belonged to the daughter that died. Starved to death. For a moment now he looked out over the orchard and I kept brushing, not wanting to see any square-shouldered manly sadness. Instead, I thought how money was like food. The smell, the way it came in portions, how badly you needed it. How hungry you got for it, that acidic longing which burned and sickened in your stomach. Firm muscular control was needed over food and money. Money could kill you, wanting and needing it and fighting its power.

In fact, I'd only seen the dead sister a couple of times. She was usually away, first at university then at a skiing resort where she went to work after dropping out of her course. One day she came up to tell me how grateful she was to me for looking after Willow. This was about a year previously. She was twenty when she died. She was pretty. She had long hair in a colour I'd jealously described to Anne-Marie as Ash Blonde. She had skin I'd called Flawless. She'd had legs you'd call Shapely.

I did not remember her as having a particularly bent and hunger-ravaged body. Even when Tam told me later that her sister had been getting to a critical stage about this time, that this was when she always smiled with her mouth shut because her teeth were yellowing, crumbling from the vomit acid, I held an image of her as enviably neat, all her messy girliness contained in a small, tight prettiness.

It was no surprise I hadn't noticed anything wrong with Sadie Fakenham; to me thin was always highly impressive no matter how medically worrying, and so faced with a starving girl I would, of course, have been blinded and green with rivalry, and felt not even the palest hint of concern.

'You can't ride her anyway. She won't be able to be ridden again,' I said when the silence between us was humming. And as I looked up I saw a red stripe that was Mrs Fakenham standing on the step, then walking the few paces backwards and forwards in an agitated, pure loon way. I wondered if she was annoyed because I was talking to her husband.

'It's funny having a pony in your own garden and not being interested in the least. I suppose when you've got advantages you don't appreciate them. Whereas you . . .'

'Yeh, kids like different things, I suppose,' I said, but mumbled into the hollow cup of hoof. I really didn't want him to talk about the dead daughter who used to have innocent times with Willow, or anything to do with hospitals or death. 'It's been a nice day,' I said. 'Hot.'

'Yes. Hot. Well, I'll leave you to it. Don't be late back for the party, will you? And thank you, Mona, thank you very much indeed. Thank you.'

'Yeh, bye.'

I felt exhausted. I wandered round to a quiet part of the gardens and sat down against the wall of the house. When Tamsin Fakenham arrived yesterday, when she pulled her hat boxes and her gowns from her carriage, when she stepped across the gardens with her crinolines rustling and the servants bending low to greet her, when she cast a glance towards the stables to see if she could remember my dismal common face, well, then, at the exact moment that Tamsin began to bewitch them all with her posh girl-person beauty, well, then, I'd've been playing the fruit machine, watching Shred pogo dancing and listening to Dad telling PorkChop how him and Cleo met: *We were just two lonely people, two lonely people*, he kept mumbling over and over: *Just lonely, lonely people*.

After a short while the 'Wild Thing' started up again, the plucking of strings by strong fingers.

It was still hesitant, uneasy and slow.

peanuts

I lay in bed with me hands behind me head and looked at the security light on Drake's factory opposite. It was Tuesday 3.04 a.m., nearly three days since the wedding. The drink had left me, I couldn't sleep. I had altered since the burglary.

I slid me fingers between me legs and tried hard to think of Tony, who was a skinny boy widely believed in current girl circles to be 'my boyfriend', but he just morphed into a moody stranger, then into Phil the Flash, then evaporated.

I had, a few hours earlier, just committed my first crime but was disappointed by how quickly the feeling of celebrity had passed. As fleeting as the joy after food.

Already I felt like yesterday's regional news.

Downstairs there was a new fruity. One brought to us by the brewery, called *Money, Money, Money*.

I could see a dark drool of lace dribbling from the drawer where I'd drunkenly stuffed the underwear. I'd come in, recounted out the saved-up money, stacked it into piles of tens, each pile coming to fifty, then laid it back in the bottom of the wardrobe. By then I hated mesen again.

Get. Thee. To. A. Nunnery, I said slowly and malevolently, in the dark night.

I'd got the key to the shop I'd just robbed off Mucky Sarah. Her sister worked at the shop as Assistant Manageress and to impress me Sarah had stolen the key. Sarah was all right, though she was mucky with lads and her legs looked like they should have a hoof on the end. She didn't have any friends either, which explained her willingness to try and impress me.

I could hear a distant rumble when a lorry crossed the flyover. I could also hear Dad's far-off shattering snores and, closer, PorkChop's crazy doped-up giggling. Then, after a while, a hush. I listened to the nothingness until it was filled by memories of sounds; the thundering of me feet in the shop and the rattling of hangers on rails. And beneath this soundtrack, the pictures in me head of me mam in that hospital bed.

When Lindy was here, if we were woken in the night from Mam and Dad's arguments, she'd come into my room and we'd invent games, like dreaming up the most horrible thing to say to some ugly bloke who asked you out. Not that blokes did ask me out, which was the reason why I could never think of anything. Lindy came up with ones like: Bloke: Do you want to come back to my place? You: Is there room under your stone for two?

For a few nights after me mam's death Lindy stayed in this bed with me. She slept on her front, her plump arms above her head, her hair falling over the edge of the bed.

The pulse of her, the sexy, bad-tempered breath, was still in the air, only the body was gone.

I couldn't get sexy so I got up. When I moved, me head hurt. I put on the new stolen dressing gown and the price tag pricked into me back.

Like the sharp fingernail of conscience, I thought gloomily.

In fact, it was not a dressing gown, it was a Galore for Girls 'wrap'. I had fourteen of them, though they were surely for sex-hungry housewives to sit around the bungalow in, smoking.

Increasingly, I felt stomach sick and hazy at the thought of old, poor women.

I also had six 36D bras in fluorescent colours. The cups stood out like they held enormous invisible breasts. I also had a whole rail of G-string bikini bottoms, though these were for girls with

30

high brown buttocks and ankle bracelets. I had nothing I could actually *wear*.

When I tried to walk I felt like I'd been run over by Bob's pony and trap. I remembered how Mucky Sarah had turned up wearing Bravo Avocado eyeshadow so heavily it looked like her eyelids had gone mouldy. She'd given me the key, then stormed off into the night. Without even a thought for the murderer.

Perhaps we had all longed to be noticed by him in some way. To be the victim of a terrible assault would deliciously confirm the righteousness of our despair.

My lipstick, which I had chosen especially for the crime, was also applied too thickly, so it looked like I'd been eating a raw steak.

Me hip was like I'd been in a car crash and in the moonlight I saw a bruise as brilliant as a butterfly.

I made a knot of the dressing-gown belt and carefully opened the bedroom door.

For the first time in me life I felt I walked distinctly; like a criminal.

In the shop I was so nervous and sickish I felt I was about to faint. At one point I think I fell over.

PorkChop's room was next to mine. Both of us now had small rooms at the front of the pub, with high ceilings and balconies overlooking Black Beck. Lindy, as a child, had PorkChop's room but when she was getting divorced and had to move back to the pub with Siouxsie she'd insisted upon having the room at the back which overlooked the car park, the biggest bedroom in the house. So Dad and Cleo had to move into her room and she'd moved into their room. Until recently PorkChop, the most enormous person in the house, lived, at my insistence, in the smallest boxroom. He never once complained, or suggested I swap with him, though it was like demanding the rabbit live in the hamster cage so the hamster could live in the hutch. On Sunday Dad and Cleo had moved back into the big bedroom and PorkChop was given the room next to mine.

I'd never been in his room, it was a rule between us. But that night the light was still on and through the half-open door I saw his white, whalish body dressed only in green-spotted underpants.

I smelt the sweet smoke of dope. He was growing up into a drugs boy.

Hanging proud over the wardrobe was his big, white shirt; by the window were a pair of polished brown shoes. PorkChop dressed like he had a job.

Ha! Fuckwitidiotspermiface.

It was nearly dawn but he was up and alert. He'd got some writing paper spread out in front of him and a pencil in his fist. He was resting on his other hand which propped him up and covered his ears. A tiny red tip of tongue curled from the edge of his mouth. From his ashtray smoke went upwards in ringlets.

PorkChop had lived at the Adam and Eve for two years. Me mam had left home two years before she died, because Dad was having an affair with Cleo. Cleo left a dignified break of ten months before moving into the pub with her son. I was used to him now and, though he disgusted me, I rather liked him too.

I knew that he was writing song lyrics down on a big pad. He did this to relax; he'd told me once when I'd caught him at it. I'd never told anyone. I'd never teased him about it.

I turned to go, then heard, in almost a whisper:

'You all right?'

'Yeh,' I said quietly, not moving so I was still hidden behind the door.

'Where've you bin? I 'eard you come in.'

'Out with Anne-Marie,' I said and the thought of me dear, absent friend made me want to weep.

'Where?'

'Nowhere.'

'Where you off?' His voice was thick with the slowness of dope. I wondered if he was concerned about me because of the murderer. Lately, some men held their women tightly to their chests like wallets.

'Downstairs. Fruity.'

'Oh.'

'What you doing?' I asked and moved slightly so I glimpsed him as he curled his fat arm over his sheet of writing paper

'Nowt.'

'OK.'

'OK.'

Something in me ripened to a blush.

On the way down I passed Dad's room. The snoring was loud, uncontrollable and apish as always when he was very drunk. All night it rocked us.

When you hear the attack warning, you and your family must take cover at once. I would rather blister and fry.

Quietly, I unlocked the door at the top of the landing that divided the living quarters from the pub and descended the stairs.

Downstairs, damp bar towels hung like veils over the pumps. The cash tray slot in the till gaped emptily. The blue curtains had been pulled too quickly leaving narrow spears of raw morning at the centre of each pair.

In a horror film a snarling face would appear.

The murderer was snoring somewhere right now.

Perhaps with his bloody fists still gripped tight round Mucky Sarah.

There were eight dog-ends in the ashtray, and round the rim of a slim glass a fleshy pink lip had bled its mark. There was no pint glass, which meant Cleo'd been drinking alone. Next to her glass was a list of sums crossed out and done again. The pen had pecked hard into the paper. At the bottom was the boxed total of £11,249.

While in Galore for Girls I was reminded of the night we caught our mam smashing up the place. Everyone was woken by shattering glass and shouting. Lindy saw her with a pile of ashtrays high under one arm and with the other hand she'd just started lobbing them at the optics, smashing right from Glenfiddich to Campari. It was May 1981, she'd just found out about Cleo and she was angry. She was tossing them like a frisbee mainly, twisting like she was doing the shot-put, and sometimes she did it in a bowling way, overarm. She was good – each optic exploded on target. Eventually Dad woke up. He came hurtling down the stairs with Jaws snarling. Then he was screaming, *Get the till, get the till.* He thought it was a burglary. It was after this he started sleeping with the cash trays under his two pillows.

Another thing was that Dad had started turning his own trousers inside out and checking the pockets before he put them in the wash. Which was a sure sign.

The bar had been cleaned to a pattern of misty moonlight swirls and the smell of Dettol lingered over the floor.

The place seemed strange, not like the same place it was when Lindy was here. Two packets of peanuts hung from a cardboard display.

Some bad part of me wanted to eat.

You had to sell all the peanuts to reveal a topless girl playing in sea water. Dad always left just two packets to cover her tits, until someone, usually on Sunday lunchtime, called out: *Go on then, Charlie, let's get 'em off!*

My darlingg you lurk wundurfool toniiiite.

Cleo'd left the knife sticking in the lemon like a dagger.

That evening I'd heard Cleo say to me dad that she was worried about me because I *appeared to 'ave no mates.*

Correct. But now I was special: I was illegal.

And I was to be, A Friend To Tamsin.

Someone had dropped a generous fifty pence into the handicapped bottle and I fished it out with a swizzler stick and then went over and turned on the new *Money, Money, Money.* It was rather nice, flashier than *Blaze A Trail* but not as characterful. She would take me a while to get to know her. Though, of

34

course, I longed for something to happen to change my life, and take me away from the pub for ever. There was a pile of coins on the display which changed colour but I didn't know what this meant yet. I got this odd feeling, like when you heard a dog barking, always in the distance: troubling, irritating.

The door to Galore for Girls had swung open with silent ease. In the darkness by nightwear I'd lit up and just the sound of *cigarette* was enough. I remember only thinking how the fact that it rhymed with majorette, launderette and suffragette proved it was a girl thing. Then I was aware of having no skills for burglary, I could not pick a lock or magic anything open with the sliced edge of a credit card. There were no cash boxes or safes. Just knickers, dresses, nighties, and I just stood there drunk in the dark. And Lindy was right, I thought, I'm nothing; a pale slug worming through black water.

It was like being in Barbie's clothing store; fragile, plastic and soon disappointing. Maybe thirty seconds later, when things were in bags beside me, it was over and I was back on the street and the door was locked and I was in between a knot of drunks weaving back from the pub.

Get thee to a nunnery, I whispered, making tight lumps of fist in me jacket pockets. Any of the men could've been the murderer. Women walked nervously with their arms folded, their heads down, their steely heels echoing quick clicks.

I played for ages that night, and while I was doing it I thought of Tony, that skinny lad, and what was the point of a broke boyfriend, particularly if you didn't really want thumb-twiddlingly bad sex and could make your own money. Then I thought of his sloping shoulder because of the paper round and how he smelt of ink, and how he was at least an almost friend.

I thought of PorkChop and how he liked fishing and writing never-to-be-sung pop lyrics.

I thought of me rotting mam and the dead Sadie.

The new dressing-gown 'wrap' was stiff and cheap and made me sweat.

I thought of the Soviet Special Forces and how soon they would tramp over our ruined country like red ants.

I had no best friend, no sister and no schoolgirl innocence to shield me. Things would be different. Still, I played 'til all me money had gone and I was sleepy and could go back to bed.

As I was going out the door, I gave in to the nasty stomach gnawing and pulled the last two packets off of the peanut display and revealed a pair of full pink tits rising up from the foaming white surf.

pepper

When I got round the back of the house I knew something had changed. Mr Fakenham was armoured up in his grey office suit, arms outstretched, his face mottled with a purple rash, glaring up at the gable window at the top of the house. I clenched the brake on my bike and skidded on the gravel just a little way behind him.

I'd been in such situations before, and since. It's like lightning – before anything happens you get still heat and an electric cracking in the air, and no one can do anything to stop it.

Mr Fakenham had seen me and flashed me a charming smile, but he didn't move. It was Thursday, after nine, and yet he was not at work.

No one had bothered to take Willow into the orchard and she was hanging her head drowsily over the splintered rim of the stable door.

Then out of the gable window Mrs Fakenham's wild face appeared. A look on it I'd not seen before; a sting in the morning air. She glared down at us like the water-spouting demons on Shred's church. Then with a ringing thud the window clamped shut and the face melted away behind small cubes of glass. Mr Fakenham still didn't move; he was staring upwards, his mouth a little open, his arms away from his side, like a figure in the illustrated Bible.

Then the thunder: first a lamp, then a white bath towel, a piece of soap, a vase, a jacket, a dressing gown, a book, until finally a jar of pink bath salts exploded at Mr Fakenham's feet. I wobbled on the bike. When the bath salts struck, a cloud of grey pigeons flew up from behind the stable-block chimney, rising into the blue sky like smoke. Willow jerked her head and moved back into the dark of the stable.

'Well, that was quite a show,' he goes, turning to me and smiling his perfect advertising smile.

I felt sorry for Mr Fakenham. Surely all women were possessed with some lunacy and men struggled stoically to rein us in. We owed them thanks for managing our madness.

'It was,' I said, but didn't look at him. I was watching every window over the broad back of the house for a glimpse of Mrs Fakenham flying by, my eyes moving from the wide French windows on ground level to the small panes of the laundry room then up to the jutting attic windows. It was already an impressive building and now the house seemed to be inflating, slowly taking in more breath. I didn't know whether to help pick things up, for fear this might make him feel like an old man who'd dropped his change in the street. I wished I could dissolve, though this had as much to do with Galore for Girls as it did with the Fakenham family.

I feared the police might have to be called.

He moved his feet through the bath salts slowly so the ground growled, then glowered at the tubs of triangular trees lined up outside the back door. I was expecting a big response but all he did was unpin and straighten a brooch on his tie. Then he rolled his neck and walked away, got into his big car and revved out the drive, waving at me and smiling.

'Good luck with the revision, Mona,' he called. 'You look lovely today, by the way. And do remember what we talked about, won't you?'

Then I noticed a girl person sitting on the edge of a flowerpot.

Her eyes were working over me like she was computing hundreds of tiny calculations.

She was making comparisons.

Next to her was a bottle of bleach.

This was the first time we'd been alone together since the time last year when she'd told me of the starvation of her sister. She seemed instantly familiar, and I thought afterwards how at that moment something within me sighed with relief and slotted into place like a bridge completed.

I noticed she had a mole sprouting a single black hair on her chin. On any other lass this would've seemed disgusting, for I hated body hair, but instead it strangely attracted me to her.

From the first real moment of our meeting I was already a criminal and she was distinctly witchy.

'You're burning,' she said, as though what had just happened was as familiar as the milkman calling. There was an earringless hole in her ear and her body was taut as an elastic band, stretched wide with anger. I noticed immediately her hands, which were clean as freshly sliced meat, a swollen pink, like they'd just been dipped in boiling water.

'I don't mind. I want a tan.' I'd figured that with a tan and a pair of heavy breasts you need not worry about independence or self-sufficiency because someone, a police officer perhaps, would look after you.

I got off my bike and laid it down in the drive. My legs trembled hung-overly and my calves were still drunkish and aching. The memories of Galore for Girls would not go away. I had told no one, though I'd returned the key to Mucky Sarah and given her a bag full of the finest 36D lingerie as a payment. Now I hoped to keep out of her way.

'Hmm, you'd look more healthy,' she said, playing with her hair, quickly winding a loose strand round and round her index finger.

'I know. Though I just blister and go red. Are you sunbathing?'

'I'm playing my guitar, of course.'

'"Wild Thing"?' I asked, but she just looked at me with cruel confusion. And then for some reason I boldly said: 'I'm sorry about your sister. Dying. It's still terrible. It takes a long time. I mean, to get over it.'

'Oh,' she said, surprised. 'Yes. I didn't know you'd remembered. Thanks.'

'What's that for?' I asked, pointing at the bottle of bleach by her side. I knew we both wanted to change the subject.

'Well, if there're lots of leftovers in the kitchen and you might be seduced by the sight and want to eat them . . .' she said, and then paused, as though gauging my reaction. I smiled to urge her to continue. 'Well, if you pour a bottle of bleach over anything as soon as it appears in the kitchen, then you take away the temptation.'

'Brilliant idea,' I said, impressed.

I liked any idea that was about covering your tracks.

'You can also use pepper. Though it doesn't always put you off. You can rinse it away, that's the problem,' she said solemnly.

I nodded.

'Anyway, you need to have brilliant ideas when you live with someone as slovenly as my *mother*.'

She said the last word like it had gone rotten in her mouth.

'Oh,' I said. I knew about the pepper trick. I'd even used it a couple of times, but not bleach.

Bleach was better.

'Don't get a job, Mona,' she said, kindly, like this was in response to something I'd told her. It was like half our conversation was happening unspoken. I'd not even admitted to myself that I was going to need to get a job.

'But I need money.'

'What do you need money for?' she said, her look betraying a quick flicker of scorn.

'Oh, things.'

'What things?'

She turned sharply towards me. She was still interested in me: her quick, girl eyes sniffing at every inch of me.

40

I wondered if she was rather fattish. She was at least a size ten, and though she did not have any unsightly chubby lumps, you could not see any bones either. She was slender, sure, but perhaps a bit too fleshy to be totally right.

'Things.'

'Like what, for example?' The way she said it reminded me of the way I'd loiter in Lindy's doorway whining: *Where you off?*

'I need some to play the fruit machine, for example.'

I turned away. Slivers of damp straw were threaded through Willow's greasy tail. I no longer felt much connection with the pony. She was becoming just an animal.

And I was not breathing properly; all respiratory action had ceased as though I'd just suffered an enormous cardiac shock.

'*Mona*,' she said thoughtfully. 'Hmm. It's not really the sort of name I'd expect for your sort of girl.'

'Who's a *girl*?' I said, snorting the word in the way she had, as though she'd said spider or lizard or rat, and I looked around like I was looking for the girl. It was a good joke and she got it and smiled, impressed; we both recognised that the word *girl* was usually an insult. My breathing started again.

'Your name's very . . .'

'I know. My sister started it. Because of me always complaining as a kid. She started calling me "The Moaner", because of me being called Lisa. Geddit?'

'Indeed. I've studied the original. It's not *that* good a painting when you see it.'

One of the first things I was to learn about Tamsin in the coming weeks was that being rich and well educated allowed her to question, pull apart and then disregard everything; she was confidently critical and cynical. This was an effective way of ensuring she felt superior to all around her. She mocked and used irony. She was cheerfully nasty. She believed she was the future.

'Me name was meant to be an innocent joke but it stuck for

life,' I said, in the self-hating way which I was to learn quickly worked well with these sorts of women.

'Like a false but evil eyelash,' she shrieked, delighted.

'Like a lonely sock, stuffed down your bra, becomes attached to your chest for ever.'

'Do you actually put socks down your brassière, Mona?'

'Not any more,' I said, smoking a fag harshly and narrowing my eyes.

'I don't need to,' she said, cupping her breasts in her hands and weighing them with a smile. They were beautiful. 'Mostly fat,' she said when she saw me looking.

My darlingg you lurk wundurfool toniiiite.

This was true. This was indeed the very problem with breasts. Though some girls did manage it: to have tits and nothing else.

I would reward Tam with one of the fluorescent bras from Galore for Girls.

'Anyway, you always lose on fruit machines,' she goes.

'I don't. They're like dogs, they can't actually tell you, but once you get to know them they all have a certain style and they communicate. Like different breeds. And if you do stuff, like count reels on your fingers. You know, like, for example you know there's three more symbols before the cherry. And you have to touch the buttons very firmly, not like they're gonna hurt you. You need strong hands.'

Tamsin held up her hands for me to look, at an angle like she was protecting herself from attack. They no longer seemed freshly boiled. Then she spread her fingers wide so I could see her white face though the pink-finger web.

'It's all rigged,' she said quietly, now playing with the dirt on the ground, then collecting a small pile of sparkling bath salts and coaxing them into a pile with her index finger.

'Only at the seaside, not normally.'

'What's the point?'

'Well, you only live once,' I said, hoping it sounded careless and philosophical at the same time.

'Once will be plenty, thank you very much.' This was something Anne-Marie might have said. I wanted to tell her more about fruities but then she collected her bottle of bleach and stood up, stretched, and just when it looked like she was gonna snap, said: 'My mother is such a mess. And I don't just mean mentally. I mean she's so bad at keeping the house *clean*. Even with the old servants, who come every day, it's still like we live in a Bombay slum.'

She sounded dangerous and angry and I looked away embarrassed.

The Fakenhams had two old people as their main servants, Ivy, who was the housekeeper, though this meant cleaner, and Paul, an old man, who was the groundsman, though this meant gardener. In addition to these two servants, they had a young man who was often seen cleaning the car and a poor, depressed girl who came to do only laundry. Someone else came to hang and unhang curtains. I wondered if they had other staff to flush the toilet and light their cigarettes. I was a servant too, in a way, though I didn't get paid. I'd only recently started thinking of mesen in that way. Sometimes Ivy brought me a drink when she saw me mucking out the stables. Once she said she felt sorry for me, the way they got me to do all that work for nothing, though I told her I didn't mind. When old Paul came to take the manure to put on the flower beds he made jokes about us all being the darkies. He said Mr Fakenham made him work like a nigger. He made me laugh. I liked him. Sometimes you saw the two servants standing in the yard waving their hands around and whispering about the things that went on in the house.

It was so rich and characterful a house; the ivy, the walled gardens, the stone lion/dog, those high thick doors, that it got gossiped about like a person.

'It seems a nice house,' I said, and thought of the disgusting food scraps turning white like fungus beneath the bleach. 'I'm right fucked off with living at home.'

Now I was a criminal I had to swear more, though in truth

I'd never been the type to blaspheme heavily. When my deeds that summer came to light many people were most surprised exactly because of me initial quietness and politeness. At most times I could've passed for an averagely damaged Christian.

'Oh, Mona, but it's so *tatty*. Look. Just look! At the dirt, even on the outside.' And she picked a ball of fluff off her T-shirt. 'But it's worth a fortune. It's a listed building, built in the eighteenth century apparently.'

'Oh,' I said. I looked at the house which towered above us. It was wonderful but also so gloomy that it could've starred on the cover of one of Lindy's albums.

'Yeh. Fuck. Jesus.'

'And it looks like my father's got a girlfriend.'

'Oh.'

'Unbelievable, isn't it?' she said. I didn't know if she meant that parents did such things, or that any woman would fancy her dad. Both meanings were OK.

'Hmm.'

'And,' she said, sticking her chin out and staring right at me, her eyes like fierce stones, 'Guess what? She's twenty-eight and his bloody *secretary*. It's a hoot. This time it's such a cliché it's an insult to our intelligence, don't you think?'

'Yes. Your 'ead's getting sunburnt. Cancer,' I muttered. I would not talk about fatherly infidelities, I refused. 'Fuck me,' I said awkwardly.

The reason I didn't find swearing and bravado easy was because I was too much of a worrier. Since me mam died, I looked at the sun and thought of black blisters, at flowers and thought of asthma, and blue sky reminded me of what was coming: the great brown mushroom cloud of nuclear fallout. But crimes would change this.

She just looked at me and said nothing, and for some reason I remembered Anne-Marie saying this was why people had sex, so there was something to do when talking got awkward. I looked down at my legs, at the dark hairs coming through round the

44

ankles, and the pads of what suddenly seemed like certain fat around me knees.

Get thee to a nunnery and thus diet.

I wondered if I should offer to help pick the clothes and books up off the path.

She was supposed to be fifteen but she seemed younger. I knew people thought I seemed younger too. I'd once heard Anne-Marie's mam complaining that I was *immature*. Tamsin seemed more like a pretentious fourteen. Still, I understood how the death of a close relative had a strangely regressive effect. A bereavement adviser told me you needed to believe in what children could believe in: angels and ghosts and heaven.

Already, from that very first moment, I believed I understood Tamsin like no one else.

It was 9.42 a.m. and the May morning breeze fluttered at our faces. Goldwell was deserted; all the suited daddies had driven their big cars into Whitehorse, all the expensive mummies were weeping tears into their yogurt and the posh little boys and girls were away at cruel schools.

I felt blissful, as though Tam and I were the only two worthy people in the whole summertime world.

Then, as I looked up at her, I had this feeling coming on like there was a coach and horses hurtling round me skull and I hadn't had a drink yet that day (except brandy, which didn't count as it was only a fancy thing, a frilly nightie of a drink).

'Do you think there's life on other planets?' she goes, not looking at me, instead grinding her heel into the ground and spinning round like a child. I laughed and she looked annoyed and said: 'Really, it's a question. Do you or don't you?'

'Probably.'

'Have you ever thought of running away?'

'To another planet?'

'No, Mona, seriously. To another *place*.'

'Not recently,' I said.

In truth I'd run away three times before, once with a girl the

45

day after her father had gone to work in Saudi Arabia. We went on our bikes nine miles to Wooten Newton, a village where we used to have a pub. It took us all day. Another time with Lindy, after my mother left in 1981, and a third time when I set off on poor, frail Willow for no reason I remember.

'It's very hard to actually get anywhere,' I said.

I really wanted to talk about women and crimes, about the next step we would take together. She looked at me, smiled in a slow, thinking way, that seemed to be half admiration and half competition. Later that day I realised I recognised this look because it was the one I was used to seeing on Lindy's face.

Then she went and sat down on the low wall again and began to play with a handful of soil she'd scooped from the flowerpot. She put her mouth close to her hand and spat on the mud, stirring it with her index finger 'til it made a smooth paste.

'D'you eat mud, Mona?'

'Not unless I'm celebrating,' I said. I could feel every part of my body working at premium rates. You had to be alert when you were with Tamsin Fakenham. Her skin was so clean and scrubbed it looked like no one else's skin ever. Not even the fawning models in magazines had this rawness which seemed to pulse with the exposed tension of 'herness'.

Watching her skin gave me the same feeling as seeing on TV the dangerous insides of a body slit open for an operation.

Sometimes when I'd not eaten all day I'd lay there at night and think of me mam's cancer cooking up in a simmering casserole of intestines. The deathly cancerous fragrance weaving pungently through the steam.

'It's very interesting on the complexion,' she said and began to smear the brown mess thickly over her face. First she covered her cheeks, then her forehead, chin, nose and eyebrows, pushing the mask right back to her ears.

'I've got an egg-and-honey-enriching preparation at home,' I said sadly. 'It's in the fridge.'

There were just two pale fleshy circles either side of her

nose where her eyelids half covered her eyeballs so she looked drugged, sleepy and sad. I was sure now I would never go back to the innocent lass who made her own cosmetics and liked animals.

'Though it's tricky because you do have to be careful of worms,' she chirped, ignoring what I'd just said.

'Ah, that'll be the complex complexion complication,' I said quietly.

'Correct,' she goes and, not smiling, got up to leave, a patch of mud slipping in a drip to the ground.

lemons

I knew criminals were often caught because some strange last-minute lunacy compelled them to confess, I'd seen it happen with disastrous consequences on films, but still, at 10.17 a.m. the following morning, Friday, I dangled me legs into the cool, mucky water of Black Beck and told PorkChop what I'd done.

'So,' I said. My voice was harsh and bitchy though I'd tried to adopt Mr Fakenham's sure managerial tone. 'I've ended up with the knicker drawer of a Mediterranean beach goddess but nowt for me to *wear*.'

PorkChop looked at me and narrowed his piggy eyes. I was wearing Brazen Lady lipstick with a dusting of Midnight Vixen on my upper eyelids. I'd learnt a few years previously that my facial type was 'small almond' or thin. The make-up gave me a seriously scowling look. I'd done my hair up in an angular style that I hoped was a bit Human League.

I sucked at me teeth and blinked confidently. 'I feel more bad about not fitting into any of it than I do about having robbed it. I'm so guilty I could *chew* me own hands off as punishment.'

We were sitting at the point on the Black Beck where it bent sharply to a triangular point like a crooked finger. It was a ten-minute walk from our pub. There were factories on all sides. Of course, being so fenced in is what made me feel so wildly free. The rawhide factory had a site down Black Beck along with boat builders, tyre yards, steel-rope makers and a caravan depot. By this stage the skins were further down the production process from cow to jacket and the smell was more chemical, the fresh headiness of newsprint or glue, less gutsy than the skinning factory.

'In fact,' I sighed, 'I might call the cops right now and tell 'em to release all those 36D beauties, slap the handcuffs round me waist and haul me in. I mean, it's like you stealing tight black plastic trousers or a pair of sports shorts, PorkChop. Ridiculous.'

He put his hands into the water and scooped out a palmful of the slimy speckled green.

My legs ached: I'd been crouched in the Fakenham garden since 6.09 a.m. hoping for a glimpse of Tam. She'd not been around, no sign of her anywhere, and there was the distinct danger she was in a library somewhere revising for her exams. Strangely, the thought made me want to bite someone.

Praying for Tamsin had stopped me sleeping and I felt half crazed and angry. I'd prayed so hard I could feel God sucking on me toes. I took a few blasts on the Ventolin, about six more than necessary and me arm went all dead and trembly and I got the heart-rush overdose. I rather like this heart-attack feeling, the same as when you nearly, but not quite, got a big jackpot win. Or when I used to eat five Mars bars at once; a sugar rush does the same.

'Oh dear, I dunno. I probably just need more practice.'

I feared me own crime high was wearing off and I was returning to my lonely girl self. I looked down into the water. Black Beck was sinking through cracks in the mud and soon the fish would be flapped up on the earth, sun-dried scaly flips of silver leather. And if Julie was down there she'd rise from the water on a plate of baked mud.

PorkChop continued to eat the pizza wedges he'd stolen from the pub kitchen. He offered me some, but I sighed and said I knew they had roughly 467 calories a slice.

'Perhaps I shouldn't have told you about robbery,' I pouted.

Still, there was more dangerous zap in the world as soon as I'd confessed. I felt like a nurse who'd just surfaced after her first invasive surgery, or a hairdresser who'd just executed her first perm. Now that I had both *done* a crime *and* told someone, well, I felt like a really real criminal.

For breakfast I'd eaten six packets of cheese and onion crisps and a bumper bag of pork scratchings. The food in me gut felt like blue poison.

Just because it was daylight didn't stop there being a murderer about.

I gazed into the dark water, thought of deep seas and fish pulsing like a girl's tiny heartbeat, how much easier it might be to breathe down there, and the beauty of wide, gently waving gills.

Soon I would feel better and then go back to the Fakenhams', knock on the door and ask for her. Perhaps show her the fourteen white G-strings. Maybe tell her of me plans for fresh crimes. She would see I was a girl of means, who could take risks, who could make something of her life, independent of her tattoo-titted sister.

Hell, yes! Crimes were surely the key.

'Anyway, next time I'm gonna take a detailed list and tick things off as I go. I've gotta be as focused about thieving as I am about shopping and slimming.'

Opposite from where we were sitting, directly on the other bank, was a Pine Warehouse and behind this an estate of new houses. You wouldn't break into the Pine Warehouse because of an alarm on the front and an open yard to both front and back, and there was no fence or bushes to screen you. The more Ventolin you took the less it worked. You could also be seen by cars crossing the flyover. Behind us on this side of Black Beck was the row of terraced houses which included the one Julie Flowerdew had lived in.

How lovely it would be to exist fishlike on nothing but air, to be one sleek weight of muscle, to have no need for hands, no need to be noticed.

Get thee to a nunnery and dissolve.

He threw a stick into the water and a crescent of ripples fanned out round it.

''ow old are you, PorkChop?'

'Eighteen,' he said innocently. I knew this, of course, and was only asking to rub his snout in what we all knew: PorkChop was a lazy, fat no-hoper, well past his prime. I didn't want him to forget this.

I gave him the special look of scornful sorrow.

'I can understand impulse. Sometimes I wanna fish when it's not appropriate,' he said.

'D'you wanna do one with me?' I said quietly, seductively adopting the voice of the girls who went 'away' to school. 'And we'll get summat useful this time.'

'And I understand about timing. The waiting for the right bite, holding steady.'

'A robbery, I mean. D'you wanna do one with me?' I spoke in a breathless lusty sigh. 'I thought you could 'ave 'alf of the stuff. Well?'

'Patience and timing and not rushing things is crucial.' He looked at me very seriously and I wondered if he too was saying these things as a kind of sexy come on.

'D'you wanna do one or not?' I yelled.

'D'you wanna go fishing instead? I could show you. Me dad's a fisherman, well, he was.'

'I know. Deep-sea trawling, blah, blah, blah. You told me.' I yawned.

Then we argued for a while.

Suddenly, it occurred to me that if I didn't change me life, make money, get successful and independent and admired, I might end up like PorkChop's dad. Of an evening he drank gin, while watching telly alone in the front room. An ex-fisherman, he had a fair bit of money, a tan and two pornographic videos.

He'd been in trouble with the police. He never got up at weekends before midday. I knew this because I'd heard Cleo telling Dad late at night.

I lay back on the warm stone and, putting my hands behind me head, I looked up at the clear blue screen of sky. Everything seemed like a funny crazy mistake: PorkChop, Galore for Girls, me mam, Lindy, everything. Only Tamsin Fakenham seemed to make sense.

'Jesus, sometimes I get an inkling that you can divide men into two camps, dangerous sexual predators and lardy losers.'

'Mona, you don't 'alf talk some nonsense.'

When I first thought of crimes and female friendship they seemed distinctly apart, but the more I thought about it the more naturally they merged together.

After a while he goes: 'How often d'you go on a spree?'

'Spree! I like that,' I said, and exaggerated for a while.

'I think I might go now, Mona.'

'Don't go. Let's go for a walk,' I said and tried to think of a joke.

'Don't you feel guilty?' he goes when we got to the top of the bank and were walking the road over the water.

I took his cool hand and held it. So fleshy it felt like holding an inflated rubber glove. As we walked I could smell the pizza gunk.

'Any of these houses could be the home of the murderer,' I said. I felt sickish which must've been the hangover. 'Often it turns out that murderers are people you know: fathers, brothers, boyfriends, headmasters, cheery milkmen you've chatted to for years.'

Get thee to a nunnery and start to plot.

We were getting closer to where Julie had lived. Years ago I'd played with her, I'd been in that house. I'd seen her bedroom with bunk beds and purple sheets and babyish wallpaper and a brown plastic potty under the bed because they only had a downstairs loo. Julie's house was in a long terrace of fifteen houses with a low wall in front and a gap where a gate had been. The windows were black, clouds hung mirrored in the glass, and you couldn't see in, though the curtains were pulled back.

Someone had taken the net curtains down. This was another thing the government definitely recommended, in fact *insisted* upon, in the event of a nuclear attack.

Her mother was standing in the alley that ran down the side of the houses.

As soon as I saw her I smelt lemons. Something cooking perhaps, or a herb. It could've been washing-up liquid or scouring fluid, or something she'd been eating.

I felt truly sick at the sight. Her mother was so much like her, though her clothes were old and different. She had menopausal grey tights, a short red skirt, a black jacket with gold buttons, her big hair curled away from her face in a furry pub-singer sort of way, and waved down on to her older lady bony shoulders. Bitch.

'Hey, hello, Mona,' she cried out. I waved and then clutched PorkChop's arm, and together we strode towards her.

She might invite me in for a cuppa and a chat, I thought. Ask about me mam, and what we were doing for the anniversary. Say about friends, how they come and go. There was more chance of being friends with Mrs Flowerdew than Mrs Fakenham, though both had the same cosmic, womanly troubles that so attracted me. Maybe these women could forewarn me, perhaps by knowing them I could stay one step ahead of catastrophe. They were the bad example I would learn from.

'Hiya,' I chirped as PorkChop and I sloped past.

'Hang on a minute, you two, you can take these,' Mrs Flowerdew said. Then she disappeared into the house. I waited, looking left and right, up and down the street. I knew she was going to get a bag of jumbly for Cleo who was collecting for the miners and the thought made me nervy. I was sure carrying jumble made me a target for the murderer. Scared, poor and tarty lasses were the main target.

And there was another thing I couldn't forget. A few weeks back at a jumbly in the Labour Party rooms in town I saw my own clothes tumbling around the table. A little white dress embroidered with ladybirds was flicked and flung. The thought made my breath come in quick catches, like the chack, chack, chack of a train.

'Give those to Cleo. I know she's been collecting.'

'Okey-dokey,' I trilled, like I was auditioning for the part of 'Happy Normal Girl Aged Fifteen' at the youth theatre.

There was a pause and I knew she was looking at me body and wondering. She looked at me wrists. She was still a mother who understood girls and the things they tried to do, though her own daughter had gone.

'How's the revising going, Mona?' she asked kindly.

We discussed this for a while, as PorkChop shuffled his feet through the dust and a white butterfly winged round our faces. Then we said goodbye and continued on our way.

I didn't want the bag. This bag of clothes ripped from all the corners of the house. Given away like rubbish. I didn't even want to carry it. I held it between my thumb and index finger and well away from me body. I walked slowly, lightly, as though carrying a bag of sleeping eels.

At the top of the road they had erected another police observation unit on a patch of rubble in front of a disused shoe factory: Sweet Feet. There were two policemen at a desk pouring tea, one opening a pack of currant biscuits. I stood there in the light so they could see us if they wished. All they had to do was look up. A skinny lass with Little Lady blue/black mascara dribbling down her cheeks and her confused obese stepbrother wandering at her side.

Hellllllllllllllllllllllllllllllllllllllllllllllllllllllllllllllllllllllllllllllllllllllllllllllp.

I dropped the bag, then there was water on me cheeks and saltiness round me mouth and skin stinging and sky was streaked purple and a chill breeze was blowing and Siouxsie cried like this: *I will not, I will not, I will not*, and it was possible someone might see me so I crouched on the pavement with the plastic bag between me knees and I was kind of choking and I put my chin on my chest and breathed in steps and gobbled up more Ventolin 'til me heart became a drum roll and then I curled goose-bumped arms round that dreadful bone-flat chest to stop it heaving.

It was hilarious!

I fancied a voddy and Slimline with a slice of lime.

The police could've seen if they'd wanted to. PorkChop could've stopped me if he'd dared. But all he said was: 'Don't cry, Mona. Don't cry.' He put a fat damp hand on my shoulders and squeezed: 'Breathe. Breathe. Breathe.'

Eventually, when I could, I took a few rippling breaths and looked in the bag. I moved the clothes aside pickily, with stiff finger tips. I could smell the clothes, their yeasty warmth, the dry stench of old biscuits, weird but still kind of sexy. Bodies had lived, itched, throbbed and swelled in those cotton skins. I could see where things had been hand-stitched, mended, darned, washed to a cheap fade, rubbed raw round elbows and knees. Which things were bargains, which cost a bit more, which had been for very special family days.

'It's all OK,' I sobbed to PorkChop. 'Except for a girl's pale blue, soft cotton T-shirt, which she must've put in accidentally, it's a bag full of lads' stuff.'

We continued on, and walked through the new estate conspicuously cuddling. PorkChop wiped my tears with his snotty sleeve.

'If I'd a pound for every tear I've shed already this year I wouldn't need to be a burglar,' I snivelled.

'Me too,' he murmured. 'But writing lyrics helps.'

PorkChop, The Musical. I thought.

Ha! Fuckwitidiotspermiface!

I never encouraged men to show emotions. Surely in the time it takes you could teach your budgie to tap dance.

We carried on walking. Without a girl person I was just a

maggoty lass with no friends and a dead mam and a stepmother who'd abandoned her family for 'The Struggle'.

A skeletal lass reduced to cuddling with her obese step-brother.

A man with no money or girlfriend or job.

No power, no success, no adoration, or sex.

Get thee to a nunnery and forget the dating game!

Then I saw that one of the houses had a window open. I checked things; no cars in the drive, no neighbours watching, no burglar alarms, no desperate signs saying 'DOGS'.

'Come on, fishboy,' I said, but he stood firm and I had to walk right past him leaving him enormous and gaping. I walked up to the window, unhooked the catch and this dark varnished frame eased open.

It was afternoon that same day, half-two, the language was getting ripe, arses spilling off bar stools and by the windows blokes had closed their eyes gently like cats in the heat. Dad's breath smelt of onions which was unusual because on Friday he always had the fish. Then I noticed there was a much reduced menu on the board, only cold food, no chips, fish, chicken or gravy because Cleo was away for the day at a miners' rally in Durham.

Debbie Courtney was sitting smoking at the end of the bar. I'd only just noticed her. She was old, around twenty-eight; two kids, married to the bloke who fitted burglar alarms. Her face was sore from the sun and the skin was smudgy round her eyes. She lived round the corner from the pub, on Baker Road, so she couldn't've been too afraid to walk home alone. Bitch.

Dad looked at me as I looked at Debbie. I wondered if the new crime was showing on me face like a thump. But when I looked at Dad he quickly went back to the paper. Men treated Debbie delicately, like she had a very great and very special trouble only they could know about. It was very enviable. Bitch.

I knew she too had taken down the net curtains and had sat

back to think on the Soviet Special Forces. She would love now, yes, yes, or never.

Some of the younger men were organising a sweepstake, folding over small strips of paper and dropping them into a pint glass.

PorkChop was not in the bar. I wondered where he had gone to curl up and tremble.

This fat, half-pissed bloke, with one blind eye, who they called Strange Dave, goes: 'You hear about those lads this morning, Charlie? Robbing that 'ouse?'

'Yep,' goes Dad. His shirt had been badly ironed. A sure sign.

'What d'you reckon about that then? Little buggers. Cunts.'

They'd been having the same conversation all lunchtime.

'They reckon they've got a good description of 'em. Three of 'em. A bloke in 'is garden saw 'em, like,' Dad said. His eyes were glassy with new love.

'Cunts. It'll be part of a bigger thing. They come in from Leeds or somewhere an' speed right out again.'

'Well, keep yer windows shut. They weren't blacks or owt, *apparently*.'

They discussed security measures for some time.

'So what's they like, these blokes?' I goes, pushing the spoonful of coleslaw that I'd been pretending to eat away from me with a swagger. I was so nervous I didn't know if the words'd come out right. I knew me posh-girl accent sounded rather weird.

'Average height, average build, young an' that. Still cunts,' goes the fat bloke.

'Did they do loads of houses on the estate?' I asked, not looking up.

'Aye, they might 'ave done others, police don't know yet because of people being away on 'olidays.'

'Is it to do with Julie Flowerdew disappearing?' I asked. I no longer felt the need to be cocky or coy. I had the bud of a personality.

They looked at me bemused. They'd all forgotten about her.

'The lass that's gone missing,' I said.

'No,' said Strange Dave, looking puzzled. 'That were murder, this is burglaries.'

And from the look on his face I could tell this was something much more interesting.

'Were they proper robbers then, or just kids?' I asked.

Different blokes happily provided me with many detailed facts about the burglary.

'Did they 'ave a getaway car?' I gasped.

'Oh aye. Sped straight outta there.'

I'd got the record player in the cellar. There was a tropical fish tank, which would've been really summat but the record player, which was slim, black and shining, unplugged more easily and, though me flesh had jellified to be as cold and clammy as an eel just hooked out of water, I had managed to untangle it.

I'd bandaged it up in a box with black tape.

I slipped off the stool and went to check on it.

The dipped wooden stairs creaked beneath me feet.

The cellar was mushroomy and cool. You could hear voices like rats scuttling overhead. An alcoholic fugitive could live quite happily here, I thought, drinking lager slops and eating the occasional peanut.

Let me buy you a drink, I had said to PorkChop when I came out of the house and he was still standing there, but as I said it he threw up.

I wondered if the cellar was suitable as our nuclear bunker, and if I should mention it to me dad.

The shelf around the edge of the cellar was sparkling with fresh spirits. I unscrewed a bottle and got a gulp of voddy, then another and another. Then I pushed the box with the record player into the dark of the furthest corner of the cellar, where the old white paint was blistered into a rash of damp bubbles, and spiderwebs hung like hammocks.

My toe was on the warm lip of the window. A seamless white

kitchen, all washed up, surfaces all clear, and the dishcloth folded politely on the upturned bowl. Then just the feeling of springing on the soft carpet, brushing past leather jackets hung on hooks, tripping over a pair of big blue slippers close together in the hallway, then clicking the bronze latch of the front door. I could see him and I beckoned. He shook his head, dazed like he'd just been in an accident, and everything about me was slow like moon walkers, drunk fathers, old dogs and I made me face into a smile. Toothily wide and anaesthetised, big enough to reach across the estate to where he stood. He would not come in, maybe thinking of his ex-fisherman father, how a criminal son would sting worse than the gin. Everything about his body said, *No, I will not.*

And for a moment I did think of ending my criminal career right there, just slipping on the big blue slippers, covering myself with the loose home-knit red cardigan and curling up in the sun on the sofa. Waiting for someone to come in and rescue me.

brandy

The next morning, Saturday, I had to hang around for three hours before getting a glimpse of Tamsin Fakenham.

There had been a mist over the orchard which had trailed a tinge of purple, like it was going to be one of those hot sagging days.

The high house shone.

Nothing would happen.

Along one side of the field lay a fresh rash of poppies.

It was peaceful, though I felt irritated and angry.

Her bedroom window had been open all morning and I'd heard a faint tinkling of music, disco perhaps, though it was hard to tell because of the chirping of birds and servants. They were working even though it was a Saturday. Paul was trundling by with a wheelbarrow, followed closely by Ivy bundled into a ball with washing, chatting cheerily to me about the coming drought. Neither Ivy nor Paul had mentioned the murderer, though I was sure they'd lately seemed more agitated.

Seeping from under the door of the stable I could see a slick of slime over which flies hovered. The smell was thick and sour. I gave a tut.

I felt angry because I looked scraggy and weird.

I was not dressed right. I'd wound a red scarf tightly round my neck, put on a rosy T-shirt with a butterfly appliquéd to the front and smeared white foundation over an encampment of spots on me chin. In places I'd dabbed on green correcting fluid.

And I was not very drunk.

And it was a week since Lindy's wedding.

At home I'd got the thought, though it was only 8.30 a.m., of having a brandy. The more I thought of it the more impossible it became to resist the idea. My saliva tasted of alcohol though I'd just woken. Me fingertips itched. I had some sort of delirium. All night I'd wrestled with a lonely panic about the burglaries. My nose bent low to the bar, I searched for the boozy perfume stained into the wood. I left the toast I was eating and edged round the bar, drank a few glasses of burning fierish brown.

On the bar a racing paper was open on an article about the runners in the Derby. Opposite was a list of beautiful equine names some of which had been circled in blue biro. They worked like music: they calmed me. Beside each circle was a cash sum: ten pounds, twenty, five. I thought of how putting all the box of saved-up money on the right horse would bring about a change in my life. Put me in the running for a new kind of life. Bring admirers and respect. Make me A Friend For Tamsin.

I rubbed a finger hard over the newsprint 'til the tip was blackened with ink.

Eventually, at around 12.30 p.m. I saw the silver car leave with Mr and Mrs Fakenham sitting in the front seats, as serious and erect as losing politicians. Then a few minutes later She passed by the bedroom window wearing a green T-shirt, her long blonde hair wound in a loose curl and clipped to the top of her high head.

It was only two days since I'd seen her but such was the joy I felt at watching her it felt like we'd been parted for months.

She was alone yet absorbed in something private and fascinating. I could see the clean and meaty smell rising off her, yet at the same time she was so removed from me it felt like I was watching her on TV.

Her neck seemed longer than was usual on a girl. She seemed like a purer breed than me. She leant her long arms on the windowsill and looked out, perhaps breathing in the smell of the oak tree or just warming her unblemished skin in the sun.

Get thee to a nunnery and ogle beautiful women.

'Mona!' she called when she saw me, and then made a swift, smooth turn from the window to come down to me. My heart lifted like a balloon. Again I regretted my whorish appearance.

'Why you looking so sad?' was the first thing she said when she threw herself on to the dappled oak tree shade. In her hand she had a wafer biscuit spread over with a thick layer of Marmite.

I knew this trick; if you ate very strong-tasting spices or spreads, it felt like you'd eaten for a long time after, though you'd maybe only ingested a tiny scrap of food. I felt Tam was very smart to have worked this out. Both of us were one step ahead of the eating game.

'Are you jealous of her? Is she more successful, more beautiful, more confident and popular?' she said, leaning forward and taking a crumpled pack of cigs from the back pocket of her tight olive cords.

Oh, the ripeness of her!

'I mean your sister, stupid. The one you said made up your name.'

'Oh, she used to be a punk and now she's a housewife. She's got a daughter, and a stepson. And she's pregnant, four months gone. Blonde hair. Breasts,' I said, and touched the butterfly which was appliquéd to my flat chest.

'Breasts! Oh dear, what a burden to have a once remarkable, fertile *and* well-endowed sister. At least my sister's periods had dried up and she had a chest like a tea tray. Though she was remarkable, I suppose. Brave.'

'She refused to breastfeed, so she kept her bosoms intact. And she still thinks she's the amazing one despite her age. Her husband's religious, born again in fact. He makes her feel like a heavenly body.'

'Indeed. Christians are often big on breasts in my experience,' she nodded, lighting a cig and blowing the smoke in a grey cone up into the leaves. 'I knew a vicar once.'

'Hallelujah!' I said, though I wasn't certain what she meant.

'Yes, it was rather good.'

'And bottoms. She's got a perfect arse,' I said quickly, to cover my confusion.

'A heavenly ass,' she said in the voice of Pamela Ewing. 'That's some claim to fame.'

'I know. Most lasses just get one or the other, breast or bottom, don't they? Well, our Lindy's got both. Bitch.'

'My sister died with neither – no arse, no breasts, no flesh at all in fact. Just grey skin and bone.'

'Oh,' I said. I couldn't tell if she was joking or not. This was the first time she had really mentioned her sister since she spoke to me seven months ago.

The sun had gone in and my arms shivered a little. I felt a quick concern about the murderer, though this was the countryside and it was Saturday, and the Fakenhams were rich which surely made murder less likely.

Rich people and posh independent women got murdered less, surely?

She was looking at me but obviously thinking of something else. I'd seen the same concerned gaze on the brows of headmistresses. I felt suddenly thick, fat and ugly.

'Well, I think your sister probably needs all the help you can give her. The temptations of the wifely flesh must be enormous. And she's so trapped, she can't let herself be tempted in the way you can. Might as well be in a coffin,' she said and I laughed nervously. 'Like my sister.'

'I'm often tempted, though I've a figure like a cheap ironing board,' I said because of the awkwardness, and the way something about her voice chilled me arms.

'I've known some very sexy ironing boards. Though admittedly none with an evil, tight-arsed sibling.'

'It's double trouble to be sure,' I said, for some reason adopting an Irish accent and nodding in mock solemnity.

'She should learn to dance,' she goes, in an even more Oirish accent, and holding her long arms above her head like a ballerina.

'Oh no. She hates dancing. She's dedicated her life to the fight against what she calls "disco crap".'

'You mean she's never danced like a true woman, in spangles and high heels?'

'No, I don't think so,' I said, cautiously, because I couldn't tell if she was joking or not.

'She can't be a rebel if she's never felt the throb of true disco.'

'I know,' I said.

'What's her problem?'

'Well, she used to go into record shops especially to scratch the vinyl of disco records with a pin or a needle,' I said and a silence fell between us and I looked up at the sunlight singing through the leaves.

'Where's yer mam and dad gone?' I said eventually. 'I saw them going off in the car.'

'Out to lunch at the Watermill Restaurant.'

'Oh, that's good,' I exclaimed. 'They must be getting on better.'

She looked at me angrily.

'Aren't they?' I said nervously.

'I think you'll find, Mona dear, that Churchill dined with Hitler in the early months of 1939.'

I shut up and fixed my gaze on the house.

If the Fakenham house was a person it would be an ancient alcoholic actress from the era of silent films, with an ashy cigarette in an ivory holder and a crude circle of rouge over papery cheeks. I wanted to say this, but knew she'd sneer so I kept silent.

'God, our house is a slum,' she said, again like our thoughts tangoed, quick but quiet, and arm in arm. 'You should see the kitchen when Mummy's depressed. The whiff of rotten food. Old casseroles she saves to make into sauces. It's nauseating. And bits of old food that drop down the side of the cooker and then mould until enormous insects come and carry them off. It's totally disgusting.' She made her hands into quick, grabbing insects and tickled them over me arms.

'She's got tattoos,' I said a minute later. I desperately wanted to continue this first true conversation I had ever had about Lindy with someone who understood. Food was a good topic, but not as good as the inadequacies of other people, especially sisters. 'So she's obviously daring and stylish.'

'Lorry drivers and workmen have *tattoos*, Mona,' she said languidly, looking up at the sky. She had pronounced my name heavily, the way Lindy used to when emphasising the meaning she originally intended. Tamsin's eyelids were drooping.

That was the first time it occurred to me she was a drinker. A true, heavy, girl drinker.

Get thee to a nunnery and make straight for the bar.

This was why she changed topics and didn't seem to concentrate.

My darlingg you lurk wundurfool toniiiite.

'But she has one on her left breast,' I said. 'A tiny ladybird crawling the gentle curve of sweet girl flesh. They tell me it's very tempting.'

Oh, praise the Lord she was a drinker!

'Anyone can be tempting, breasts or no breasts.'

'But not everyone can be satisfied,' I said in a high American accent with a cheeky smile that I instantly regretted, assuming as it did a sexual confidence I did not possess. It was meant to be *Dallas* but it hadn't come off. Tam didn't laugh. She saw the falseness of the statement even before I did. I was no harlot.

She sat up and stared at me angrily.

'You smell,' she said suddenly. She edged her own firm bum over the earth towards me and sniffed at the skin on my arm. Small kitten breaths which trotted up towards my armpit.

I felt a rough response was required.

'Blood and guts from the fucking rawhide factory,' I said, sucking on a cig. 'It's a leather tanning factory near our pub. Or grease from chippy in the arcade?'

'Holy shit! It's brandy,' she yelled, her eyes wide with admiration and her mouth curving into a wide, full-lipped smile.

I'd recently realised, through incessant watching of American soap operas, that a Big Mouth was essential if you were to be truly attractive to men. Thin lips were a burden equal to poverty. I wondered if there was a widening operation whereby they cut an inch into your cheek and folded the skin outwards to form a wide, raw slot. Or if you could transform in the comfort of your own home, if inserting the bottom of a milk bottle into the mouth each evening upon retiring would do the trick.

'Wait there,' she said and she ran into the house.

I looked from the light to the shade.

I reached into me back pocket then took a drag on the Ventolin.

Sitting next to Tam was like cuddling up to a blowtorch and all tender thoughts got blasted aside. Only now she was gone did purple fears of the burglary seep through.

A moment later she reappeared with two glasses and a decanter of strong-looking liqueur.

'She'll be jealous of your oddity. She'd probably like to be so full of freedom. Of the way you play the fruity. Of your looseness,' she said and poured two drinks, then lifted a thread of hair off my face. 'The way you're more of a doer than a thinker.'

I wondered if she was going to kiss me.

Or hit me.

'She'd probably like to think of herself as the sort of person who takes risks in life, but look what's happened to her. A fine-arsed punk girl, turned dumb wifey with snotty kids. I *hate* women like that.'

'Me too,' I gasped as the alcohol scorched me throat.

'Jesus, what use are perfect tattooed tits if you're washing up all day? Whereas you, Mona, have all the time in the world to make your life as exciting and unusual as possible. Cheers.'

'Yes,' I said. 'Cheers.'

I wondered how she managed to understand Lindy so well without ever having met her.

Tam's skin was so healthy-looking it upholstered her face like an expensive fabric. Though sometimes when she smiled her mouth looked sort of horsy, her teeth a millimetre too big.

I felt scared and guilty even thinking it.

The brandy was snaking through me like a disco dance.

I finished one glass then poured another.

I was becoming the person I wanted to be.

'It isn't the first girlfriend he's had,' she said, stroking her fingers through the grass. Catching my confusion, she added, 'My father. I mean, he's even had a thing with a girl who came to help my mother after she had one of her weeping weekends. She was from an agency called Little Helpers.'

'In more ways than one,' I giggled. 'Wow, what a bitch though.'

'Yes. He seems to like women who work for him. It's like . . .'

'His dick is part of the attractive bonus package?'

'You've got it, Mona. You understand. Wait there,' she said and vanished again.

She'd gone up to her bedroom and turned the disco music on very loud. It whooshed through the sunlight and shimmied the leaves on the trees. When she came down, grinning, she stood before me with her arms outstretched. 'Dance,' she said, but not like it was a invitation, like it was an order demanding immediate ecstasy.

I found I could provide it.

I danced.

We galloped around the tree and twirled so hard we ripped up the lawn. I wiggled, making curves where I'd never had curves before. Delighted, I ran around on tiptoes like I was wearing high heels.

'What will you do that's remarkable, Mona?' she said panting, as we threw ourselves down on the grass.

'I'm gonna put a thousand-pound bet on this year's Derby,' I said.

The grass was more than green, it was thick and oily and sang like emerald paint, so bright and pure it was rubbing off on me skin.

'It's a plan. It's all worked out.'

As soon as I said it I knew this was now what I had to do.

She looked genuinely impressed.

'Well then, that Lindy is shortly going to have something to be very jealous about, isn't she?' she said and blew a slim ribbon of smoke in my face.

And I melted like butter in the amazing heat of the confidence she gave me, drinking more brandy and saying more contemptuous, sneering things until drunkenness overtook me and I was falling asleep against the tree.

vodka

It was that same Saturday night we held the first Miners' Social in the pub and I was standing at the bar with Phil the Flash. It was 10.30. p.m., the room was steaming with blokes, smoke in a swirling sheet overhead. We'd had quite a bit to drink, me on vodka, Slimline and lime, Phil on bitter.

I only drank Malibu with friends.

I'd managed to eat only one bag of crisps all day which gave me both a feeling of great joy and an unsteadiness like I was on board a ship.

The music was a fusion of disco and country and western. The lads were putting the disco on the jukebox and there was a fat woman paid to sing country live and loud into a microphone. Dad, who tonight was dressed as a proper barman in a snow-white shirt, shiny blue trousers and slim black tie, pulled at his cuffs and said there were more of them than us.

A lot of the people there were teachers and it was hilarious to see them in their freaky casual clothes. No wonder they had to become teachers, we laughed. All night the regulars had eyed the miners and their supporters like cattle, though this calm was deceptive; if you closed your eyes the sound in the room was like fighting and I liked the anger in the air. Perhaps we all sensed there could be a murderer among us.

I saw Dad wink at Debbie Courtney, who was alert and

giggling at the far end of the bar. I wanted to stub me cig out on her terracotta forehead, put a match to her beige hair.

'Oh, darling,' Phil goes and he reached for my cheek but missed and clipped the side of my nose instead. He was now so drunk his head hung like a donkey's and his mouth was puffed up and slurry like he'd just got back from the dentist's.

'Hey, Charlie,' Phil said, suddenly ignoring me and leering over the bar towards me dad and shouting above the rousing country that was tearing through the room. 'I've gorra joke for yer.' He pronounced it jerk.

'Go on,' said Dad, delighted.

'What happens if you play a country and western record backwards?'

'Dunno, Phil. What happens if you play a country and western record backwards?' Dad grinned.

'You find your dog, your truck gets mended and your woman comes back.'

I liked a man who could tell a joke, and I blushed with pride that this man was taking an interest in me. Still, my new girl person confidence meant I didn't have to show it, so I left them laughing and watched the room.

There were more women in the bar than usual. Cleo, who was with her new friends from the Labour Party, smiled over at Dad, sadly, as if now she noticed the stain in him. It was a smile of apology, like she'd just decided what she'd do with the rest of her life. When the talking got going these women leant forward on their bar stools, as if huddled round a cauldron, and Cleo hugged her knees with girlish excitement.

Earlier that evening, when we'd all be having our tomato soup and were watching the ITV news, she'd looked dreamily at Arthur Scargill and said softly: 'Hmm. It's the Brotherhood of Struggle.' PorkChop said: 'It sounds like a fucking puff band.' Then his mam stood up and said: 'Why do you all treat me like this? If you really want to know I'll bloody well tell you. I think it's 'onourable that the man's right in there when things aren't going to plan,' she paused, then with tears in her eyes continued saying more revolutionary things. I felt tearful too, and angry, and wanted to close the curtains and lock the door in case anyone were to see the terrible sadness emotions trembling through our room. Then there was a quiet coolness all around us as we listened to the sound of the sun fading our soft furnishings. Finally, she quivered and, calm now, said: 'If you are lucky enough to find somewhere you want to be, then you should be there.'

You couldn't help what you liked in a man. Or a woman for that matter. Women could fall in love with billy goats and honestly believe they were telly stars.

You could meet a crazy girl and truly believe her to be your saviour.

When I looked round, Dad was straining over the bar, his face close up to Debbie's.

Phil told me to stand up, then to turn round. 'What d'you weigh?' he said.

'Nowt.'

'You what?'

'Nothing. I weigh nothing,' I said, and could sense me voice going high and scratchy.

'OK, sidown, 'ow tall are yer?'

'Five feet two inches,' I goes.

'What colour are yer eyes?'

'Greeny brown.'

'OK. Good. You ever 'ad blonde 'air?'

'In another life perhaps.'

'No, silly, I mean, would you dye it?'

'If the money was right I might,' I glittered.

Then he said to put me hand up under me chin and smile, then to put a hand on me cheek and smile, then to cross me chest with the hand over one shoulder.

My nails were Plum Shimmer and especially filed.

Dad was watching by then, sly out of one eye. For a moment

he and I eyed each other like poker players. In that moment I wondered if Julie's murderer was in the bar. If Dad knew. He was too busy to speak but just his concentration on me was enough to give me a screeching headache.

I wondered if the full make-up look looked wrong.

Then Phil tapped his chin and asked Dad for a sheet of paper.

'Put yer 'and on there,' he goes, and I did. Then he asked Dad for a pen and goes, 'Spread yer fingers out,' and I did, and he started to draw round me hand, like when you're at school and bored. Then, when there was a pause in the crowds at the bar, I felt a stabbing on me shoulder and Dad's face bursting into mine.

'Don't act like a tart. D'you 'ear me. People don't like it.'

Then Dad goes to Phil: 'There's enough puffs in this bar tonight to open 'airdressers.'

'Aye, watch the bum bandits,' goes Phil, the man who I was soon to learn fancied himself as a poet.

No one was mentioning that it was not the bum bandits we had to worry about, but rather a man who liked teen-age girls.

Phil said to put me other hand on paper and he did the tracing again. I enjoyed the tickling of the pencil round the webby bit between me fingers. Then Phil took off his glasses, folded them over on the bar and started to make a little square in front of his eyes with his sausagy fingers.

I looked away and in the kitchen saw PorkChop making a roast tatty sandwich, picking cold potatoes out of oil in the roasting tin and thumping them down between slices of white bread. Sometimes I forced mesen to watch people eat. It was a kind of punishment.

I took a big swig of the voddy.

Strangely, though, crime made me less worried about food. You needed to be hollow to commit crimes. It was a requirement of the job. For women. You did not see fat women on Wanted posters. You could be fat and MISSING. But never fat and WANTED.

Phil goes to Dad to get us the same again and Dad goes: 'She's 'ad enough,' and just got Phil a pint. I saw a touch of the look of hatred in his eyes and when Phil turned away to look at the first of the miners speaking, Dad pointed a finger in me face and clenched his teeth.

OK, once, it was true, I woke up next to a man from our bar. I remember nothing, he was smiling, stroking the hair back from me forehead. It was morning, sunny, warm, and I was on his settee and I was naked. I still saw him in the bar sometimes but he was not there that night.

I left the wobbly starfish of fingers on the bar and went for a wander. As soon as I stood up I felt like I was falling over because of the drink. I banged into the table which had been put up for selling badges. A kindly woman leant over to steady me and asked if I was all right.

I wandered over to PorkChop and a group of blokes he was with. One of them, called the Turtle, perhaps because of his eczema or his scrawny neck or his too small eyes, goes: 'Did you 'ear what they found when they were looking for that missing lass?' and through the roar in the room suddenly everyone in this small group was listening.

The way some of the young men talked about the murderer reminded me uncomfortably of the way they spoke of sporting heroes.

The Turtle stood aside to let me in to hear his story. He shook his head and puts a look on his face like he was ready to drag out all the details. 'Well,' he goes, 'they'd asked five blokes to comb alongside of Black Beck, like. Just along where the lass lives. So they're going through all this long grass and stuff, and just when they'd got to flyover end and thought they'd found nowt and was gonna go off 'ome, then,' he paused to let his voice drop to a whisper, 'they sees this carrier bag. It was right full of wet soft stuff, like.' The Turtle stopped and lit up another cig. 'Anyways, so they poked at it with these rakes coppers gave 'em. They didn't open it but kept prodding it and looking, like. It appears there's all this red squelchy stuff inside.'

I got a pain in me head. The Turtle was going on about *summat dripping against the inside of the bag*. Then about *coppers*, then, *evidence*. I thought I might faint.

'When police come they won't touch it without rubber gloves on. They move towards it very slowly. Another couple of coppers hold back the crowds who've come to watch.'

He describes how *people keep coming out of their 'ouses when they know summat's 'appening*. I put both hands over me face which is red and burning like a fag end. I close me eyes and breathe, breathe, breathe.

Then he throws back his head and laughs.

'When they lift it up they see it's not evidence at all. It's a bag full of rotting old schoolbooks. The ones you write stuff down in. Turns out to be about a hundred red books and the red is the colour coming off of the card on the covers and the heaviness is 'cos they're all pulpy and rotten.'

All these men were around me, laughing.

Suddenly, I got the sense that before too long I was gonna be the kind of girl who went for older blokes. With money and cars, who bought all the drinks, took me to the seaside, drove drunk. Murdered me maybe, in a lay-by somewhere, up an alley, dumped me in a quarry or in a discarded rusting fridge.

The problem with boys was that they were wet clay; you'd leave fingerprints on their face, every smile you gave them got dug into their skin like a name in tree bark. Getting off with blokes like that, sex and stuff, was OK but anything more, I mean doing really exciting stuff, was like trying to light a fire with damp leaves.

For those things a murderous man or a sharp smart girl was better.

Breathe. Breathe. Breathe.

A miner's wife was up to speak. I listened. I liked her voice, soft and urgent. The way you'd like to imagine a true lover talking of their need for you. She spoke of hardship. How these blokes came into her living room, threw the furniture aside, rolled the carpet up and took it away in a van. She said how this was the first time she had ever spoken in public. I understood her because I too no longer wanted to feel fainty-hot and afraid, but longed to move in the cool air of a manly public life.

As I was going out the room Phil the Flash, who was still slumped at the bar, grabbed me. Oh, poor, weak, helpless men. He sucked on his fag and his voice was like mucky sea water rasping over pebbles. He still had the starfishy drawings of me hands in front of him and he points to them, and goes: 'Come and see me next Friday, Mona, at the Cinema Studio.'

'OK,' I goes, saying the words in a whisper too, though I didn't know what our conspiracy meant. I imagined the Cinema Studio in a black-and-white Sunday afternoon film, a place of lights and space and crescent-shaped steps.

'Promise me, darling,' he goes, his eyes fallen shut, his lips lolled open in a slobber.

'Promise,' I said and then for some weird reason I kissed him, wet and sucking on the side of his stubbled cheek.

'Keep it a secret,' he said.

'I know all about secrets,' I whispered and kissed him again.

'Oi,' I heard Dad say, as I went out the door. 'There's a nutter on the . . .'

Loose. Free. The midnight was blue as new jeans. It had been eleven hours now since I'd drunk brandy and danced with dear, dear Tamsin. How would she think of me now, away riding my bike drunkish with speed and the attention of men? Real men. How true that even ironing boards could feel desire.

I was fleeing, I was free.

With this feeling inside me I could ride into the graveyard to visit me mam. Or I could if I weren't dying of asthma, too drunk to remember the Ventolin, me chest splitting with the will of breathing. So instead I did some thick flat singing because I was drunkish, and the bike curled across the road like a crazy bird.

I did not like being alone. At night what sometimes happened was I dreamt me face was pressed up firm against this black iron grill, a gate maybe, or a railing. My head was too heavily caked with make-up to lift away from the painful, crushing ironwork, and the grill was too solid and heavy for me to push through to the other side.

For a punk girl this inner gloom would've been stylish, but for a disco lover it felt like failure.

The moon hung in a thin arc like the clip off of a fingernail. Passing Julie Flowerdew's house I could see the TV flickering though the curtains were closed. At the bottom of the flyover was a gully, a ditch of weeds and dry stalks which had been trampled down by the men. We used to slide down this snowy slope on biscuit-tin lids, or if we'd been out whoring we'd get a drop off above and crawl down with bent backs so no one in the neighbouring houses could see us.

What would Tamsin Fakenham think of that? Ha! I dropped the bike and walked along the dark gully. I could sense Tamsin near me, though surely she was several miles away. I walked bent because of the not breathing. There were no sounds only distant traffic. There was no sign of where exactly the books'd been found, but it was very close to Julie's house. The heat had baked the earth and cracked it up like dangerous ice, but when I sat down it was warmish and instantly I wanted to sleep.

I worried that now Lindy was gone from the pub I'd never be able to sleep again. To sleep with someone every night, as I had with Lindy those nights after me mam died, to be fitted warm into their holding arms always, it seemed such a perfect thing.

I could feel a heat on me neck, like Tamsin was breathing behind me.

The thing about silence was that it could make you feel you

were dissolving. I was always fizzing, fizzing in my forehead, my fingertips, my tongue, and when there was only silence I was like a common Disprin in a glass of clear water, dissolving, dying of breathlessness.

Eventually, this concentration made me see our mam and then feel very ill. I got up and walked a few yards, then kneeled down. I pressed me hands together and lifted me chin. Me prayers always started with 'Oh Lord' and then a list of schemes I wanted help with. They were always about being independent and successful and popular. About surviving.

Then I threw up, and the flare of sick bubbled and bleached my throat, then my nose and the backs of my eyeballs, but I felt better too.

When I lifted me head up this strange girl was pacing towards me. Then towering above me muscly and thick as an athlete. I was panicked with embarrassment for my shabby, cracked-up family who were only across the road.

I was sure she could smell them.

'I've been waiting for you,' she said angrily. 'For hours and hours.'

'I didn't know you were coming. You should've come into the pub. How did you get here? Did you walk from Goldwell?'

'No, stupid, I got a taxi.'

'Are you OK?'

'No, actually, no. I feel like a metropolitan American business-woman trapped in the life of a rural English spinster, if you must know.'

'I know, I know what you mean,' I said excitedly. She was wearing glossy red lipstick; Blame the Flame perhaps. She had wanted to come to the party. She'd longed to see what 'real life' was like. 'It's so true! We have to become who we truly *are*, not who others want us to be,' I babbled.

'Indeed. What's that smell?'

'What smell?'

'That awful bloody stink in the air.'

'Oh, that. That's Hoggins. It's an animal skin factory. I think I told you about it. It makes leather.'

'How simply dreadful.'

'Sorry.'

'Anyway, what you said about my father and his attractive bonus package penis is so true. I've been thinking about it. I mean, as Marx said, it's the bosses who do the fucking and the underlings who get fucked.'

I wanted to say something razor-sharp but nothing came to me.

'How did yer mam and dad get on at dinnertime?'

'It's none of your business,' she said furiously. 'How dare you pry into private family matters?' I mumbled apologies and then she softened slightly and said: 'I don't want to talk about it. I'll tell you another time. It was simply terrible.'

'OK. Sorry.'

'Men are so . . .' she said smiling, continuing to walk slowly, troubled, 'weak.'

'They are easily fooled,' I said. 'Women can beat them at their own game, because of the way they are so absolutely one-dimensional.'

'What are we gonna do?' she said. She had a silver halter-neck top on and shorts. Her breasts were like church bells and she saw me looking and smiled: 'Mostly fat,' she said.

'We have to make some money. That is the main thing,' I said quickly, feeling the words weakly evaporate into the night. 'If we are to have any purpose. We mustn't be needy. Or live in poverty. And if we are to have any chance of becoming who we truly are. That's the thing now, you see, isn't it, to have money and power? You have to be like your father, not like his *secretary*. To have a public life, that's the thing. To be known and recognised. No longer to be hidden away in private with *babies*. I mean, like my sister.'

'Oh, Mona, darling!'

'Blood, sperm, milk, hell! Women are forever hidden away in the darkness making or mopping up vile body juices!'

'Oh, Mona!'

'You see, we have to be publicly recognised for *something*, anything. Anything but be hidden and private and forgotten.'

'Kiss me, stupid.'

'Oh, Tam, I've missed you so . . .'

For a while there was just night and kisses. Then she said: 'If truth be told I'd be truly happy working with animals and helping old people. Elderly poodles in a third world country would suit me fine.'

'With a chest like that I'm sure you'd be in high demand.'

'I can't stay now. I've been waiting out here for you for ages and I simply can't bear the smell. But come to see me tomorrow.'

'Tomorrow.'

'Tomorrow.'

'Tomorrow.'

We said this over and over 'til we felt stoned with little kisses.

mint

When I arrived at 2.06 p.m. the next day I saw the van. On the side it said 'Northern Lights Theatre Company'. A woman got out, old with green baggy trousers, big hoopy earrings, flip-flops and her hair short and feathered. She hugged Mrs Fakenham at the high front door. Then two men with over-tight jeans and glossy hair slid open the side of the van and went into the house behind the women. They'd've made Dad laugh.

Five black bags of rubbish had been left on the roadside and a bonfire pyramid of wooden ladders, chairs and broken children's toys covered the far end of the drive.

The blinds were down. Like someone had died again.

I went into the orchard to see Willow. Really I was playing for time. I walked her round in circles in a daze. The reins slipped between me fingers because of the sweat. I stumbled. I'd had a few drinks to calm me but not many.

I thought of those delicious hexagonal coin push machines you get in arcades. That throat-catching tension as each coin slides nearer to the edge, mounding up, up, up. Gambling games understand this feeling of being right on the very edge.

In this slow Sunday daylight it seemed there would never be a minute of the day for the rest of me life when I did not remember that feeling of PorkChop over there in the distance and me burgling the quiet little house. The feeling was sealed in me like a shipwreck in a bottle. Perhaps crimes were an illness that needed a long period of recovery. Or perhaps they were a hangover that needed another strong quick fix to make you feel ready again.

I tied Willow to the gate and only the taut rein stopped her head from drooping to the floor. I was pretending to be engrossed in brushing her when Mrs Fakenham, the woman and the men came out the back door of the house. They were carrying three suitcases, a potted plant and two cardboard boxes. They got into the van. No one waved. They drove off. Then I was alone in the silence and I was shivering, at the point of dissolving.

I looked around for Paul or Ivy but perhaps they'd been allowed this Sunday off.

I kept brushing and polishing, me whole body bending into pony curves of muscle and bone. Being alone with secrets was a double desolation.

Then I heard screaming.

At first I thought it was to do with the burglaries and just in me head and I ignored it for a moment, but it was real and the sound was roaring and tearing. Then I saw this peculiar posh girl running towards me. She looked like she hadn't run before and her face was crunched with panic and concentration like someone doing the egg-and-spoon race. I gave one look then turned back and stared into scabby pony fur.

Tamsin. Like a face from a horror film.

'The fucking cat,' she said panting, pointing to the tree next to the stable. Expensive white shorts, a green T-shirt with a logo on, bare feet, a bracelet round her ankle. Her flesh had a baby's healthy swell. She was no lard pot sure, but those vital statistics might stretch from a delightful thirty-six to a saddening twenty-six, thirty-four; definitely more fattish than I would've been comfortable with.

'What?'

'Up the tree.'

'Oh.'

'It's gone crazy because of Mummy going, I imagine. I saw her from Daddy's office. She can't get down. Stuck. Look.'

'Yeh. I can see. It's scared,' I said and thought how Tamsin said all her words like she was singing them in the school play. I also feared she was one of those people who pretended to adore animals to disguise her dislike of people.

'Oh, *fuck*,' she said crisply, like she was crunching into an apple. 'I knew as soon as she was out the bloody drive something had to go wrong.'

'I'll get it.'

'No, don't, it's dangerous.'

'It's OK. I like dangerous,' I said.

To impress her had so quickly become my reason for getting up in the morning and now here was my chance. I noticed there was sweat coming out all over Tamsin, and it was glistening, silky, like juice from meat. I could even smell her.

I took my sandals off, walked over the hot stone and put one dirty foot on the cool green bark, the sole sliding on the dusting of lime. I was very scared of climbing. The tree was a thick sycamore. In summer it rained a sticky drizzle of sap over the roof of the stable.

With one hand I pulled myself up. Despite the sore thigh, and my shoulder which was aching and flaming hotly where Dad had poked me, I eased into the tree as smoothly as I had into the little house.

'Perhaps I should ring the fire brigade,' she called. 'Demand they send muscly men.'

'I'm OK,' I said. 'It's better we try and get 'er, she might panic. You need to be very light to do this, muscles are no good.'

'Don't you eat much?'

'I never eat if I can help it.'

'Perfect,' she said with a definite purr in her voice.

I was deep in the leaves.

With each move me bruised thigh moaned with a pain that

yelped right down to my feet. But it was cooler and there was a smell like ginger and in spite of the aching I was climbing quickly, flies butting my face. The terror of my second crime was pumping through me like sour liqueur.

'Be careful. You're delicate. Don't forget you're a girl.'

'But with a cruel joke for a name, don't forget. I'm all right. I used to do ballet.'

'Me too, but I got too fat, what happened to you?' she called up into the tree.

'It used to make me fall asleep. In the middle of a trot across the stage I'd come over all dozy.'

Below me I saw her smiling and then wiping a too-fleshy arm across her pink forehead. She was glowing with excitement. The tree seemed to rear up and meet my face; below, the ground was throbbing in an earthache.

'Maybe you should come down and I'll pay someone to do it. There must be professional cat-catchers. Dog-loving unemployed people with ladders.'

'I'll get it, don't worry, Tamsin. The unemployed can be very tricky about their ladders.'

'So I've heard.'

What would she do if I threw mesen to the ground?

Surely she would love me more?

I wished I had a cigarette and instead I breathed in the moist tree air like I was smoking it. The Ventolin was a long way off in the basket of the bike. On the horizon was the glossy brown worm of a river. Twenty miles away in this direction was the sea. I saw two church steeples and four red dots of combine harvesters. I tried to imagine what my country would be like after the nuclear attack. I hooked me legs over a branch that rocked with me weight. Brushing flies away, I lay me flat chest down, rested me chin on the bark and, camouflaged like that, stretched me hands out to where the cat had frozen in porcelain terror. I could just about touch her. I was in danger now, but I cared not.

I heard a crack but the branch did not break.

Far away I thought I could hear her screaming.

'Here, pussy, pussy,' I whispered and the branch rocked.

With me fingertips I felt the cat's muscled neck and then in a rush, flailing, I lunged and grabbed her towards me. Far away I could see Tam bouncing in a thrill, holding out her arms towards me. Through the hoop of her sleeve I saw her armpits, raw glossy pink. She was expecting something. She loved seeing me in danger, I realised later.

And because of this I decided to throw mesen out the tree. When I was about ten feet off the ground I held the cat to me chest, closed me eyes and lurched forwards.

After the knocking stabs of pain, the crashing of twigs, disco lights in me head, I was on the ground bleeding and Tamsin had her brown arms, her varnished, upholstered, expensive skin, wrapped around me.

'Oh, God. How damaged are you?'

'How long have you got?' I said with a wink in my voice. I was alive.

'As long as you want, darling,' and she kissed me, a gentle cool fingertippish touch on the lips. 'Let me get you some tea.'

'I need a cigarette. And a brandy,' I said.

Our second kiss lingered there like a dab of cool water.

In the kitchen, as she put plasters on the cuts, she offered me fresh coffee. I said, for a bad joke, I'd prefer stale tea. I felt like I'd been shot in the head and more of my skin was torn than I had at first realised. Still, Tam was mightily impressed.

'My father's so disappointed in me. He wanted me to be a war reporter or a doctor, that kind of thing, but I'm scared even going on a ferry, and swoon at the sight of blood. I haven't turned out at all like I should have.'

I knew that whatever was wrong with Tamsin neither of her parents wanted to be around it. They'd both fled from her.

They'd sent her away, and then when she'd returned they'd gone away. She knew this too.

Even the cat would vanish the next day and not be seen again for the entire summer.

'Never mind. You do have wonderful tits, a most enviable asset.'

'I suppose they'll get used to me,' she said sadly.

'I suppose they will,' I said, not knowing if she meant her tits or her parents.

The warm kitchen smelt musty, with a thick lick of rottenness, as though the bin had not been emptied. Next to the fridge, milk in a bottle had sunk to a dark cream. On a noticeboard was a picture of Sadie the dead daughter. She was smiling, looking happy and not too thin. She was, in fact, an infuriatingly attractive girl and I had to look away, feeling, for some reason, strangely angry. There were plates piled up round the sink, unwashed, and dirty plants which had shed leaves deadened by the heat down on to the draining boards. There was a pile of wet towels steaming on the stove.

I imagined this old womby smell rubbing off Mrs Fakenham in damp balls and I shuffled my feet. I saw that the cat had five bowls of food, each day a fresh one on the floor, without the collecting of the old bowls.

'If you're wondering why the kitchen looks like that of a student squat, well, it's because Mummy's been on a twenty-four-hour lightning strike. What I didn't tell you was that when they got back from the Watermill Restaurant yesterday, just after you left, it turned out Daddy had told her he was leaving.'

'No!'

'Oh, yes. And what's more he's told her he's in love with the sexretary.'

'Oh, God. I'm so sorry, Tam.'

We smiled at one another.

'You're the toffee round my apple, Mona.'

'You're the batter round my fish.'

We smiled again, harder. Then Tam got up and sighed: 'Mummy says I can get Ivy in to clean up, but I haven't got round to it yet.'

The sight of the cat food suddenly made me hungry.

'So when's he off? Your father, I mean.'

'Oh, he's already gone.'

'Where?' I gasped, barely able to contain my excitement.

'To live with the sexretary in Whitehorse.'

'It's all happened very quick,' I exclaimed, biting me lip and blinking fast.

'He's had a *carpe diem* moment, apparently. It's Latin, Mona, and it means damn everyone else and do what the hell you like. My mother and father swear by it.'

'Sounds rather fun,' I said smiling, but she ignored me.

'Though I can understand his desire to get out of this stinking place.'

I'd never been looking around the rest of the house, never been invited to, but I imagined many cupboards, cellars, cobwebs, moth-eaten jumpers and milky larders. Places where Ivy was too frightened to clean.

The floors of the corridors were heavy stone and the doors were high and solid wood. In one corner of the kitchen was a witchy rocking chair with a worn-out cushion. It seemed to rock even when no one was sitting in it. Hanging from the high lampshade were two varnished curls of flypaper, pitted with flies like raisins in toffee. I thought then if dear Tamsin did offer me anything to eat I definitely wouldn't take it.

No wonder smart Mr Fakenham had done a flit.

There was a pile of money on the table and a sheet of instructions in Mrs Fakenham's stuttering handwriting, the ink faint, breaking down in the middle of words.

Oh, please, Lord, save me from mad old women.

I looked at the pile and quickly estimated at least a hundred pounds.

I noticed someone had left a dog-end drowning in a bowl of muesli.

'So you're looking for a job?' she asked.

'I'm not any more. I'm not bothered about a job. I don't want one,' I said. I wondered later, when everything was over, why I never told her in the beginning about my crimes. From day one I felt I was related to her, and I realised later this was exactly the reason I never quite trusted her.

'Are you revising, Mona?'

'No, not at all. I 'aven't done one spot of revision. Don't intend to. How's your . . .'

'Don't. That's the last word on the subject. I won't ask you any more about your revision and you don't ask me about mine.'

Just her presence made me braver. She put the tea in front of me in a cup and saucer and handed over a packet of cigarettes.

'It's herb tea. Mint. Mummy drinks it to relax her. I don't know if it works. Do you like it?'

'It's all right. Thanks.'

The herb tea tasted like summat you'd drink by accident when you were very drunk.

'You're so brave. And you've been so kind to dear Willow,' she said. I smiled, blew smoke down into me cup, in a careless masculine way. I couldn't tell if she was patronising me or not. I didn't want her to think I cared about ponies. I knew for sure that her words were like the church clothes Lindy wore – they did not in any way show the person she really was.

Rich, successful people never reveal what they think. This is a key to success.

She asked me if I wanted any food and then started making me a sandwich. She put four After Eight mints between two slices of bread and handed it to me, seriously, without a trace of humour.

'I don't mind looking after her,' I said in a gobble, the bread

87

and mint making a gluey brown paste in my mouth. 'Though, of course, I'm not interested in ponies any more.'

This was the first thing I'd eaten for many hours. The strangeness of the food laughed away the sin, which was of course (smart Tamsin), the idea.

She wiped her hands wearily over her face (her hands were attractively bony, and had none of the slight fattishness of the rest of her). She seemed tired and upset.

'I'm so glad not to be at that bloody school any more.'

'Me too,' I said through a mouthful of goo.

'You know, darling, they wouldn't call me Tamsin. They used to call me Tamla Motown just because I liked very different music to the rest of them.'

In truth, I thought she'd got off rather lightly; at our school they'd have called her Tampax.

She had a few tough briars chewed into her hair near the skull. She noticed me looking and made her slender fingers into a wide comb and dragged them from her scalp to her shoulder.

'What's wrong?' she snapped.

'Your hair looks painful,' I said. This was an instant and honest statement, there was something about her body which seemed to be hurting.

Get thee to a nunnery and thus heal thyself.

'OK then,' she said, after considering my face carefully, and with an angry snap walked to the kitchen drawer and removed a pair of heavy iron scissors, the sort made to cut rind off bacon and tails off oxen. She came towards me slowly, the blades open like a beak. The scissors were as long as my forearm. Sunlight sparkled on one blade like a star. Her footsteps were heavy on the stone floor, and regular as the striking of a clock. Then, standing a foot away from me, she began to cut into the hair. The scissors made a rusty crunch so she had to pull on the reluctant hank of hair and saw. There was a creak before the thick slow snip. After several more raw clips the scissors seemed to loosen, and the creak became a gentle scrape.

Gradually the hair became a blonde nest on the floor.

The cutting was going closer and closer to her scalp 'til some of the hairs were no longer than an inch. Where the iron blade rested on her neck was an angry red groove. She lifted her hair up high to cut it and a nobble of skull bone was revealed.

I suddenly thought how easy it would've been to kill her then. Just a quick thump of her mother's marble rolling pin (which lay cradled on a pine stand by the sink) against that pale head. One lock of hair hung like a tail from the neck of her T-shirt. Her face was changing, becoming less sophisticated, more childlike, less disco. She looked like she had donned a disguise.

She looked ungirled.

I knew then that we would be together and it would be extraordinary.

'Am I right in thinking you've got a sister?' she said, laying the scissors gently on the kitchen table. The ends of her short shorn hair were curling up giving her the rough boyish charm of an angel.

'Yeh. I told you all about her. Lindy. Tattooed tits, heavenly arse, you remember,' I replied, puzzled.

'And are you the brave one and Lindy the timid one, same as Sadie and me used to be?' she said, not acknowledging our previous conversation but instead lifting transparent single hairs from her shoulders and letting them float in light curls to the floor.

'No, I'm the scared one, and she's the brave,' I said, though I didn't know if this was true.

The room felt cold. I looked round for a clock as I suddenly wanted both to leave immediately and stay for ever.

I was noticing the way the left side of her hair was up much closer to her ear than the right side, so it looked like she had one leg shorter than the other. I smiled to mesen because this was rather cute and then I saw her look darken in annoyance.

'What a way to spend a Sunday,' I smiled.

I knew I should go but was too scared. Surely the burglary showed on me like measles.

'When's your mam back?' I said. I noticed how strong her newly revealed shoulders were, damp and firm like a swimmer's.

'It's hard to tell. She's gone to be in a play. Last night during the crisis she called up her old lost friends in the theatre and, amazingly, she's persuaded them to let her be an understudy in a play in Scarborough.'

'Brilliant.'

'At least the role's appropriate this time. Some mad old English bag abandoned by her lying husband. Of course, it could all be another of Mummy's fantasies. For all we know she could be smoking and drinking gin in a seaside B & B.'

'How long's she gone for?'

'Well, assuming she *is* in a play in Scarborough, then if she falls out with everyone like she used to, then she could be back in two days. If she falls in love with the director, like she equally often used to, then she could be away for years.'

'Oh, blissful freedom!'

'The day after tomorrow when I've finished dealing with all the household duties, I'm supposed to be travelling to stay with this fat old auntie but I'm not going,' she snorted. 'She's about ninety stone, with inch-thick eyebrows.'

'But won't they investigate? Won't they check if you've arrived?'

'No, stupid. I've thought it through very carefully. This morning I've rung and told the aunt that I need to do extra revision so am spending a couple of weeks with a school friend at her home in the country. My parents would've been suspicious, as I don't have any friends at the school, but my aunt thinks it's all rather jolly.'

'But what if . . .'

'*If*, which is unlikely, Mummy or Daddy remember about me long enough to ring my aunt, she'll have to tell them, I suppose.

But by then it'll be too late. And as long as we're careful, and don't answer the door or phone and stay well hidden, they wouldn't know where to find me anyway.'

'Tra-la!'

'I know, it's marvellous, isn't it? I should work for MI5.'

'So, what are you really going to do, Tam?'

'Stay here with you. All summer long.'

I knew it was true.

When you hear the attack warning, you and your best friend must take cover at once.

The sunlight made the moment seem suspended, our words as light as the dust which rolled in the afternoon air. I was getting a headache. It seemed to be brought on by the powerful brown smell of rot which hummed around the kitchen. It was a similar smell to the rawhide factory. I noticed all the windows were firmly shut despite the heat. Suddenly, I had to have water and I wandered to the sink and pulled the taps on into a noisy gush. A great tent of water hammered down into the bowl. I put my hurting head low into the sink and slapped handfuls over me face.

I could feel her behind me watching. I was still bleeding on my shoulder and forehead.

When I felt better I went back over to the kitchen table and sat down, the water running over me cheeks and down me neck like tears.

'No, really. What are you really gonna do with the summer?'

'Oh, I've got a plan,' she said and tapped the side of her nose and smiled. 'Is your arm hurting badly?'

'No, it's OK,' I said, though I realised I'd been rubbing at an ache all the time I'd been talking.

'Your hair looks good. It shines,' I said. 'D'you wanna see in a mirror?'

'We don't have any. Mirrors.'

'Good idea,' I said immediately. I knew instinctively this was the tip of a conversation I didn't want to have.

I knew one of the things women hated most was the sight of other women being looked at. This was why women hated models and Page 3. Jealous.

Or maybe it was the heat flash. Maybe the government had now ordered the removal of all household mirrors. Very possible.

'Sadie was obsessed with viewing her disgusting dying body from every angle in all the mirrors in the house. In the mirrors she saw a blubber pot. My mother threw them all out when Sadie finally slipped away,' she said with a smile in her voice.

'Oh,' I said.

The phrase *slipped away* made me think of a successful burglar, a hero in the annals of crime. Or a callous boyfriend. In my mind thieves and cruel lovers definitely had something in common.

When people asked about me mam, *if* they ever did, I never said *slipped away*. I just bounced the word DEAD.

'Yours looks rather lacklustre,' she said, smiling. 'Your hair.'

'Lack lucre more like, I'm broke,' I said coolly, with a gangster's smile. I would reveal to her the box of saved-up money later.

'Here,' she said, not laughing at my joke but handing me the heavy iron scissors from the table. 'You'll feel much better. Changing your style is a good cure for poverty.'

Though my shoulder blazed with pain I cut into the hair purposefully. Maybe because of the heat this cutting of hair changed the room and everything in it, like the taking off of clothes.

My brown hair looked grubby against her blonde.

Where hers had made a fluffy girly pile mine looked like a seedy barber's sweepings.

I cut the side strands with careful snips, measuring them in line with the furry pads of my earlobes. In time my neck felt cool and embarrassed.

'You're wonderful,' she whispered, pushing the shearings with her foot, edging the piles of blonde and brown hair side by side. 'I adore the way you'll do *anything*. I was really so terribly impressed with you risking your life for the poor puss. Now we'll be friends for ever.'

Instantly, our mingled hair looked criminal. Like wigs torn off and flung by fleeing raiders, or the erotically tossed disguise of strippers.

'Have you got any real drink?' I said. I felt loose. Ready.

'Real drink?' she said surprised, like she'd forgotten the brandy we'd drunk under the tree.

'Like Malibu or vodka.'

'Indeed, I will change for cocktails,' she said and went out of the room.

Far off down the hall I heard her feet running.

Then above were faint steps like jackbooted squirrels dancing in the attic.

I felt we were very alone.

She was right. For her I would do *anything*.

After a long time she came down wearing full disco gear, her make-up like lights on glass and her body frosted with a glitter of clothes.

'You look very, alive,' I said, dazzled by her TV beauty. I wondered if we were going to dance again.

'I hope that I can get that woman Ivy for tomorrow. Then the kitchen will look so lovely and clean,' she said smiling.

'I like your outfit.'

'Thank you. I do try. I think alive and clean is important, don't you?' she said. We were speaking like we had just met at a society ball. 'At school when they'd bored of calling me Tamla Motown they used to call me Disco Queen.'

I'd never asked her what had gone wrong at school, since Mr Fakenham had referred to problems she'd been having. Instinctively, however, I knew it had to do with the fact that no one liked her.

'That's good.'

'Oh, it wasn't a compliment. I read *Vogue* when they read *NME*. I was trying to be like Sadie. I was very posh. A red lipstick person. They didn't like me for that. Come, let's go into the sitting room.'

'Just on your lips or all over?' I said, following her down the dark corridor.

'Just the face, though they still found it hilarious.'

The sitting room was white and green, with so much window it was like being in the endless open air. Above the fireplace hung a large photo of Tam, Sadie and Mr and Mrs Fakenham: full colour, softly focused, smiling.

The nuclear family before the war.

She gave me two glasses and asked me what drink I wanted from a silver trolley. She said I should have a double because I'd already had double the excitement of a normal day. I chose. Tamsin poured a vintage brandy mixed with Bacardi. The smell was worse than normal, a kind of medicine, and it was soaking into all the richness of the room as though through a Christmas cake.

It was nearly evening and I was calming down, forgetting. Me lips tingled, me throat burned, I wanted it never to be night again. She poured me more straight away. Oh, I like it here, I like it, I thought. My fingers touched my neck and my new cut shocked me. I played with the jagged edges of hair. My new identity should keep the police off of me for another few days at least, I thought. I sighed with cruel adult cool.

She was folded in a chair, her knees up near her busty chest, her white hair curled and frizzed. A few minutes ago it looked like a knot of sheep's wool barbed to a wire but it was changing now into the lush curls of a golden retriever.

In the sitting room it seemed like we had lived together for many years. That this was our home. That soon there would be a photo of Tam and me smiling in technicolour above the fireplace.

'Thanks. That's better. Are you gonna miss your mam and dad then? It'll be strange being all alone,' I said, pulling at the back of my head with a finger and thumb.

'I want us to have music. Music and dancing is what we need,' she said, gazing around the room not listening to me. Then she looked over and nodded, 'But I've got plenty to be getting on with.'

'What's this plan then?'

'I can't possibly say, honeybunch,' she goes.

Her words were like tinfoil; they shone and they covered things up. I spent a few minutes pleading with her to tell me because like Lindy I knew she wished to be begged for information.

'Well, did you see that money on the kitchen table?' As she said this she reached over and poured my glass full again. 'Well, that's for painting the house. We're going to cancel the painter who's starting next week, paint the house ourselves and keep the money.'

We.

She smiled at me over the rim of her glass. Like this was such a brave plan.

'There'll be a cancellation charge,' I snorted, disappointed. 'And we won't get paint at cost. And we'll 'ave to buy brushes and stuff so it could come to more in the end.'

'I know, ten per cent, I checked. I've costed it all. Plus once all this muck is cleared we'll sack the servants, and supplement our income with the wages that Mother's left.'

'Do you know 'ow to paint?' I said. I felt anxious for Ivy and Paul and didn't want to ask any more about their fate.

'Er, no, that I do not know,' she said, and I laughed so suddenly the brandy spilt from me mouth, because she said it in her dad's gruff managerial voice. 'But I can assure you that we will fully furnish ourselves with all the skills required before undertaking the task.'

She leant forward laughing and I saw down her T-shirt her white breasts braless and swinging.

I closed my eyes and lay back on the sofa.

'Be careful not to bleed on our furniture,' she said sternly. 'It's calfskin and very expensive.'

Then she picked up her guitar and was patting the strings.

Her skin seemed no longer boiling red, but white and cold.

My darlingg you lurk wundurfool toniiiite.

'I like your "Wild Thing",' I said.

'What's "Wild Thing"?' she said with a snap in her voice like a sneer.

'That song. The one you're always playing.'

'Oh. I don't know what that is. I usually just play disco records. This tune is the only thing anyone's ever showed me how to play on the guitar.'

And with that she put her cool candle fingers to the chords and started, biting her lip with concentration, to play 'Wild Thing'.

water

In true crime stories what you should be given are the many cool days, weeks, months of tedium: of toast-making and tea-brewing, in between the furnace moments of blood-boiling criminal activity.

And the throat-catching moments when you feel yourself stepping off a coastal shelf, sinking, suddenly, sickeningly into deeper trouble.

It was teatime on Monday 1 June and Lindy was in jogging bottoms, her hair scrapped back in a tight ponytail. She looked at me as if to say, *What are you wearing?*

I had a woollen hat on to cover me new hair and though I knew she suspected something she stayed silent. She could never bear to acknowledge there was anything noticeable about me. All her curls from the wedding had gone and the blonde bits in her hair'd gone frizzed orange and brittle so she looked clownish.

I felt delighted she was looking so ugly.

'Thanks for coming,' she said solemnly. 'I wanted you to be the first to know. That's why I telephoned you.'

When I put my arms round her for a fake hug, I felt the bumps of her aged spine. She leant into me like an old person, curling her back, stretching her neck and offering a dry cheek for a kiss. Her white foundation smelt damp, like wet pottery. Against my chest her tits felt deflated and saggy, like balloons a few days after the party.

Ha!

Not even a desperate murderer would pick her out from the crowd.

Her life was private, sticky, menstruating, lactating, ovulating.

Soon the menopause would come galloping round the mountain towards her.

The room smelt of TV.

Siouxsie and David rushed up to me shouting, 'White rabbits, Mona, white rabbits,' because it was the first of the month.

'So when's the bloody woman taking her leave?' I said, trying to make it sound snide and ironical in a Fakenhamish way.

'We don't know. Dad just said she'd told him the other night, after that Miners' Social in the pub, and she would be gone soon.'

'Oh.'

'She said she'd realised when she was listening to the miners that she'd changed. She was no longer the person she used to be blah, blah, blah. That she felt a solidarity with the miners' wives that she didn't think Dad understood blah.'

In truth, at first I felt fine. I had perfected a way of not caring about feelings.

As we talked Shred watched us miserably. He was sad about Cleo leaving. In his sunshot world we were all attached to summat, like the electric rudder on a bumper car, and he could not imagine those for whom the car was chugging out of the fairground and off over the rubble.

'She's packed. She's 'ad 'er bags packed for a few weeks Dad said.'

'Sensible, I suppose,' I said. 'She'll need a pit helmet and a canary.'

Shred smiled at me sadly. Shred had a new job at the council and his tar-black hair was gelled down like a painted busby on a toy soldier. Shred had earned his name when his hair had been marmalade-coloured.

'Can you still crimp it?' I asked and sighed; how shabby their little terrace was compared to the high glory of the Fakenham house.

'Not for work, no, we don't think so. Too much of a risk. But for weekends, yes,' Lindy said proudly.

'I like your suit too, Shred,' I said and he undid the jacket and gave us a twirl. The suit made him look small and plasticky. He'd got his bullet belt on. He'd got cowboy boots on and the leather strand with David's first tooth on round his neck. In his ear he still had the tiny bone earring. 'You could go to a disco in that. It's suave.'

'He won't be going to no disco!' Lindy yelled. Shred sloped off.

She was proving very easy to provoke.

'You all right?' Lindy said when Shred was out of the room. If I was a cat I would've arched me back and bristled. 'You seem shorter. And you look pale. And really tired.' She gave me the look of sorrow, as though she was certain my life was to contain many terrible things. 'It's just you look real grey. You eating? Are you sure you don't want to stay? You're not gonna go all bony again, are you?' Lindy put her chin on her hand and leant forward.

I shook me head and looked away. Tam was so lucky her sister was dead.

'And another thing,' she said, shaking her head. 'You know that fucking Debbie Courtney?'

I nodded. She smiled. I was sure I didn't want to hear what she was about to say. I knew from the way her eyes were shining bright that she had saved this up. She smiled even wider. The silence boomed like a fanfare.

'Well,' she said, flicking open the lid of her fag packet. 'Well. She's moving in!'

'To the pub?' I gasped, unable to conceal my emotions for the first time in a year.

'Yep. And,' she said, wide-eyed with delight at my dismay, 'with her two kids. *Two kids! Boys!* Can you imagine our dad with two small boys around the house all day? I mean, look how long it's taken him to even *talk* to PorkChop.'

'Oh.'

'And have you seen that woman's sperm?'

I looked at her confused. How much worse could this story get?

'Have you? Have you noticed? She's a fashion hazard. I haven't seen a perm like that for years. Make sure you keep your distance or you might catch a bad hairstyle,' she said, and then smiled her most vicious big-sister smile: 'If you haven't already, of course.' Then she patted my woollen hat and walked out the room.

Bitch.

I remained watching the sun sparkling the dust for a while. Lindy had taken her net curtains down too, though it was odd for a former anarchist to act so swiftly on government advice. Outside it was clear and sunny but the windows were dappled with sandy dirt and so smeared and dusty that everyone walking by seemed the same: grey-haired, haggard, wifely.

I wished she'd offer me a drink of lager and lime, or voddy like she sometimes did. I thought of the small bottle of Southern Comfort I had in me bag ready to drink before bed. I longed to be drunkish.

'Is PorkChop off with her?' I asked, when she returned.

'Doubt it,' she said, smoking hard on the stub end of her fag. 'I mean, would you want that soft tub of lard with you if you were embarking on a new life?'

'Yeh, I guess not.'

I wished they'd put some music on.

Tam was surely right about the despair of Lindy and the dependent life.

'Did the police find anything?' I asked later.

'What?'

'Along Black Beck.'

'Oh, I dunno. I've not had the radio on,' she said bored, as though a missing, maybe murdered, girl was a very obvious and tedious topic of conversation.

'Do you think there's any hope?' I said.

'I'm not interested,' she said firmly. I knew she was dismayed and amazed she'd acquired no starring role in the drama. 'We've got our own problems to worry about, don't you think?'

In silence we focused on our great misery and misfortune.

We were quiet for a long time.

There were piles of ironing tilting on all the chairs in the room and I thought how later I'd tell Tam that being pregnant struck me as a damn good excuse for a holiday. How she'd laugh.

It went on like this for a while. Lindy then made a long speech about how I should get a job with her at Frink's.

'I'll let you know,' I said wearily. At Frink's they had hand-written signs around the glass bottles of cough mixture which said: *Nice to look at, nice to hold, but if you break it we call it SOLD!*

'We should get her a leaving present,' Lindy said. 'I'll get it and you'll give me half the money.'

'OK,' I said, not knowing if she was joking. I was losing the scant ability I once had to judge people correctly.

Where did parents go when they went away? I imagined a great transportation terminal, zinging with fluorescent strip lights, where they all gathered, clutching suitcases, their dream destinations scribbled on the scraps of cornflakes packets. I thought of Mrs Fakenham in her seaside B & B with her potted plant. I pictured Mr Fakenham in a tiny kitchen at the other side of Whitehorse starching his white shirts by candlelight.

That afternoon I'd been into the arcade and seen a new poster on the wall saying 'MISSING'. It was black and white and so damn ugly, her looking all spotty and fattish, that I was sure many people thought she'd deserved to be slaughtered just because of the way she looked. If only they'd put out a different photo, slimmer, more smiley, people might've responded. As it was she looked like she had no money. She looked weak and dependent. Therefore, it was no surprise no one was wondering where she was except me: at the bottom of Black Beck or under a pile of pallets in a factory.

I knew I really should be thinking about Cleo but for some reason it was easier to think about Julie Flowerdew.

Then Lindy went by and I smelt a spicy stroke of Poison. She collected the tiny green samplers, which you only got given if you looked smart and had no kids with you. She used half a sample a day, morning and night. I sprayed some on once in a shop but it was like fly spray.

Debbie Courtney in the pub! Now it was decided, I would never return.

A lorry rumbled by outside and the windows shook like corrugated iron.

Cleo would soon be gone and I felt I was set apart from all of this for ever.

Their sadness emotions would never touch me.

'How's the 'orse?' she said when she came back in munching a biscuit.

'Lame. I think she might 'ave to be put down.' I'd slipped into this way of being with Lindy permanently; of making everything seem worse than it was. Like drinking, lying, robbing and not eating, it made me feel better. She seemed so much happier when she thought my life was going extremely tragically.

I noticed Lindy had a new photo of me mam in a decorated china frame on her new sideboard unit.

'That's a nice photie,' I said. She turned and smiled at it.

'I like to look at it,' she said quietly. 'I'll get you a copy if you want.'

I nodded, then asked for a glass of water.

'It's nearly a year,' I whispered.

'Feels like yesterday,' she said, still looking at the photo. 'In fact, it'll probably always feel like yesterday.'

For a while we sat there thinking of our mam.

When Shred came down, he was tall in his inky jeans and ripped black T-shirt, his hair sticking up again like he had a finger in a socket. When he was sitting in his chair, Siouxsie and David went and climbed up on his knee. For a while everyone was as quiet as animals, grazing on the silent TV.

A wildlife film was on, showing a pack of felines ripping apart a bloody carcass.

Tyres rubbering over tarmac were like the rumble and hiss of waves.

Our lips were apart, our eyes wide, loving, loving the screen.

It felt like we were praying, for the safe, sunlit lives of the blondes on the adverts.

If you are lucky enough to find somewhere you want to be, then you should be there, Cleo had said.

chilli

So there I was a-knocking on her door.

'And so punctual!' she said, flinging the high door open and stretching her arms wide. 'Come in, darling. I've prepared you some brunch.'

I walked in and put Lindy's tattered tartan suitcase (with the punk rock stickers) by the wooden umbrella stand. I'd packed as though for a month in a holiday camp; a camera loaded with film, summer dresses, shorts, a bikini, high-heeled shoes, a couple of records and enough face creams, sun lotion, razors, brushes, make-up, cotton wool and perfume to beautify a thousand 'small almond' faces. I'd also packed Julie's blue T-shirt that Mrs Flowerdew had given away in the jumble, and my box of saved-up money.

'It's an amazing house, Tam,' I whispered, for it was even more wonderful inside the front than the back.

'Oh, I guess so. If you fancy living like Charlotte bloody Brontë.'

The floor inside the door was patterned with black, white and brown tiles and ahead the carpet was a silvered meadow of dewy grass. The curtains were thick and shiny as quilts. Oil paintings showed hunting scenes and oblong pigs. On low mahogany tables ornaments and little silver boxes shone. In front of me, at the bottom of the great fan of stairs, like an oily puddle of black paint, was a baby grand piano.

'Don't look so confused, darling, she was a writer. It's a *joke*. She lived in this dreary parsonage with her glum father and her weird sisters. And she never got to meet any boys, and she went on and on about it in all these hilarious bloody novels.'

Tam had an excitable parentless twinkle in her eye. She had the tape measure round her neck like a fashion decoration. Early that morning I had telephoned and detailed my hopeless situation and she had told me to fear not, but to arrive on the dot of 11.00 a.m. She'd sounded thrilled.

'*Quelle horreur!*' I said, but Tam was now sashaying off down the corridor, swinging in one hand the blue bottle of bleach. She moved with the swagger of a model slinking down the catwalk, and all she needed to complete the look was a little pug on a diamanté leash.

Dog-like I followed her into the kitchen. The room smelt so delightfully of fresh baking that I expected to find a rosy-cheeked grandma in a spotted headscarf skipping around with a wooden spoon.

'I asked Ivy to come in and clean up and do the shopping ready for your arrival,' she said, seeing me sniffing the air. 'I've told her we're spending the day together revising. The poor little creature's even baked you some fresh bread. I'm hopeless as a hostess but I guess I'll learn. Now that I've got you to look after.'

'I'm easy to care for. Just crack open a bottle of gin and throw in the odd scrap of dry toast.'

'It's so awful being a woman,' she said, sitting herself up on one of the kitchen surfaces and lighting a cigarette. 'And being expected to do all this cooking and cleaning and scrubbing and polishing. No wonder women all go doolally.'

'It's a good job you've got Ivy.'

'Hmm.'

'Have you heard from your mam? Has she started doing the play?'

'Though, of course, after the triumph of communism,' she

continued, ignoring my question, 'well, then women won't just be in the kitchen. They'll be able to do absolutely everything. They'll be working down the mines and on building sites. They'll be dustbin women and armed killers and sewage workers.'

'Oh, yippee. I can't wait.'

'I mean it, stupid. You wait and see. Imagine how grateful poor old Charlotte Brontë would've been for those opportunities.'

'I just mean I'd rather lay around on the settee looking at magazines.'

'Well, on your fat nylon arse be it. God, Mona, don't you know communism is all about helping *your* sort of person? I mean, people like *me* are fine. It's people like *you* who'll be liberated.'

I took a fag and, exhausted after only five minutes in the house, sat down at the kitchen table and rubbed at my aching head. Tam made harsh angry sucks on her cigarette and sighed dramatically.

After a good long while she got down and took from her back pocket a pair of yellow rubber gloves which she pulled up her arm with an angry snap.

She started banging about throwing down pans, clattering cutlery and slamming shut the fridge door without saying a word.

'Do you need any help?' I said, but she ignored me.

Eventually, she produced a plate from the oven and said: 'Here, I prepared this earlier. Eat. Then I'll show you to your room.'

It was an incredible thing. Hidden deep in a mound of Smash mashed potato was a nest of melting liqueur chocolates, huddled like baby mice. To give it that required scorching taste she'd dusted the pile of food with a thick layer of chilli powder.

'What is it?' I asked as politely as possible.

'It's a chilli-chocolate bomb, stupid. I invented it. I hope you like it.'

I ate it.

'It's marvellous, darling. Well done.'

It was indeed the sort of food the English nation would have to get used to eating once the planet had gone atomic, the Emergency Feeding Plan was implemented and the little plastic spoons were distributed.

'It's yummy, pumpkin,' I enthused again. I noticed she had a rather disgusting habit of smoking while I was eating. She rested her fag on the edge of my plate and watched the ash crumble into the food.

'Now for the grand tour,' she said, walking out of the kitchen. 'Come on, follow me.'

'Do you mind me coming to live with you?' I asked as I trailed after her up the stairs, chewing on the chocolate potato goo and dragging my tartan suitcase behind me. She was still wearing the yellow rubber gloves and her hands flashed by her sides like a pair of attendant canaries.

'You wouldn't be here if I minded, would you, stupid?'

'There was just no way I could be at home now Cleo's left,' I continued breathlessly, hurrying to keep up with her. 'If you'd ever had the misfortune of seeing my stepbrother you'd understand.'

'In fact, I expected it. I'm sure that Cleo woman ran off with the miners, and my lascivious father started loving the dumb sexretary simply so we could be together. There is a divine meaning to all these things, Mona, believe it.'

'Father agreed I needed a few days to absorb the changes.'

I'd started calling me dad *Father* so that he too sounded like a character in a book.

When we got to the top of the stairs she turned right and stopped.

'This is the master bedroom. Scene of many masterful acts of hatred, loathing and betrayal. There's the en suite bathroom.'

I stood in the doorway panting, looking where her yellow rubber finger pointed. An enormous oval bed was spread over with a glossy floral bedspread which matched the curtains. Through the bathroom door, which was open a few feet inside the room on the right, a salmon-pink newspaper was spread out in front of the white toilet. The bedroom was primrose and a great window looked over the sunny green garden.

'Your mother has some lovely things,' I said, looking at the leather sofa and chair in the corner of the room, and the jewellery boxes on the glass-topped dressing table. I counted three photographs of Sadie in the room, some of her alongside Tamsin, some solo.

'Have your mother and father not got that much money then, Mona?' she smiled. She knew me mam no longer existed, though seemed to have forgotten.

'Well, I suppose they just spend it on different things,' I muttered, following her into the bedroom and over to the window where she stood looking out across the garden.

'Hmm, like communism,' she said, pulling her yellow rubber fingers through her strange hair, and giving me her best thinking look. 'Under communism there is a complete realignment of priorities, you know. They don't have ace cars and top washing machines but they do have food and clothes and non-stop central heating. Whatever the hell they need to stay alive.'

For the first time I noticed the Fakenhams had three tennis courts behind the high hedge. Markings in the orange clay indicated a match had recently been played.

'Really, I might be a communist,' she smiled. 'What do you think?'

'When you grow up?' I smiled back.

She looked at me sternly and did not smile.

'I bet you're brilliant at tennis, aren't you, Tam?'

'Of course. I was a Yorkshire champion years ago.'

'I'm very good at ping-pong.'

'Well, it's similar. I'll teach you.'

The countryside, so perfectly decorated with its blues and greens, was watching us and grinning. The tall garden trees, their tips whiskering the sky, were swaying in celebration and, above, little white clouds gazed in appreciation of us wonderful girls. From this window, which looked south beyond Goldwell, you could see no roads, people or houses, just the rising smile of earth, fields, hedges. The rich had better views. The humming green washed a few feet into the bedroom, soaking us, two new shoots, in sun and breeze.

'It's so different to the view from my window which is all factories and mucky old Black Beck,' I said quietly.

'Yes, I suppose it is pretty here,' she said. 'If you like this sort of thing. Which my mother and father obviously don't or they'd be here, wouldn't they?'

'Maybe they just need a break from it. It probably gets exhausting having such an amazing life.'

'Come on, dopey,' she said, shaking her head and turning away from the window. 'I want to show you right round the house.'

The corridor was dark and smelt of polish, but the carpet was a trampoline I wanted to bounce over. Ahead of me Tam was tapping her yellow gloves on each door she passed. 'That's the first bathroom. That's the first guest bedroom. That's another guest bedroom. That's a junky storage room. That's the third en suite guest bathroom – you could go in there. Would you like your own bathroom?'

She hurried on. Her questions, I was coming to realise, were really just remarks.

We passed another set of stairs leading higher up into the house.

'What's up there?' I asked, showing the keen interest of the most cultivated guest.

'A few junky rooms and a strange place where Mummy stores all these props from crazy amateur dramatics productions she's been in over the years.'

It sounded fun and I wanted to see, but she was marching on and offered no more information. At the bottom of the corridor she turned right, so we were now facing the back of the house which looked east, over the stables and Willow's field. There were three more closed doors.

'That's Father's office, scene of red-hot telephone sex with numerous sexretaries over the years. And that there's another guest bedroom. And this.'

Here she stopped. She was standing outside a closed door.

'This is Sadie's room.'

'Oh.'

I stood beside her and touched the cool skin of her arm. She was looking down at her feet, blinking.

'Could I see inside?' I asked quietly. With me mam, I liked people to take an interest in her, and her things, even though she was gone.

'OK,' she said, putting her yellow glove slowly on the door knob and gripping it for a moment. There was a sinister squeak of rubber against porcelain. 'But don't be shocked. The thing is, Mother has insisted on keeping it exactly as it was when Sadie was alive. It's a bit spooky crazy really.'

'I can understand that,' I whispered. 'It's quite normal. I didn't want anyone to move any of me mam's things for ages.'

'OK. Ready?' she said and I nodded. And slowly she squeezed open the door.

It was the most beautiful room, light and fine, and buttery sunlight poured over all like Devon cream over a fancy cake. A single bed was shrouded with a lacy white quilt, and frills fell in a foaming ripple on to the floor. On a round bedside table a single book waited, and next to it a glass of clear water. There was no dust. All was polished. Against a high bank of pillows a cluster of ashen-faced china dolls rested. On a dark wood chest beneath the window, which stretched almost from floor to ceiling, abandoned teddies stretched out their arms hopelessly. An oval dressing table, with a glass top and full skirt, displayed bottles of perfume, make-up, jewellery and a brush.

A silver brush still soft with golden glossy wisps of girl hair. But worst of all was in the corner: the only mirror in the house; a full-length antique, tilted back proudly on its stand, reflecting endlessly only dawn, sunlight, twilight, darkness and the high wardrobe opposite.

'Oh, don't cry, Mona,' Tam said, annoyed.

'I'm sorry. It's just that I know how awful it must be for you.'

'Yes, it has been awful. But now it's much better because I've got you here with me. Oh, please just stop it. I don't need you going all bleak and desperate like everyone else.'

With that, she marched out of the room. I stood there for a moment alone. I walked over and looked for one glance out of the window. Below was the place I had waited for Tam last Saturday morning.

So, out of this window she had watched me.

I turned and, collecting my tartan suitcase, gently closed Sadie's door behind me.

'Next, Mona, proof that you don't have to die to go to heaven,' she said when I caught up with her at the bottom of the stairs. 'You'll like this one, darling.'

'Oh?' I exclaimed brightly.

'The cellar. Rows and rows of dusty bottles of booze just waiting for girl drinkers.'

'Oh, paradise.'

She turned left at the bottom of the stairs, and pattered past the baby grand piano and along a narrow corridor. She turned a key in a slim door and descended the stairs.

The damp cellar walls were great slabs of glistening stone. I could smell a cool mossy greenness like a night walk in a thick garden, though the light we were coming into was bruised dark with deep wine purples. I bumped the suitcase behind me as we creaked down the stairs. At the bottom Tam stood still and silent, and when I turned her face was rigid and deathly as a waxwork. Surely before her she could see her sister, her hair blondely sparkling through the gloom.

I could hear a slow dripping and the air was spongy and moist. I felt like a goldfish: damp and dizzy. I did not want to concentrate for fear I would see Sadie too. I could feel me eyes beginning to prickle with tears again. Willow. I would think of Willow. But it did not seem to be even the same lifetime in which I'd looked after a posh family's pony. My days with Willow were a hazy childhood memory. The animal was still out there somewhere, but I no longer wanted to look for her and if her carcass was being feasted on by vultures I'd not have noticed.

Then it was chilly and Tam rubbed her gloves together so they made a spooky clucking.

I reached into me pocket and took a few blasts on the Ventolin. It was a risk because I knew Tam hated weakness and vulnerability.

'You look ill, Mona,' she whispered, and then in the darkness touched a rubber finger to my cheek. I realised then that she treated me the same way Lindy always had: like I existed solely for her personal entertainment.

'Your skin's all white and cauliflowery,' she sighed. 'And you look half dead. You look like you live in a hospital.'

'Me mam,' I said and then stopped.

'I know *Mam. Mammy*, no really, I like it, it's nice. I like the way you talk. All gruff Yorkshire.'

The smell was soily, like we were deep under the earth.

'Sorry, it's the dark. And seeing Sadie's room. It reminds me of her and what happened. When she died.'

She looked at me suspiciously.

'It's nearly a year,' I added. 'Since she died. Me mam.'

She pushed her bottom lip out and blinked rapidly in a clownish imitation of sorrow.

'I still think of her,' I said and smiled. 'But it's OK.'

I smiled again so she didn't feel awkward, the way people often did when you mentioned it. People sometimes assumed you were encouraging the confession of agonies on their part.

The air was heavy, almost wet, like a cloud of tears was about to break over us.

'Well, never mind,' Tam said, walking off into the deepest clutch of dark at the centre of the cellar. Then turning suddenly, defiantly, she said: 'It adds to your *je ne sais quoi*. And men will simply love it. They much prefer damaged women.'

'Oh, yes.'

'Go on then. Choose what booze you want,' she said and then ran off up the cellar stairs so I was alone with my suitcase, breathless in the dark.

I slid three cool bottles from the wooden rack and carried them upstairs.

When I emerged from the cellar she was sitting on the top of the baby grand piano smoking and swinging her legs anxiously.

'Right, if you think that was scary, Mona darling, you better get ready for what I've got to show you next.'

'What?'

'Wait and see. Leave the wine there.'

I put the bottles on the piano top, but because she had not ordered me to leave the suitcase I continued to drag it across the hallway. A slant of shade dimmed the hall now and we crossed from the light into the dark. Immediately to the left of the front entrance was a white door, closed. An ancient black key with a looped end poked from the lock.

'You ready?' she asked. She stroked my face.

I nodded. She turned the key between gloved finger and thumb.

The slowly opening door made a tiny yelping creak. She pushed it wide and made a gesture for me to walk under her arm, as though we were country dancing. I entered the room first.

It was cold. That stony old cold that drips over you in churches.

In front of me was a great rink of glossy chestnut, a table

so big it would have served for snooker. In the centre was a three-pronged gold candlestick holder. Nipped in close, so their backs nudged the table edge, were ten chairs. Behind the table an ancient dresser decorated with blue and white plates loomed. There was nothing else in the room.

'This is the dining room, Mona,' Tam said solemnly. She had closed the door behind us, and was now standing against it, barring any exit.

'It's beautiful.'

'No it's not, stupid. It's the most terrifying place in the house.'

'Oh.'

'Can you imagine sitting at this table every evening? No one talking. Sadie not eating. Daddy dreaming of the sexretary, Mummy stiff with all her lost opportunities. The vicious scraping of knives and forks, night after night.'

I thought of us sat round our TV taunting PorkChop, our teas wobbling on our knees.

I shivered. The room was surely so cold because since Sadie died no one had entered here. It had been sealed up. A mummy's tomb.

On the table, to the left of the candlesticks, was a round glass object; it glinted like petrolled water, purple-blue-yellow, a flower displayer perhaps, or Mrs Fakenham's crystal ball.

Tamsin walked away from the door. She was coming towards me. She had the little black door key between her finger and thumb and began rubbing it slowly against the edge of the table. She looked down at the table and I saw her dangerously doubled there in the mahogany's mirrored pool. Then suddenly, so I bristled with surprise, she turned ferocious, bent low, geared all her energy into her right arm and began to make a great scribble with the tooth end of the key right across the table.

'Urgh, ah, er, urgh,' the face in the table groaned.

'Tamsin!' I gasped, then put a hand over my mouth to clamp the shock. She had the movement of polishing, but the searing sound of frantic scraping. Her teeth were clenched and she had a haze of wet over her wide eyes.

Then there was a blonde snarl of curves, angles and lines seared through the dining table, like the finest speed skaters had just performed a breathtaking routine.

That evening, after we had drunk the dusty bottles of thick red wine, and despite a leaflet which had been pushed through the door yelling 'WARNING DROUGHT', we decided to take pleasure in a deep, hot bath.

Tam put candles round the bathroom and dragged the turntable up on to the first-floor landing so the thumping disco rippled through the steam.

Then came the time for us to take our clothes off.

Very slowly, Tamsin disrobed. Because she insisted on keeping her yellow rubber gloves on, the procedure was agonisingly slow as she fumbled with buttons and zips. First her socks, then her pale blue cardigan, then her smart white trousers, then her pink T-shirt. After she had taken each item off she folded it carefully and placed it in a pile on the bathroom chair.

Slowly, her nakedness was revealed. Her skin so creamy you felt sure the gentlest stroke would leave a white lick on your fingertip.

When she was down to just her pink lace knickers and matching bra she turned away from me, softly pornographic, suggesting not showing. She reached a yellow gloved hand round her back to unhook her bra. Then, first looking shyly over her shoulder, she turned coyly to face me.

Was Tamsin too fat? Hard to tell. She had two pert buttocks and those breasts. Breasts so full, and pinker than the rest of her skin and strangely translucent towards the nipple, so they looked as if they'd just been blown out of bubble gum. But the rest of her was long and slender: her hips made just the gentlest of curves, her plump calves smoothed into sinewy ankles, her ribs were nicely visible, her waist cut in tightly. In any boy's book, she'd do.

'Your turn now,' she said nakedly, folding her arms so it looked as if someone had pinned a yellow rubber rosette over her chest.

I tore my own clothes off as fast as I could. I stood before her with an apologetic grin and me hands clenched into tight fists. I looked down at me breasts and thought of them photographed. Them appearing in a magazine. I thought how, hey!, they would have to offer a magnifying glass free with every issue.

She gave me a long wolf whistle and then collapsed in a fit of giggles, before throwing herself into the bath without further comment.

'Look, Mona, if you hold your breath, open your eyes very wide and go rigid, you can play dead underwater. Watch. It's great fun.'

I tried it and nearly drowned. After she had stopped laughing Tam turned the music up and told me to stand in the bath and dance through the steam. I did and then later, just beyond the bathroom door, where the music was loudest, I galloped up and down the corridor practising my latest routine.

Romance.

A time did not come that night when Tam suggested we go to bed. She did not show me my room though I dragged the suitcase around with me awkwardly. Neither did she show me her room. Instead, she made me a pepper and cold baked bean sandwich at 1.00 a.m. and just when I was yawning and rubbing at my eyes, she said: 'Don't go getting all tired, darling, there's no sleep for you tonight. What we're going to do is sleep through the sunshine hours and dance through the darkness. What d'you think?'

'Whatever you say,' I yawned.

'We can't take the risk of people discovering us, so we'll live like wise owls.'

'Okey-dokey.'

'You're too nervy, Mona. You should smoke more.'

'Yeh,' I said and took the lighted cig she plucked from her mouth for me. The filter was wet and soft and stuck lightly to my lip.

'I mean, we have to be so careful, because what if someone tells my father that they've seen us here? I'm supposed to be holed up in the countryside with my hair in plaits and a pencil stuck studiously in the corner of my mouth.'

'Oh, no!'

'But, you see, if all day the curtains are drawn and the doors are locked, they'll just think I've gone away as planned.'

'What if they see us during the night?'

'They won't, stupid. Everyone round here's in their sweaty beds by 10.30 p.m. And we'll be careful, of course. Anyway, that's when I'm going to be doing the painting. Night painting. Much more pleasant painting in the cool moonlight rather than the daylight sun. Don't you think? In fact, I think I'll start now.'

I still found it hard to tell if Tamsin was joking and using irony or if she was being serious. But she disappeared and returned twenty minutes later wearing a pair of dungarees and her hair covered in a scarf. She was carrying a knife in one hand and a long flat tool in the other. It was 2.16 a.m.

'Now I'm going out to the shed to find a ladder. You stay in here working on your betting strategies for winning us some money. I want you to learn about all the finer points of gambling so that we can't lose when we start to make money. Meanwhile, I'll go outside and start the painting.'

Eventually, she had a ladder up against the side of the house and was scraping at the paint with her knife. She was only a few feet up the ladder, because she was too afraid to go higher. She started on the east wall, at the back of the house because she thought this would be less suspicious should folk come prying.

Though I was supposed to be in the kitchen, focused and

keen, I spent my first night with Tamsin biting my nails and staring out into the blackness.

When she had been gone some time I went upstairs and stuck me head out of the second bathroom window and called through the darkness to her: 'Say cheese, darling!' and snapped a few photographs with my camera. She looked annoyed and upset. She was pounding away with great force, like she was exercising a hated body. She was wild-haired and breathless.

She'd made little scabs in the paint where she'd knifed away, angrily. Gradually, paint began to come off in patches and lay in moony flakes around the back garden. She was keen to start the new colour before all the old paint had been removed and soon descended the ladder and went to find a tin of pink paint which she then began to fling on to the walls.

'Go on, darling,' I called encouragingly. 'You're doing wonderfully.'

'It's exhausting,' she yelled back through the chilly night. 'But I'm relieved to be tidying things up.'

At 3.48 a.m. she came back into the kitchen and threw the tools on to the table, followed by the headscarf. She looked furious. Beneath the gloves her hands were callused and sore. Her beautiful bubblegum breasts were heaving like she was about to start crying.

'I'm off to bed, now. Good night,' she said and disappeared, slamming the kitchen door behind her.

I sat there but nothing else happened.

When my head against the kitchen table began to ache I decided to sleep on the rocking chair. I pulled a tea towel over my chest, put my feet up on Lindy's tartan suitcase and clenched my eyes 'til morning.

sausages

'Where've you been?' she asked angrily. She pulled the rubber gloves up making an elasticy slap. She folded her arms and pulled her chin in.

It was Thursday 4 June and we had been living together three whole days. I had been out into the town to have a bet (unsuccessful), though it was supposed to be the middle of the night for us. She'd been waiting for me, and she was smoking anxiously. Her hair had gone back to the crazy sheep-wool frizz.

'We've been under attack while you've been out. I had to get up. I've been awake all day. It was awful, bright and sunny, and you weren't there. I nearly called the *police*,' she hissed, jutting her chin out at the beginning of a sentence and snapping it in at the end. 'I don't want you going out without telling me,' she yelled. 'Do you hear me? You really are a very selfish person, Mona.'

She played anxiously with the tape measure, which she now wore hung round her neck at all times.

I noticed how glintingly scrubbed everything was, how the taps shone, the floor squeaked if you pushed a toe over, even the white tiles had an icy freshness, like the place had been tongued clean. Perhaps Ivy had been round.

I felt a sudden nut of anger in me stomach. Then longing. I had confessed to her that I felt both happy and scared

when I was with her and she had said: 'Isn't that the defi-
nition of the most exciting stage of love? One without the
other leaves you bored or desperate, stupid.' Which I thought
was smart.

I had been promoted to sleeping beside her in her bed, and
though I was given very little space, and she was wrapped tight
in the blankets and sheets while I shivered at her side, it was
still much better than the kitchen rocking chair. Her bedroom
was neat, with books and a desk and expensive paintings on the
walls and soft, adult lighting. There were objects from Africa
and a weird carpet hanging on the wall.

'I had to go put some money on,' I whispered quickly, though
I was no longer sure anything she said was true. *She nearly called
the police.* Tomorrow was exactly seven days since the burglary
of the little house with the big blue slippers and the home-knit
red cardigan and the shiny kitchen.

'Did you hear, darling? I said I was under *attack*.'

I didn't know what she meant by 'under attack', but it made
her sound like a foreign country.

'I had to win us some more. So that when we put the bet
on there'll be plenty.' My voice sounded like I was hearing
mesen played back on tape for the first time. We talked often
about the Derby Day bet, because this was the only thing we
had to aim for. We were failing to find anything purposeful to do.

'If we ever do put the bet on,' she mumbled, slumping one
shoulder in a gesture of forgiveness. I looked at my feet and
then up again. My face was burning hot; the sun was so fierce
it steamed the tears from your eyes.

She had laid a row of shining knives out on the table, curving
in ascending order.

'We will. Trust me, Tam.'

'You sound like a husband in an American TV drama.'

'Hey, honey, I'll make it all right for you, I swear.'

'Your accent's terrible. You shouldn't have left the house

without asking me. It's not safe. And it's too hot out there. It's not natural.'

'Honey, that's why I always carry my ole hunting gun,' I said and patted my arse and gave her a slow, irresistible grin. I fixed the grin on me face until it became a bit scary.

We scared each other regularly, without admitting this was what we were doing. It helped the boredom.

She turned away from me and rubbed at the last knife in the line with a soft, lemon-coloured cloth.

'Stop it. Be real.'

'Honey, I wud do nuttin to ever hurt you. My liddle ole apple pie.'

'Don't!'

'I'm sorry. I won't do it again. I'll not go out again without asking you.'

But she was not looking at me. She was looking over my shoulder, and her face was freezing into a look of great pain.

I felt suddenly fattish.

'They're back! Run!' she screamed. I twisted round in panic but could see nothing. I could hear shouting. I followed her in a scramble into the hall, our feet shocking on the stone, towards a door. The shouting voice was like a crazed bingo announcer, fast and flat.

Was it the fat old auntie?

Then I was alone in the dark hallway. Despite my tour, the house still felt unknown. There were still rooms with high wide doors I'd not entered. Doorknobs, keyholes, locks smoothed solid with centuries of ivory paint. Each floorboard had a creak so individual and unapologetic that even those planks of wood seemed like fierce characters.

Then she was there behind me, unreal, romantic, smiling, and she pushed me in first, then came in, in front of me, pulled the door shut so we were in musty grey darkness, my nose in her hair, her back pressed against my dreadful chest.

Her face was up against a bunch of coats on the back of the door. I feared she would smell the sausage slice on me breath.

A tiny place, of muck, wires, old carpet and behind the pant of our breathing was the clicking of electricity.

'All afternoon he has hounded me. And I was alone. No one to help me,' she whispered. She was speaking into the door, a row of five planks in front of her face, and I was speaking into the back of her head. I wondered if she was smiling her mocking sneer.

'What?' I murmured. I could hear him now, he was mad, this man who was out there, he was saying terrible things that you'd think he would be ashamed to say to a girl who went away to a major educational establishment. He was demanding money. I imagined his moneyless, old, saggy face munching the words.

It was old Paul the gardener. I sucked on me Ventolin as this was the only stimulant I had: no fags, no booze. I wondered if it might be worth suggesting we search the cupboard for some glue.

'Men are not frightening, they are losers, we have to remember that,' I whispered.

'Tall Paul. That bloody old servant. I don't know if he's harmless or not. I could've been killed. He wants his wages, but it's all gone, spent. He keeps ringing up. Or knocking on the door. He could murder me.'

'Sorry. I've been out making money, honey,' I said. I could not imagine the humiliation of Tam knowing about my recent loss.

'Imagine if there was your nuclear bomb now.'

'We'd be OK in here. We'd survive.'

'Would you like it if I let you put some blankets, cans and bottles of water in here just in case?'

I couldn't tell if she was sniggering or not, but I decided to risk it. 'Oh yes, let's, Tam! We could line it with books for extra safety.'

There was a pause. I pictured that beautiful orange mushroom against the blue sky.

'Have you been eating?' she said, sniffing, but not turning round.

'No,' I said. 'Of course not. Your swell home cooking is the only thing for me, honey.'

'Sausages,' she said and looked down sadly. It was true I had eaten a deliciously evil sausage slice while I was out.

We were scared. But we could not acknowledge this because we had nowhere else to go. If I breathed in a certain way it scared her more, sucking in deep from my stomach and saying nowt. I realised I liked scaring her, seeing her body alter with fear. This was a satisfaction Lindy had enjoyed when I was small, and now I felt that singular pleasure in terrifying another. Also, I was learning that you could make people act in a certain way by altering your own behaviour. She knew this too. You could do this with just one another, you didn't have to be part of a crowd. I thought how the smell of me this close, mingled with the dust and dead insects, must have been like rotting underground.

'It's like being in a grave,' I said.

'Sadie and I used to play in here,' she said. 'Well, not exactly *play*. She'd lock me in and tell me there were snakes crawling round my feet. She'd hold the door pressed shut until I begged for mercy.'

'Lindy used to make me stand in a bucket with a lollipop in my mouth and sing pop songs to her friends. Only when I scored a perfect ten was I allowed out of the bucket.'

'When Sadie got very ill, if you said anything even slightly cruel to her she'd faint, fall to the floor like a leaf dropping from a tree.'

'Bitch,' I said.

'Yeh,' she giggled.

'Ssssh!' I whispered, reaching an arm round her neck and pressing my finger over her lovely soft lips. We were friends again. 'I used to pretend to be dead if Lindy slapped me. I'd crash down on me knees and make her think she'd killed me. I'd lay still for a long time. Up to half an hour. I got very good at it. Even if she pulled me around and bit into me skin to make me come back to life I could appear stone-cold dead.'

She giggled but not for long and her breathing was quick and scared, hearing the sound of Tall Paul changing as he moved around outside the house.

'You look a lot like Sadie standing in this dark cupboard,' she whispered. 'She was thin and bony like you.'

'Do I?' I said, blowing the words gently on to the back of her neck.

'A bit scared in the eyes. The same straight hair as you used to have.'

In truth, despite what I'd heard, I always pictured Sadie as a healthy-looking Swiss girl like Heidi. This was how she'd seemed that day of the flawless skin and the ash-blonde flowing hair, and how she looked in all the photographs around the house.

'It was only later I realised just how much courage it took to live like her. How brave Sadie was to *dare to die*,' she said, pronouncing the last three words dramatically like she was on stage.

'Brave as a little ol' button, that there gal. How brave to *dare to die*.'

'To dare to die,' she said. 'It sounds so romantic. Like a film.'

I tried to imagine a Cambodian Sadie: her blonde hair falling out in bunches.

The banging of a man's fist against the door was distant but strong.

She backed a bit closer to me and I saw there was a bald patch in her hair where she'd scissored too close. She could've turned and kissed me, licked every fold of me.

'He can't get in, can he?' I whispered when the breathlessness and the anxiety and the closeness were becoming unbearable.

'He's the gardener, for heaven's sake. He's a *servant*, Mona! He wouldn't come in unless *I* let him. I'm still in charge.'

'Good. Someone needs to be in charge of things.'

'Did you win?' she whispered, moving her arm back and resting her hand on my thigh, not in the usual way of excessive love, but in a way of checking I was just a harmless girl.

'Yeh, I won. Plenty,' I said in a mysterious way, like my winning was the start of something. That I had a power she couldn't quite understand. Something so unexplainable it made people very interested in me.

I was trying to appear manly.

'It's so exciting!' she cried.

'Yes, yes!' I screamed, screwing shut my eyes and clenching my fists.

That cupboard was *exactly* the sort of place the government recommended you take shelter in, in the event of a Soviet attack.

'Then soon we'll be able to put the bet on,' she whispered, giggling, and turned around so she was facing me. 'I'm glad you came back. I thought you'd run away.' She took my hand and stroked it. My scraggy wrists are always the bit that give me away. To women. Men never notice. She held my thumb in her fingers and stroked her own smooth thumb slowly over my tiny wrist.

'Hands make me think of fruit machines,' I said quietly. To be back talking of fruit machines seemed a great relief.

'Shall we run away to a land of endless fruit machines, Mona?'

'I told you, you don't get anywhere when you try and run away.' I could see thick cobwebs stretched across the corners of the dark cupboard like locks of grey hair.

'Remember this,' she goes. 'Remember this feeling of being together in the bunker.'

'Yes. I will.'

'Always.'

'Always, honeybunch.'

'I want to do something fun tonight, when he's gone. Let's do something fun,' she said and tottered round, in the way Lindy and I would if we were pretending to be the fairy on the musical box, 'til she was facing me, breathing her scared warm sighs in the musty darkness. 'I'll measure,' she said, flicking the tape measure from around her neck like a whip.

'I'm so glad you're here with me. I'm so glad not to be alone with Lindy gone and Debbie there, and me mam's anniversary coming up.'

'Neither of us really have sisters any more, do we?' she said, measuring. 'We just have one another.'

'I know I should be a solo success but I long to have no will other than yours.'

'If you've won plenty of money, you clever old thing, let's spend it! Let's not let these terrible men ruin our fun.'

'Let's get braver,' I said as she tightened the yellow tape round me waist.

whisky

We tried for a long time that night to think of something brave and exciting to do. By then we were bored and gloomy. In the end Tam decided we would go to Tall Paul's house and sort this thing out for once and for all.

Tam led the way.

We exited through the courtyard.

How tight and safe we were then, ringed on all sides by garages, stables, outhouses. It was being so rich and powerful that allowed Tam to feel so incapable and weak. It was being loved so strongly by my family that allowed me the insolence to believe, with fierce certainty, that they did not notice or care about any damn thing that I did. I was surprised Father had neither objected nor tried to contact me for three days. I felt sure he had abandoned me for ever.

We were giggling and fizzy with a midday/midnight energy though it was a good mile walk to Tall Paul's house, and we'd been awake for over eighteen hours.

Tam had told me Tall Paul lived on the poor side of Goldwell. Well away from the beautiful country homes was a small estate of neat council houses, politely concealed from the eyes of the silver-car commuters by a pick-your-own strawberry farm. Just before the council houses was a row of eight terraced houses where Tall Paul and his family had lived all their dreary lives. The quickest and most witchy way to get to his side of the village was overland.

We bounced and ran, skipping and striding over moonlit mud and bracken.

The night air was cool and refreshing. We crossed fields and squelched through a damp clutch of woodland. We turned our fear almost immediately into hysteria so soon we were speaking in accents, me in Oirish, her in Russian. We sniggered and drank from a little bottle of whisky that clever Tam had found hidden in her father's study, and let the fiery brown drip down our chins. We wiped it away with our fists.

I wondered, in a sudden panic, if the bitch had a private stash of booze that she was keeping from me, and then banished the thought.

We clutched hands (Tam still wearing her rubber gloves) and skipped in our loose wellington boots.

We had a purpose.

'The thing you'll never understand, Mona, is that when you have servants you are never alone. Your every move is watched. Since I was a baby I've had people watching over me. There's always staff poking around. And because you're always on show you always have to look right and do the right thing. It's such a pressure. I mean, with you it's so different; no one cares if you head off for days. No one cares if you look like a gyppo and don't wash and get all scrawny and half dead. But for me. Well, hell, to be always watched by common people. I mean, it makes me feel like the worst sort of cheap TV.'

'Oh, you poor, poor darling.'

Every few hundred yards we kissed 'til our faces were sticky with booze and if you'd put a match to us we would have instantly ignited.

It was pure romance now.

And yet almost immediately this loving change occurred, we distrusted each other. That same night before we went to Tall Paul's I believed Tam had been out spending, though she'd not admitted this. She'd spent the servants' wages on chocolate, crisps, biscuits and cigarettes, which she'd secretly piled in the kitchen cupboard. I knew because I heard her rustling.

In turn I had been into her bedroom while she was out on the ladder. There were no clues to her revising, though I was sure this was what she was doing. I had to be quick, so I went through her drawers like a rat, but everything was neat and correct, and there were no clues to what she was getting up to. But her handwriting! It was irregular and messy and she pressed hard against the paper like a child. The script tilted uneasily to the right, as though the sentences were on the point of keeling over, suddenly flat on their face, like a drunkard or a dead man.

Still, I believed we could distrust and be scared of one another and yet be utterly, madly in love.

The terraced house in which Tall Paul lived had a red door, two upstairs windows, one downstairs, a bell and, caring not one damn about the forthcoming nuclear attack, grey net curtains.

We hammered on the door, giggling so hard saliva dribbled from our lips, and a light went on in the upstairs window. I hummed 'Wild Thing' and Tam screwed her face into a look of concentration and waggled her fists fast and loose like a drummer.

We danced on the doorstep because of the booze. The night seemed felty and close to our faces, like we were hidden, wrapped in a dark blanket.

A few lights were still on in the neighbouring council estate and Tam said that if you sniffed hard enough you could smell their aluminium teapots and marrowfat peas.

The fat old woman who opened the door was holding tight to the bottom edge of a pale blue cardigan which she had pulled on anxiously over her nightdress. Tam hooked her thumb into the waistband of her lovely olive cords. The old woman's puffy ankles had swollen over the sides of her slippers. As soon as the door was open Tam secured it with her booted foot. Tam's beautiful skin glowed as a blush rose over her. The old woman had a doughy grey face and a few thick hairs which made an almost beard on her chin. Body hair so appalled me I wanted to punch her.

And I was shocked by the sight of her. I'd never seen an ugly old woman in a nightdress before. Even in the cheapest catalogues they had the sense to use nubile blondes to model the pink flannel nighties. Though they are essential to the food chain, old women, like insects, are too repulsive and best kept unseen.

The village was quiet, the house had that musty silence of sleepers, but I fancied there was a steel band thundering in me head.

As Tam talked, the rattling pace of her sentences and the rigid set of her shoulders betrayed her fury. The fat old wife smoothed at her grey hair, then tried to iron wrinkles from her brow. She sniffed and then leant backwards slightly, reacting, I realised later, to the inferno blast of whisky on our breath.

'So basically, tell your husband never to come back to our house. He's fired. My mother and father have been informed and they agree entirely with my decision. And furthermore, a spot of advice for you, I suggest you investigate your husband's rather prurient interest in teenage *girls*.'

'A girl's gone missing, you know!' I butted in. I had not intended to speak but now I'd unexpectedly started I was unable to stop. Tam's cruelty fuelled my own. 'And, and the police are looking for a bloke who could be a murderer, *a killer*. So going around knocking on windows where lasses live isn't a very good idea, is it, eh? Someone's gotta be the killer. Well, eh? Don't just stand there yer, yer stupid *cow*.'

Tam touched my arm and took over the speaking. I had a headache and wanted to sit down. My heart was fighting to get out of me chest. A breeze had got up and Tam's voice tailed off towards the end of a sentence. It was 4.34 a.m. Tam was keeping a tight, cruel face but I needed to snigger. At first, the old wife looked confused, then her spine straightened and her lips puckered and she was quickly angry: but before she could say anything Tam raised her flat palm and said: 'Don't argue, please. Just tell him.'

'And take those net curtains down, you stupid old *woman*.'

We turned calmly to walk home. The paving stones seemed quite squishy, like we were walking on pillows. The moonlit greenhouses seemed to crack like ice. Behind us there was a wide-eyed silence, and then the old wife was calling out. A sound like a bundle of dry twigs snapping. Other lights went on in bedrooms down the terrace. Me hand was shivering so hard I could not even squeeze the Ventolin. The village suddenly seemed very noisy; dogs barking, cars, wind, doors opening. I touched a wall to steady mesen and it felt feverishly hot like the whole village had turned to boiling flesh.

The whisky was gone and, in what was to become a familiar feeling that summer, I felt sure that imminently some annoyed adult would appear, to chastise, or even physically beat us.

But no one came.

pork

Pink light came in through churchy stained windows and made blushing shapes on white walls. The studio had that chemically sweat stink of a cheap hairdresser's. I sat on a slippery white settee and waited for Phil to make the coffees. Far below in the marketplace was the gentle thronging of sound that was families innocently wandering.

It was Friday, the day after the night we'd visited the old woman. I was deliciously dissolving: I'd been up all night, and had not eaten for many hours. Phil had been scoffing a roast pork sandwich when I arrived. I watched a pigtail of pork fat he'd left curled on a white paper bag and thought how much more controlled and capable I was than him.

It turned out I was to be a hand model. Phil had decided that me hands were the bit of me that *work*. He was right. The studio was at the top of the cinema. He said he'd opened it especially for me. He said he did *special projects with special people* on Fridays.

I felt me hormones do the cancan.

I had spent an exhausting age that morning scraping hair off of toes, legs, armpits, belly, bikini line and other unmentionable areas. I was now covered in so many rashes and scrapes and dots of blood that it looked like I'd fallen off me bike at a great speed.

I wondered how much cash I'd get paid to contribute to the

box of saved-up money. I feared not much: I was the world's first titless topless model. My nipples were inverted like tiny belly buttons.

Phil came in carrying two mugs and a blue velvet tray of rings. His pink bottom lip protruded and fluttered as he blew breath up over his face.

Sober, he was still fatty round the edges, wobbly like a Labrador. There was something different about him though; he'd got spray on his hair, a kind of high-strength fixing gel which kept the thinning hairs swept stiffly back over his head.

How dear Tam would've laughed.

But perhaps not, because she did not know I was coming here. It was the fourth day of our living together and she'd said that as long as I asked she did not object to me going out. So I'd requested permission to leave the house, under the lie of going to put a bet on. I could not tell her the truth because the growing belief between us was that all men were powerless losers. We made hilarious jokes about them and I told embarrassing tales about PorkChop, Shred and my father. Tam in turn assassinated her own father's reputation viciously: *How do you get a father to change a light bulb? Put it above his secretary's bed*, or *How do you know if your father's lying? His lips are moving.*

'Ha! Fuckwitidiotspermifaces,' I yelled, to her delight.

Phil had a New Romantic-type white shirt on with frills round the cuffs. He put the coffees down and wiped the sweat from his brow with the back of his hand. There was a joke lurking in his desperation to be fashionable. He squeezed up next to me and told me how he didn't just do weddings, kids and families, oh no, he did plastic lunch boxes for a kitchen company and birdbaths, greenhouses and sheds for a garden company. He did clothes. He did cars. He did miscellaneous photos for catalogues. He was going to be very successful. He wiped at the sweat that ran like rain down a window over his face.

I pitied him even more than I now pitied every other man I knew.

Then I was looking at his hair for other crazy details, and it did seem probable that he'd got a dye on because the roots were darker than the main hair and it was more than just sun bleach. And he had an earring, a tiny figure on a hoop. I wished I had a girl by my side, a wolverine, to help rip all this to shreds.

When he looked at me it was uneasily, like he wanted me to reassure and understand him.

He did beautiful women, he said.

'So this is your first time modelling?' he said and I nodded. I didn't like the way he called it that. I thought of how Lindy and Tam would cackle if they knew. I wished I'd had a drink. For a few minutes he quietly looked me over seeing if there were any other bits of me body he could use.

Without the drink it was not the same. Not even the foodless hollowness was enough to make me feel strong.

Then he told me to go into this grubby little kitchen that smelt of cabbage, and scrub me hands with this nail brush and put on the varnish he'd left on the side. He patted my bottom, slap slap, as I went by.

There was muck, damp around the edge of the sink, soggy flecks of skin or bread. There were droppings of food on the lino floor too, crumbs and dried-up reddish sauce stains. I imagined how upsetting Tamsin would find this typhoid kitchen dirt, and I gave a dry retch in connection with her. He heard the retch and thought I was exclaiming in delight and so he called out that he'd picked the nail varnish out specially for me and bought cotton wool and remover.

I looked at mesen in the dirty kitchen mirror. The first mirror for days. Me skin was dry and blotched from the booze and crime, and me make-up looked like summat a child had drawn on with crayons. Me face was too 'small almond' and me shorn hair too straight and brown.

Whenever I thought about police and the cackling old wife, me breathing stopped.

For a while I had fun pointing me fingers like a lady. I was posh as a Fakenham girl. Me hands were on a red velvet cushion with a hot light above. It was cheap stuff but it felt serious on your hands. You had to keep posed hands very still, fingers soft, not stiff, and wrists loose and relaxed. In the drowsy, steaming heat I made a dream of someone putting a ring on me finger and going in a whisper: *I want you to be my [pause] wife.*

If you got married people didn't say things about you being uninteresting. They expected it.

'Good girl,' he goes while he bent down, eye to the camera. 'You're lovely and slim.' His squarish glasses made a clumsy clunking noise up against the lens. 'Perfect. Lovely. Good girl. Relax.' He came over and positioned me like I was plastic.

Being looked at by Phil was making me feel both elated, and ugly. I kept remembering stories Tam had told me about her sister. I could picture Sadie clearly. So unwilling to eat she had the body of a baby bird. She grew younger as she got older, her breasts disappearing and her bones warping like wood. In the last three days Tam had told me many tales of the sister who'd died, so now the intimacy between us felt like the stifling heat of a muggy day.

For example, how when Sadie was getting weighed in the hospital, naked as a skinned rabbit, she clutched coins in her fist, or bunches of keys, to make her heavier. For the last month she was on a glucose drip. Sadie spent more time in hospital than Florence Nightingale, Tam said smiling. Sadie kept crisp packets folded in her diary and into these she'd spit chewed-up food she didn't want to swallow. The food turned into hard brown pellets and stank of bad breath.

I did not feel I could tell any similar stories about me mam dying. I wanted to but it was still scattered crazily inside me, like an enormous, highly detailed jigsaw puzzle with a million pieces, that I could not solve, no matter how many times I returned to it.

'Me dad wouldn't like me doing this,' I goes.

Though in truth Father was already fading in my mind, and if

Tam and I had any philosophy it was probably to do whatever fathers would most hate us to do.

'Ooh, it's harmless fun,' he goes. 'But maybe you'd better not tell 'im.'

I said nothing because I wanted him to think that I just might.

Perhaps soon Tam and I would be joking up this whole damn thing. I was still not certain how far Tamsin went with her cruelty. The thought thrilled me. We still had so much to discover about one another. Some girls were like kindling, if they rubbed too close together they could set everything ablaze.

Phil looked at me in a hot smiling way. Me hormones leapt off a tall building.

Then I remembered how Sadie kept vomit tied up in supermarket carrier bags. How she smuggled them out of her bedroom in her patent leather handbag.

It was not a bad look Phil was giving me, just something he put on for the job, like me being all shy and polite with the Christians at the wedding, and now all soft and pretty when I was doing modelling. Work made you like that. With the right job I could go overnight from an asthmatic flat-chested underachiever to a hard-nut bitch in heels and leather.

I would, hell, I would!

'Lots of girls help me out,' he goes, his face hidden behind the camera. 'You got a boyfriend, Mona?'

I shook me head. Surely there was no way back to boyfriends and snogs.

For a while neither of us said anything. Once I did ballet and was in some kind of show. I had thick flesh tights and some long pink ribbons that me mam had sewn on to me ballet shoes. You had to point one foot and make your fingers curl above your head and just stand there with all your ribs and bones showing. Mam and Dad there together, watching me. I could feel everything trembling with the stillness and the attention but I kept it up and held still for ages. It was a long time ago. It was around five,

six, seven, when I was happy with stillness and quiet, blonde
hair getting brushed, Lindy, five years older, putting her cheek
against mine to have the school photo taken, the patter patter of
soft ballet shoes on wooden floor, reading a book, watching me
mam, warm water in a plastic pool in the garden and most of all
a nylon vest and everyone from my class running across this hot
sand into the sparkling sea.

'Wakey-wakey,' Phil goes. We'd finished two trays of wedding
rings and a pink tray of friendship rings and were now doing
some silver signet rings. Pictures to display the innocent prettiness of topless jewelled girls.

'I'm OK,' I goes. I tried to stay awake by making sordid
discoveries about him. When I was with men now I often
kept me hormones under control by snuffling out details to
sneer about after. This was the most fun thing, working out
the inadequacies you could exaggerate later: the lad from the
supermarket with the banana-shaped Adam's apple, the lorry
driver who had wax glowing amber like a traffic light in his ear,
the old man from the brewery whose chest hair grew in the shape
of a grin.

Perhaps Tamsin would want to know these details. Could she
picture them and giggle?

Later, he made me stand in front of a fan while we tried to
make me nipples hard but it just made me goose-bumpy and
instead he was going to touch up the nipples later.

'It's freezing,' I said. We were doing topless half-moon spec-
tacles now. 'And I'm getting double vision.'

'Think of summat that would make you very 'appy.'

'Putting my clothes back on. It's giving me 'eadache.'

'You know,' he goes, standing up and putting his hand on his
chin, 'I am seriously thinking of entering you for a photographic
competition. Just you. Something classy and 'ighly competitive.
Now I don't say that to all my lasses.'

'If you don't 'urry it'll be called "Cross-Eyed Girl with Hypo-
thermia".'

Foodlessness was making me delirious. I could have bought something in town, though since the incident with the sausage slice to eat without Her felt like a major betrayal. Tam had not offered me anything all night and this combined with the modelling made me feel light-headed and angry. It was, of course, good for your figure but it made me so tired me eyeballs were fizzing.

'Cheer up. Relax. You are sheer poetry, Mona.' He pronounced it *pooetry*. 'You inspire me to great rhythms deep inside. You could be a great man's muse. Do you know what that is, a muse, eh? Now relax and think of the flow of poetry. A muse . . . is a lady . . . or girl . . . of divine . . . beauty who . . . inspires genius . . . in men. Now relax again.'

He'd not reacted to me leaving home though I'd told him. Neither had he mentioned the starvation or the bloody scars on my shaven skin.

He bent towards me and touched my forehead. He smiled in that pleading way that meant he wanted me to smile back. Men needed women more than women needed men, I was realising.

'OK? OK. I'll take advantage of you just one last time,' he said and he got another tray off of the table. 'I'd like to do a couple of necklace shots taking in your 'ole face if you don't mind, lovely? You've got a right pretty face. OK, now touch your 'air. You think it is so beautiful. Hmm. You want me to love it too. Imagine it's a flowing river streaming over your shoulder, wetting your breasts, a rippling river of sunshot silk.'

'Watch out Pam Ayres,' I said, bored.

'My photography *is* my poetry,' he said, not joking.

When it was over we stood opposite each other and he gave me five pounds. I let him kiss me. His hands flicked up and under me dress, quick and confident, like he was shoplifting. He rubbed at the sore bony patch where me pubes had been like he was tickling the dog, and then plucked at me nipples like he was picking fluff from his jacket.

Still, I liked doing the modelling, it felt like an independent career.

Then he turned me round and started fingering around me arse, which was summat I was definitely not prepared for. The light in the room didn't change. I heard an aeroplane. It all happened very slow like a car accident. It didn't exactly hurt but it made me squirm. There was time to notice things to mock but it was not a laugh-later situation. We were both so hot and slippy his hands slid over me like we were in the bath. His breathing had a tiny yelp in it. Then he took his hands off me and turned away and lit a fag. He did not offer me one.

I was aware of a new part of me body, and I didn't like it.

'You were very good. Professional.'

'I didn't have to do anything,' I said, pulling me cardy tight around me chest. I felt muzzy. I stamped me foot and scowled. I would not tell anyone, not even Tam. Never. I felt like ripping what was left of me hair out in handfuls.

'That's a mark of a real natural,' he goes. 'D'you fancy doing any more modelling?' We discussed this and he gave me a date. 'D'you wanna see some of t'other more arty stuff I've done?'

I didn't really but I said yes. I wanted to go home and have a bath. He showed me his stuff and eventually he got to girls, or bits of girls. There were sock models and trousers models and all other bits of people, mostly carved up in individual sections, like cuts of meat. Some girls had faces. Pink, round, soft, blonde, blue. Tiny Tears sort of faces.

Lindy could've done faces. Sadie Fakenham could certainly have done faces.

I took a few blasts on the Ventolin. I wished I was drunkish.

He said things about how lovely the pictures were and how he'd made all these ordinary girls look lovely and feminine. Of course, that was the problem with modelling; being looked at, measured, photographed, observed, made me feel feminine, but feeling feminine made me feel anxious and ill.

And I still didn't really know what feminine was, apart from tears and pity.

'That's Julie Flowerdew,' he goes and points at this pale blue T-shirt.

'Where?' I said, though strangely it didn't seem unexpected. It was like her name never left me; I was always waiting for news of her.

'There,' he goes and put a fat finger on the T-shirt picture. 'Girls' T-shirt and vest top, £4.99. It's terrible. She was a nice lass. Quiet, but a nice lass. Where do you reckon she's gone?'

'How?' I said. His fingertip, the one that had just been else-where, had left a large, greasy print on the photo. I was reminded that men were not just losers as Tam and I liked to imagine, they were also dangerous animals who hunted, murdered and concealed.

''ow what?'

'How did you know her?'

'I saw 'er in the street. I know 'er dad. I asked if she wanted to do some modelling.'

'Oh.' I didn't believe he'd asked her dad. Phil had a look of wasted youth and sexual desperation that dads didn't trust. Though they liked his jokes.

He was a murderer! Yes, yes, he was!

No, never, never, he was just a man. A dad. Breathe. Breathe. Breathe.

'So where d'you reckon she's gone?'

'Dunno,' I goes.

I wanted to kneel down in a cool, quiet room and pray. It was just a blue shape and it could've been any girl.

'This was about a year ago. She only did a couple of days with me. To get some extra money to buy that trumpet.'

'Trombone,' I goes.

'Yes, trombone,' he said, shaking his head and closing the case. 'Will you come again tomorrow then?'

'Beg me.'

'Please, my sweet darling beauty.' And he bent down and kissed me hand in a way like he was trying to be funny, pretending we were in a tap-dancing film. I rather liked it. Men were easier than girls to have a dumb easy time with. Then over his face came this sad look again, like he needed me to look happy, to make him feel good again.

Soon he, like every other man in Whitehorse, would be painting his windows in white emulsion and crouching under the stairs with his tins and his wife and kid. We all had to love now, now or never!

Later, when the kissing and arse fingering had stopped, I was out the door and down the stairs. I raised me fist with relief.

Get thee to a nunnery and scrub thy foul skin.

The stairs were cold concrete, like ones they might have in hospital or prison. Though I was crying (my traitorous eyes showing an emotion I would not allow my brain to consider), I imagined it as a romantic escape and me running down into warm safe arms.

Instead, I ran into a fruity, waiting for me to one side of the entrance. It was turned off, sleeping, because the cinema was shut, but I just plugged it in and the lights flickered. It went do-dede-loo when it came on. It was ancient and called *Treasure Trail*. It reminded me of old *Blaze A Trail*. The plastic was scratched and it had no special features so most of my skills were what my careers teacher, when making a different point, once called *woefully underutilised*. Some lights weren't working but it was a precious thing and it liked my lovely Sunset Sheen nails as I stroked it and fed it.

The afternoon had taught me something: men might be losers but they were still very menacing and we forgot it at our peril. Tam and I had to be alert to this danger

Eventually, after four pounds, the fruity paid out with a slow, low clumclumclum.

salad

Tam decided we would go over to Whitehorse and visit her father's girlfriend. It seemed to me, after a mini bottle of Malibu and a bottle of red wine (for this is what I'd bought with my winnings and the money Phil had given me), a very good idea. It was Saturday so there was a good chance she'd be in.

'I could give you a croggy on me bike, Tam. I know a real quick route between Goldwell and Whitehorse. I've been riding it every night for over three years, after all, haven't I?'

Tam looked at me disdainfully, drunkenly.

'We are delivering revenge, not groceries, Mona.'

'Oh. Yes.'

'And I suggest you wear one of Sadie's sweet little skirts, rather than bike-riding jeans.'

I took another wad out of my box of saved-up money and called a taxi.

It was the first time we had been out of the house together since our trip to Tall Paul's wife. Tam had hinted that one night we might go out to a proper disco, though she had not mentioned it since, and I knew better than to pester her. Like Lindy, if she knew I wanted something badly she'd take pleasure in denying me.

Bitch. I did not trust her, and sometimes thought of her in this way now.

It was 6.17 p.m.: very early morning for us.

'Depending on who you speak to, Mother or Father, Nina Fisher is either *a scheming damned little whore bitch*, or a *highly intelligent and motivated young woman*,' Tam said. She was sitting right on the edge of the taxi seat with her legs crossed and her hands delicately placed on her knees. 'She's a Virgo,' Tam added.

'Girlfriends, eh,' I said, shaking my head very slowly. 'Have these women no idea? My father's bit wouldn't know a good man from a mound of manure, or a Manx cat.'

I could not really believe we were actually going to Nina Fisher's home.

'She's got a first-class degree in business studies,' Tam said solemnly.

'So what? That won't help when the heat flash comes,' I sneered. 'We'll all fry; mistresses, spinsters, wives, widows, girlfriends, murderers, adulterers, killers, kidnappers, all annihilated as one. Whoosh!'

'And her own flat. A new little car. A Peugeot. One of those new bob haircuts where they style it high up at the back, leaving a sleek wave over one eye. She's got a natural curl which makes it easier to blow-dry,' Tam said knowingly, and demonstrated by swirling a finger around her head.

'Like Princess Di?'

'Hmm. Only in glossy black. And she wears these wide-leg black trousers, in hundred per cent wool, with a sleeveless black silk top.'

'Oh.'

'Sadie's got her hair the same way.'

She didn't fluster. I did not react. I looked out of the window and tried to breathe in a regular, unconcerned, independent woman sort of way. Perhaps it was a slip, perhaps she did not intend to use the present tense in connection with her sister. Sometimes, though less as time passed, I used the present tense about me mam.

I let the sentence float and settle in the junk-room part of my mind where I now heaped all unsettling phrases, thoughts and emotions.

'And she's got a drink problem. So my mother said. In fact, Mummy said she was a *drug addict*.'

'Oh,' I said. Being a drug addict was of course on par with being a pioneer of early aviation, or a saloon-bar hussy straddling the tables in a speakeasy.

We both feared Nina Fisher was exactly the sort of exciting, independent, modern, out-of-control woman we both longed to be.

I imagined her as the thrilling type who winked at strange men on buses and then led them home, spellbound, for movie sex.

The countryside blurred by. It was a short drive by road to Whitehorse, a route which would take us past our pub.

Tam chatted to the driver and he rewarded her with smiles and winks in his rear-view mirror. This was the first time I had seen Tam playing cute and loose with a man. She was very good at it. The driver turned Radio One on loud and began to smoke recklessly and drum on the steering wheel. I saw for the first time that Tamsin Fakenham was a true bewitcher of men.

Of course, her successful flirtation combined with the previous day's modelling made me feel sad and ugly. Me hair was growing more wildly than expected, outwards and upwards, giving me the permanent look of just having tumbled out of bed in shock. Which was how I did get out of bed every day at the Fakenham house (for the way she kissed and stroked me in the night now was like a rare drug, the effects as yet unknown, and I often woke up hungover and scared).

'Perhaps she'll give us some money. Then you won't need to be a gambler. You never seem to win anything anyway,' Tam mused, lighting a fag and not looking at me. 'It's my father's money, after all.' The driver let Tam smoke, though there was a big sign forbidding it. He would probably have let her rip his taxi apart with her teeth, as long as he could watch while she did it.

Neither of us was mentioning if Mr Fakenham would be there at Nina's. I tried to imagine him curled up in a chair with a bag of chips, watching the Saturday sport.

'What are you thinking about, Einstein?' she snapped.

She was angry with me for going out yesterday, and suspected something. I was very close to telling her but knew she'd get it all wrong and refer to Phil as my *porno boyfriend*, and say something like she could just picture him: a white suit, moustache, a pile of gold rings on hairy fingers.

We were coming up to Black Beck. It was two weeks ago today since I left with Lindy in the little cart. I felt a stomach sink of homesickness.

'Oh, look, Mona, it's your funny old pub.'

'Christ,' I said, shaking me head. 'Thank fuck I'm free.'

I looked at her and laughed, gazed at her 'til the pub was behind us and the homesickness became usual drunken car sickness.

'Stop here,' Tam said to the driver. And the cab halted and growled outside a large terraced house. We were in the old town of Whitehorse, a comfortable distance from our pub. Here lived the sort of folk who did not drink in our pub; teachers, social workers and high-class sexretaries, who painted their doors glossy colours and attached big brass knockers and window boxes.

'Wait for us round the corner, please. We won't be long.'

The driver grinned and said: 'Yes m'lady,' trying to be funny.

We knocked on a shiny red door with a dolphin-shaped knocker, and then pulled at the hems on our little skirts as we waited. Luckily, we were well drunkish.

When she opened the door she looked exhausted. I realised she was humiliated by the love that had been inflicted on her. I wondered at the time, and in the few days after, why she never told anyone about what we did to her. She told not the police, or the staff at the hospital, or any friends or relatives who could come and avenge the attack we made on her. Amazingly, she did not even tell her lover what his daughter had done to her. She was in the early stages of an obsessive and destructive relationship with an older and more powerful man. Every odd and dangerous thing that happened to her was strangely expected. She stayed quiet because she was lessened by the love she suffered. She was ill with her love for Mr Fakenham. She did not think straight. She thought whatever happened to her was really what she deserved. It was a punishment for losing her independent mind to love.

'Can we come in?' Tam said.

Nina Fisher recognised her. In one hand she was holding a glass of silvery wine which gave off gentle beads of bubbles, in the other an all-white menthol cigarette. It was a relaxing Saturday. Perhaps she'd been trying to recover from love by flicking through a magazine, or painting her nails, or donning a peanut-and-herb exfoliating mask.

Nina's breasts were round and light and natural as full sails. Looking at them billowing beneath her white silk blouse calmed me. She had shoulder pads and a pair of loose tapered trousers which matched the blouse. She had an olivy all-over tan and honey-coloured hairs on her sleek arms.

'I've come to talk about my father.'

'I see. Well, yes. I suppose you had better come in then,' she said, looking out over our heads across the streets. Then she looked up into the sunny sky, like a person checking for rain.

We went into the narrow hallway of her luxury ground-floor flat. There was no sign of Mr Fakenham, though I'm sure Tam had expected to see him in a suitable dadlike pose: in front of the TV with a newspaper in his hand and a glass of Scotch: *Hello, girls, jolly good to see you both*.

Nina tried to speak in a neutral businesslike accent, but I could detect a common rasp to her vowels. She had bettered herself through a career. She was telling us how she thought it would be 'wiser' if we spoke to Mr Fakenham.

Silly cow.

She did not think she could 'help us'.

'We don't need *help*,' I sneered.

Tam was looking round at the impressive furnishings. In the distance was a dining room with an open door. Nina led us past this door and into the back room. I looked in and saw on the table a row of little silver fishes arranged on an oval plate. A bowl of salad was decorated with the tiniest tomatoes. Places were set out for six people. This was the sort of occasion you read about; it was a 'get-together'. She had money and lovers and bright furnishings from shops. She was hosting a Saturday-night dinner party for a few close friends.

She didn't need to read magazines because she lived in one.

But it would be cancelled at the last minute because Nina Fisher would, in about half an hour, be in casualty at St Anne's Hospital. At the exact moment the guests were due to arrive, she would be floating away under the anaesthetic.

We walked on. It was a big flat. On the walls of the hall were jolly holiday snaps of lonely but loveable men and women who all looked like they worked as catalogue models or travel agents. They were in bars, on beaches, at parties blowing hooters, or dancing in the dark with sparklers. The house even *smelt* of holidays. Nina Fisher, we both realised, could've starred in her own made-for-TV drama: *The Mistress*.

People were speaking, a radio perhaps or maybe Tam, but I couldn't hear anything because of the sudden clattering noise in me head.

The back room had framed photographs on the walls of smiling foreign peasants crouching in sun-shot alleyways. It made their stinking poverty look highly appealing. There was no evidence of the runaway dad. She had antiques and a white linen sofa and china lamps. She had a cluster of drinks decanters and a slim black stereo system. It reminded me of the one I robbed from the little house, on that day that seemed so long ago.

She was twenty-eight and lived alone. I looked over my

shoulder and saw a glass-topped coffee table with a weird circle of beach pebbles in the centre. She was thirteen years older than us. Nina leant against the ornate fireplace and Tam stood opposite her. I positioned mesen next to Tam. I felt like we were in a play and I had to remember me lines. I felt a sickening terror. I knew I would be judged on this performance for years to come. My future success would depend on it. I felt there were thousands of people out there watching. I could hear Tam's heartbeat, I was sure. I straightened my spine and lifted my chin. There seemed to be a long pause. I was waiting for Tam to say something lashingly smart. She was about to dash bloody Nina Fisher to the ground with the inferno force of her quick girl-person wit.

But no. I looked stealthily out the corner of my eye and saw that Tam's chin was trembling and her lovely long lashes, the ones she had combed so carefully with Summer Azure mascara before we left the house, were wet. Around what the magazines called the 'delicate eye area' red patches were appearing.

'Leave my father alone,' she muttered in a babble. Her words were quiet and sounded sticky.

'Bitch,' I said, to try and back her up. I could not bear to see Tam brought so low.

It was incredible.

Nina Fisher looked down at her shoes which were flat black pumps. She put her lower teeth over her upper lip and blinked several times. The ash dropped from her cigarette down on to her smart red rug. On the wall behind her was a large chrome-framed photograph of a black man playing a trumpet.

Nina Fisher was now crying too. It was terrible. I could hear a little river of tears gurgling through the room.

We learnt much later that Mr Fakenham was in a hotel and already preparing to return to the Fakenham house. He missed his family too much to be with her. He had lasted only six days away.

Then I hit her. For her tears as much as anything.

I really, really hated the endless juices women made.

It was only a slap but it was so unexpected that it hurled her towards Tam. Tam caught her neat little head in her hands. I think at first Tam was trying to stop Nina hitting herself against the fireplace. Tam gazed at me, frightened, she looked like someone who'd caught the ball in cricket without knowing the rules of the game.

'Bitch,' I said again, but now in a urging way. My feet were moving. I could truly think of nothing better, though I was aware this level of repartee was inadequate. 'What you staring at?' I added.

Then Nina began to fight. I think she said 'please'. Tam held tight to her head, her fingers twisted in Nina's glossy black hair. Nina was bent now like a goat butting against a wall. It did look rather funny, the way she struggled. I could see white flashes of Nina's scalp through the glossy black. She was backed like a cow, her spine arched and bovine. From this unappealing angle she looked rather fattish; her womanly haunches jittering; her tits hung down like udders.

Then Tam did an extraordinary thing. I thought she was going to kiss Nina, then I was sure she was going to whisper a caustic threat. But no. She leant down and bit Nina's ear. It was done quietly and carefully, like someone incising the corner off a packet of peanuts. Nip, rip.

Then Tam staggered backwards letting Nina go, like Nina's head was suddenly burning, scalding hot. Nina opened her mouth and no scream came. She looked like she was sucking in the air of the entire room. I knew that in her head she was alone. We were not there. Her eyes were stretched so wide it was unnatural. It was like her eyes were giving birth to a new type of pain. Her hands were held up six inches from her ears like she was hearing screeching music. I noticed outside the window a hanging basket and a patio potted with plants; a bee bouncing above the flowers.

Then I looked at Tam. She too was frozen into this bloody,

unforgettable, new moment. She had a pea-sized piece of Nina Fisher's ear lobe on her lip. It was a bud of pale sweetcorn. No, whiter. It was ashen, and strangely greasy, like a piece of crisp, but I wanted to cup it in my hand for it looked so tender, so alive still. I felt sorry for it. There was a bloody print around Tam's mouth. I had no Ventolin and was getting breathless.

I looked around as calmly as possible for some booze. On the mantelpiece I saw Nina's glass of pale wine, the bubbles still bubbling. I leant over and drank it down.

Then Tam wiped her mouth with the back of her hand, saloon-bar-drinker style, and the little lobe, the white pearl of flesh, the piece of woman, fell away.

'Let's go home and have a shower,' Tam said, reaching for my arm.

I saw her stretch out across the room to me, over Nina Fisher's head and her enormous fingers were throbbing and she was groping, like she was eyeless. But she was smiling now, her breath caught back in a gasp of expectation, like she was blindfolded and staggering in a thrilling party game, looking to bump up against someone new and exciting.

And I was there for her, I pulled her to me. She was panting, then swallowing hard and wiping a flushed, trembling hand over her mouth. I remember her lips were grinning but her eyes looked like she'd just been shot.

And then we left, calmly, slowly, just as the real screaming started.

The eager driver was waiting for us. But after just a few hundred yards Tam was sick all over the back of his taxi.

vinegar

'Hold it there and thrust your pelvis out – like you believe it. Be obscene!' Tam shouted, annoyed.

It was 3.06 a.m., Sunday, the next day, our mid-afternoon. She was teaching me to play the electric guitar and I was not responding as well as I should've done. She had three guitars, two acoustic and one electric, she also had fuzzboxes, amps, plectrums and tambourines.

She might be cooler than Iceland but still no one liked her at school.

She said she was supposed to be having music lessons, but it was too hot, and anyway now she didn't want us going out. She'd said she'd give me the money she'd saved by not going for her lessons to put in the box of saved-up money, which I had proudly revealed to her.

We did not mention Nina Fisher or her torn ear.

'You're good,' she yelled. 'Keep trying. Don't give up. We'll show 'em.'

We had decided that night that anything men could do we could do better. Becoming experts at electric guitar was our latest plan. I thrust me hip out and sneered. She clapped. After much practice I could thrust, sneer, tap me foot and nod me head. All I could not do was play the instrument or sing, and just the weight of the guitar hurt me shoulders and ached me arms. It was too masculine, I was too thin and frail for the guitar, and I'd have preferred to listen to spangly girl singers and dream.

We had spent an hour that night taking shadowy photos of one another in various seductive poses.

Tam had forbidden the windows to be opened for security reasons. Though Tall Paul had not been back since we visited his house, Tam insisted we were still in great danger from him and Poison Ivy, who lurked in the bushes and spied on us both day and night. Tam said I had to stay indoors *'til things had settled down.* Tam had heard the servants rustling through the foliage like rats. They were after a glimpse of her. While she danced naked in the bath, she would call out to Tall Paul who, she believed, was out there slobbering for girl flesh. The chance of us *settling down* seemed slim.

Our steam and body heat hung in the house stale and warm.

Girl flesh fermenting like yeast.

The flies no longer became pitted in the flypaper but bumped into our faces as we slept – together, hot or cold, unhappy or ecstatic, I couldn't tell. Only Tam was able to go outside, after midnight on the ladder to do painting. Even then she'd made a promise to me that her feet would not touch the hostile ground, which was why she came in through the back bathroom window. Witchlike. Three hours of painting each night was essential if the grime on the house was to be cleared away, she'd declared.

I was wearing Sadie's white ra-ra skirt which pinched me waist and her red boob tube which made me chest look like a pillar box. I was glad Mrs Fakenham had removed the mirrors, glad that only Tam was witness to my strange, grave-robbing look.

'You're wonderful,' Tam yelled. She seemed more impressed with me now she knew about me cruelty, and now that I could scare her she respected me more.

Still, I knew we had to put more fuel on the fire if this addictive confidence was to continue.

The wide window frames rocked with the sound of the bass and my ghoulish singing.

We'd started forgetting to eat, even the strange food.

Instead, we counted our money.

We planned to run away.

We discussed people Tam knew who lived abroad who might hide us.

We talked of growing old together.

Everything we thought or saw supported our dark vision.

Silently, we wondered when the police would come to speak about Nina's ear.

We often discussed how *other people* got to be so *dumb* that they couldn't see the world with our clarity.

'That old cow, Tall Paul's wife, never came back, did she, eh?' I said, smiling. We had bored of guitars and were slouched across the kitchen chairs watching flies. 'You were so right to go round there and state our case. I bet that made him think. The bastard.'

Somewhere, I feared our new confidence was based on nothing but the lazy flame of extreme unkindness. And I badly wanted it to evolve into more than this; I wanted it to be clever, witty, admirable, for us to be like people in a book or on TV. I wanted people to recognise our power, celebrate it and think we were a cool, finger-snapping, hip-swinging success.

I hated the idea of just being averagely mean and bitchy.

'Hmm. Poison Ivy said that old woman, his wife, is in hospital.'

'Oh.' So that was why the wife had not complained about us and Paul had not been to do the gardening.

'Yes, apparently anyway,' she said, waving her hand around her face, like she was swatting away a fly. 'Who knows if it's true what servants say.'

She was bored and it shrivelled me. I wanted to excite her always.

I dared not ask what the old woman was in hospital for. Nor

did I know if Tam's cruel aristocratic stance regarding servants was meant to be humorous or not. Sometimes now, if I failed to get her jokes, she would bend her face very close to mine and say, very slowly and quietly: 'That is called *irony*, Mona darling. And it is *funny*.'

Eventually, I asked as languidly as possible: 'When did you see Ivy?'

'Poison Ivy? Oh, she came round. While you were out on Friday, doing whatever secret thing it is that you do.'

I dared not ask why Ivy had visited and did not want to discuss Friday, so we went back to drinking.

I tried not to think of Nina Fisher and Tall Paul's wife in the hospital, yet whenever I closed me eyes I thought of the ward where me mam died, but instead of me mam in the bed it was Nina, no longer in her silky white suit, but naked. Her tanned slim body writhing in silent agony against the white, white sheets.

Later, at 9.05 a.m., when we should've been tucked up in bed but were in fact in the middle of a particularly complicated dance, the phone rang. It was Father.

'Lord save us from ordinary people,' I whispered to Tam while Father was speaking.

Father sounded softer, more tender, like words expressed in a letter. He was a lonely and sad dad. Secretly I was thrilled to hear from him, though I mumbled into the phone, sighed, sniffed, pretended not to hear him so he had to repeat himself several times, and then did not answer his questions.

After he'd been talking for a few minutes, Tam came up behind me and pushed a spoon of warm custard between me lips.

'Like a dog,' I mumbled.

'Good,' he said. I knew he wanted me to say summat to make him feel better. Then he said: 'I'd like you to come 'ome now. We are all missing you. You 'aven't even given Debbie a chance yet. I'd like you to be 'ome by this teatime, please. And I 'ave to say that if you don't . . .'

Tam began to rub a spoonful of the custard over me cheek and it felt like being licked with warm tongues. I wondered if me dad could hear her breathing, though he just continued talking about how much he missed me and how he wanted me back.

'I love you, Mona,' Dad said quietly. 'And I miss yer mam, even though we weren't still together. Even though I don't always express it right. She was a good, kind woman.'

Tam and I knew it was better with the thought that someone might be listening. We had started to get slack because no one could be even *bothered* to oppose us.

Tam unzipped the ra-ra skirt and it slid to the ground. She had the custard all over me chest now. It smelt yellow. It came over me like sweet paint, some patches thick and clotted, others like clear varnish. It was very funny. Dad said he'd heard of a job going for me. Tam pulled the boob tube down so it clung round me skinny hips. Dad said he'd decided to start giving me weekly money to help me get settled. Tam pulled the boob tube further down so it was round me knees, and I couldn't've walked away even if I'd tried.

I liked the thought of someone watching us through the trees.

I liked the idea of our private perviness made public.

Ha!

I wanted to shock with the power of a brick through a window.

Dad said that on me mam's anniversary him, Lindy and me would go to the grave. He said he knew it was an important day for me.

I lay Father down on the narrow mahogany telephone table and let Tam lead me up to the shower.

She was meticulous about how she washed me, because of her hatred of dirt and smells. She wanted every crack and crease of me soaped clean. She was even more concerned about cleanliness since the incident with Nina's ear. She washed me with her soapy fingers, and then her flat hands, no flannels or sponges. She washed me hair.

Father was down there having to listen to this. Ha!

When I got out of the water she dried me very slowly, starting with each toe, then a thin ankle, a calf and a thigh. She thought I was losing some weight and later that day she said she would measure me to be certain. I felt delighted. She rubbed round me thighs so slowly me back was almost dry by the time I was lying down on the bed. She practised sucking deep in me. We had perfected everything else, kisses and touches and all, but this – she did it for a long time, her face buried in me. Her lips made little whispering sounds. I thought of how she had chomped off Nina's ear. I could see the little flesh dot on Tam's lip. She sucked into me like someone guiltlessly eating a delicious rich meal. It felt like me skin could hear and taste and see. Me eyes were closed and the only sounds were of the country and the birds.

'Let your Soviet Special Forces come watch this,' Tam chuckled.

'Oh, honey, this love could stop the war.'

'Darling, the soldiers of the world would be far too astonished to fight.'

It took for ever, then we were ready to start for ever again, and I led her back to the shower and started the whole thing over on her.

Later, still Sunday but now afternoon, there was a distant knock at the door. Blissed out, I ignored it for as long as possible. We were both in bed, it being 3.14 p.m. and so the middle of the night for us. But the knocking got louder and more insistent and I slipped away, leaving Tam sleeping. If it was Tall Paul I would rather handle him alone. If it was Poison Ivy, surely she would remember how she used to be my friend. If it was the old fat auntie I would claim to be a common serving wench, and never to have heard of her lunatic niece.

If it was Nina Fisher I would hold her hurt head and soothe

away her pain. Put a slick of lip gloss, Sleekly Simple perhaps, on her crying lips, clip a golden earring, a healing crucifix maybe, over her savaged ear.

When I woke it sometimes took me a few minutes to remember I was a cruel and angry criminal. Occasionally I forgot and opened my eyes to tender thoughts.

At first I hid behind Tam's heavy bedroom curtain and watched cautiously out of the window. Below on the step was a person with black shining upright hair and a fishnet top. This was not Tall Paul. It was not Poison Ivy, Nina Fisher or the old fat auntie. He was the same shape and size as my stepbrother, the monstrous PorkChop. He was holding chips like they were the only friend he had in the world. He looked glum and gave a puzzled look all around the courtyard, then moved backwards 'til he was staring, shocked, at the battered half-pink house. He had a necklace and some muck on his face which looked like make-up.

I felt thrilled; at last we had a worthy enemy.

I went downstairs quiet as a spider. The house was thick with afternoon warmth. I stood still by the umbrella stand and listened for police, for the scuffling of boots and the clicking of triggers. Now I knew men were not just losers but maniacs too; even that blubbery PorkChop seemed threatening.

'I've brought you summat, Mona,' he said in a quiet voice, hooking a fat finger through the letter box so he could be heard. I was sick with embarrassment for him. I thought sadly how he would never know sisterhood and its many joys.

'I brought you summat,' I said, mimicking his whine, and then crumpled down on the black and brown tiles and buried my face in me hands. To be related in law to that! I fancied I could hear Tam breathing.

I thought wildly of death.

'Can I come in?' he said like the fat kid who's not invited to the party. He looked terrible in the daylight so fat and drunkish and uncoordinated. He would never be my lover. I sat down in the hall and waited for him to go.

He was a failure even as an enemy.

Then: 'It's a card, for your birthday,' he shouted. 'It's your birthday now, Mona. 'appy birthday, Mona.'

I stood up and had to press my hip against the wood to ease the stiff lock loose.

'What's happened to you?' I smirked. He had thick eyeliner, frowning on his upper eyelids and gunged into his eyebrows too. His blusher was purple and red clots of lipstick stuck on his lip like someone had smashed him in the face. He looked like a horror-movie version of Lindy. And a bit of him looked like poor lost Cleo, which made me want to weep, and therefore punch him.

Bastard.

'How did you know where I was?' I whispered. The house was altered by his presence. He brought in with him the breezy daytime world, and I knew now nothing would seem the same again.

'Dad told me, of course. Everyone knows. He's right worried. We all know where you are now. And what yer up to. Living 'ere with a posh lass.'

'What's up with that?' I hissed. 'She's a friend. We're revising. Tell that to *Dad*.'

'That's not the version going round our pub!'

'And what is the version going round *our pub*?'

My whispers were shrill and vicious, his were teasing and jokey. Mine came from the private, bloody world of girlfriends, his from the breezy public world of bar-room boozers.

I could smell her womb juice on me fingers. Her sweet vinigariness was similar to that rising off the chips.

'More X-rated,' he said and started to grunt with laughter. 'More revolting than revising from what I've 'eard. More snogging than studying, some might say.'

'I'm surprised you know what snogging is, PorkChop.' I

said this sarcastically, which was a wonderful new ability I had.

All confident, cruel girls can afford lashings and lashings of sarcasm.

'I know what it is,' he said softly. He'd put on more weight since I'd been gone, and now his belly lolled in two thick rolls. He pushed by me and came into the hall. Secretly I was rather pleased to show off the splendour of my new home.

'It's different in real life, you know, from how it is in *songs*,' I sneered. 'Anyway, what d'you want?'

'Nowt,' he said. He was opposite me by the door with darling Tam sleeping upstairs. I saw him glance over longingly at the baby grand piano, then up at the oil paintings, the vases, the crystal bowls and ornaments. I smiled. Neither of us spoke. We were not close enough, bound only by law, to be cruel to one another this intimately. Then I saw he was more drunk than we were, but lagered which was a different drunkishness.

Side by side, me stick thin, him inflatable, we were a comedy duo.

The door was still open.

'Done any more robberies?' he asked with a nervous grin.

'You look a right berk,' I told him, ignoring his question. I'd learnt from Tam that cruelty was an effective weapon against sadness. I'd cried much less since I'd known her. 'Where've you been?' I asked, sneering down at his trousers.

'A club. In Leeds. I only got back this dinnertime.'

'Jesus!' I sighed.

There was a pause and I could feel cruelty coming over me like a cloud crossing the sun. 'Penned any sad songs lately, Elton?' I said with a smile. 'Hey, that piano'd suit you a treat, wouldn't it, eh?'

'Hey, shuddup,' he said softly, and the cloud passed and I felt the blush of my unkindness.

'You got any tips for the Derby, Steve?' I said. This was the first time I'd ever called him by his name and he looked suspicious and shook his head, then said: 'I'll let you know if I hear of any.'

'Please do,' I said, though I no longer knew if we would put the bet on, if it was a realistic possibility or not. Then he said: 'We'd better go now. Yer dad's waiting.'

And then before I could slit his throat with the silver envelope knife, in the doorway Father appeared.

'Away!' I yelled and tried to close the door. He pushed it open. In one hand I saw he was carrying a tool box, like he intended to unscrew every lock to get at me. He was now inside the hallway too. I couldn't speak, so stricken was I with horror and shock. I should have known that if ever he were to come for me it'd be after closing on Sunday dinnertime.

Then PorkChop's chips were tempting me like greasy little demons. Crazily, I shovelled them in, the delicious grease enhanced by the girl muck on me fingertips. PorkChop put his hand hard on my tiny wrist. He gripped and pulled me up. I pushed up against his body.

This was it, it was all true, everything we'd ever thought about men, come true.

They were evil and dangerous.

I screamed for Tam: 'Tam, help me, help me, darling, help!'

I cracked open in a thunderstorm of tears.

She came, drifting richly, drunk and sleepy, floating down the great stairs. At first she looked annoyed with me, but this was not irony, it was real. I screamed and struggled. She ran and I reached. It seemed a true tragedy and the purest injustice.

It was romantic.

We were both yelling and flailing.

The umbrella stand fell over. A china bowl smashed. A bouquet of dried flowers exploded into dark confetti.

We liked it.

PorkChop shook her off and she slumped to the tiled floor dramatically clutching at her arm. 'He's attacked me!' she shrieked. 'That fat bastard man's attacked me!'

'Don't let him, honey. Don't let him take me, darling,' I yelled.

This united dam-burst of tears was in fact a delicious relief: it reminded us we were little girls.

From this moment on we no longer felt like we had any adult responsibility.

'I'll love you. I'll wait for you,' she panted, as I was carried kicking and crying from the Fakenham house.

Of course, separation is to romance what champagne is to parties.

ice cream

That first night, Sunday, Tam came looking for me. I liked to imagine she'd walked barefoot, weeping, from Goldwell. All night she held a vigil on the wall of Black Beck. I screamed her name from my bedroom window and flung myself against the walls and threatened to jump. Debbie wanted to call the police, then when Father refused she suggested they tie me to the bed with bandages. I told them I abhorred them all, though in truth I felt me emotions lasted no longer than a few moments before being replaced by their exact opposite.

Father had to come in and restrain me when I tried to leap out of the window.

I yelled. I did not want any of them to touch me. I'd adopted a new posture which I hoped indicated my flesh was wrapped in barbed wire, and they laid hands on me at their peril.

The whole house crackled with my wild power, as in days of old when kingdoms were rocked by the madness of goddesses.

Father wrestled with me and then at dawn on Monday went out to tell Tam to go. I could see them speaking, my beautiful Tam besides my odious father. Eventually Tam left, walking backwards as she went, waving.

Weeping, I went and lay on my bed with the white satin jewellery box that me mam had bought for my eighth birthday. With a small golden key I unlocked the box and the tinny tune began, and the tiny ballerina, who lived most of her life imprisoned in darkness, sprang up and began her arthritic pirouette on scarlet pointes. She was two inches tall, very thin, with a silver tutu and black hair in a bun. She wore a faint scowl on her painted plastic face.

Later, when Dad came in to talk to me, I just slowly straightened my back balletically, lifted me chin, then turned away.

In the morning Debbie swore at me and then began to cry herself.

I liked her anguish.

I felt easily superior, wronged, misunderstood and, most importantly, deliciously jailed: surely the style of the best revolutionaries.

And I found to my delight it was much easier to be a heroic freedom fighter when under house arrest with your stinking family, than when living free, in luxury, with your girlfriend.

It was all rather lovely being back at home.

And though they had forbidden me to leave the house, or go into the bar during opening hours, I was allowed to miserably potter around the kitchen, and I still had my dear fruity to play through the night.

Often I caught Dad watching me, and sometimes he tried to talk to me. When I arrived home after the kidnapping the first thing I had noticed was a woman's turquoise cardigan hooked over the stool at the back of the bar. It was the feeling you got when overnight they changed the actor playing a kid in one of your favourite soaps; you felt a wave of grief, then wanted to turn off in protest at the artifice of it all, but knew also that in just a few months' time you'd have forgotten the part was ever played by anyone different.

And though I abhorred Debbie, Father idolised her. Often I caught him flashing her a curious look. It was a gasp of surprise. Like a child's joy when ripping the paper off a surprise present. Oh, wow! He couldn't believe it! He'd got exactly what he wanted! Debbie was new: he loved her.

There was indeed one very good aspect to Debbie; she was an

A-grade housewife. She delighted in cleaning, ironing, washing and cooking the greasy gut muck men and bad g.'. love to eat.

And she used a powerful fabric conditioner for bed linen so I dozed with my tinkling ballerina in a bright summer meadow. The six nocturnal days with Tam had left me exhausted.

My father did not have to put locks on the doors, or screw bars across the windows because I was happy to take a refreshing break from Tamsin in this rather familiar and comfortable hotel.

And though I would never, could never, admit it, it was rather nice to be back with Dad and PorkChop.

At last, like a fatigued film star who retires to a Swiss spa, I was 'away'.

It was pleasant to have me clothes freshly laundered and ironed and placed in a pile on me bed.

And though of course I was refusing to eat anything in the presence of my family, in private I was overjoyed, after the last six days of famine, to feast on chocolate, crisps, pork scratchings, chips, bacon, and the pies and pastries that Debbie kept Tupperwared-up in the fridge.

On Tuesday Debbie hit me. She had come into my lair carrying a hot plate of scrambled eggs and a mug of Ovaltine. She sat carefully on the bed and said, with a confessional raise of eyebrow and a tight smile: 'I know what you're going through.'

'Debbie,' I said, snapping my jewellery box shut, and trying out irony on her for the first time, 'I think you and I are somewhat *different*, darling.'

She hit me. I let her. I liked it.

My weeks of lunacy training had served their purpose. I was now no longer just a girl, nor a wife and mother like Lindy or Debbie, but uniquely, famously, myself. My family recognised me as a force. As a woman with a dark mystery who you had to be very careful around. You had to think what to say to me before opening your mouth. You had to consider every action in case it offended me. The manipulative, posh-girl techniques I had learnt from Tamsin created a humming power around me, which would surely, when presented to the wider population, transform into allure, desire, irresistibility.

Dad told me he loved me, said I was all he had left of how things used to be.

I took long hot bubble baths and no one disturbed me for hours.

Debbie bought library loads of women's magazines, and I curled up in bed and read, sucking through packs of Debbie's cheap cigarettes, and regularly shouting down for cups of tea.

During the afternoon I put my pillows on the settee and with only my ballerina and a family pack of choc ices for company, lay watching our extra large TV.

The sounds from our bar drifted up to me like a lullaby.

I could easily have run away and returned immediately to dear Tam. We could've escaped across the Channel in a bathtub and set up home in a Parisian forest. And of course now that we were torn apart, I'd returned to loving her passionately, and feared constantly that she was with the old fat auntie eating roast beef and confessing.

Though, in truth, being apart seemed only to have heightened her love for me.

In my pocket I had a letter from Tam. My maid, PorkChop, had discovered it in the post on Tuesday and brought it to me. In the strange leaning scrawl, it said:

Dearest Mona Lisa,
  Don't be sad. They don't know what you are thinking, so fear not. Soon you will be back with me. Smile and think of when we are together. Conceal your true desires from *THEM*, keep your dark heart for *ME*. I am waiting for when you are able to come back. I will wait my whole life and become immortalised in legend. I will not leave the house 'til *YOU* return. My hair will grow, cobwebs will overtake this lonely abode, bluebirds will sing to me sad songs, bees will make a honeycomb of my heart, and *OUR* love will turn into a fairy tale.

But if you return then *WE* will show them how strong and true we have become, and how purposeful we can be. *YOU* know what *I* mean. With endless *LOVE*,

Tamsin Ruby Fakenham

I wept as I read her letter to my ballerina.

'That,' I would soon sneer at Phil, 'is *pooetry*.'

I worked on my letter to her for many hours. I wrote a five-page letter about every thought I'd had since we parted, then in the end I just put:

Dearest Miss T,

I want to prick my finger and sleep for a thousand years, until YOU wake ME with a kiss.

Loving love Miss Mona Lisa

I was very pleased with it. I even wrote it with my left hand, in the hope it would give me a characterful trembling weirdness.

At closing time, as I hung from my balcony, weeping and listening to my sad records, a rumble of drunk men gathered beneath my window and gazed up at my tower. They laughed and whistled and called out insults and endearments.

I'd never been so noticed.

At 4.15 a.m. on Friday I found a pair of binoculars at the back of me cupboard and trained them down on to Black Beck. I was looking for Tam, then for a long time I was looking for bodies.

I was sure someone was down there dead. But where?

In less than one week's time a body would be discovered in Black Beck. It would be lifted from the weeds by a single kindly man. The body would already be marbled white, grey and blue like a statue.

Of course, inevitably, my five-day leisure break came to an end. And as swiftly as it had begun.

On Friday afternoon, as I rested with my ballerina in a chocolately slumber, I heard Dad whisper to Debbie: 'Don't worry, she's calming down now. She's almost back to normal. Lindy was a bit this way as a teenager, but she's settled down and look at 'er now! Mona'll turn out just as good.'

Just when I was thinking he hadn't come I saw the headlights on his car. It was a sports model, but old and rusty with a jagged flash of orange down the side. *Ha! Scalextrix car driven by Subbuteo man*, Anne-Marie would have said (I still thought of her, though I was a different person when I knew her). He was parked so the car was just peeping out of the shadow that marked the entrance to a deserted factory; he had his seat slugged down so low it was hard to see his face. The engine wheezed anxiously.

It all looked wonderfully criminal.

The pub had proved no Alcatraz, I could easily have slipped down and unlocked the door, but instead I'd Houdini-ed mesen out the tiny toilet window to thrill-up my escape.

Surely I was now a woman who could entrance any adult male. I was rather like pretty Nina Fisher when she ensnared Mr Fakenham, or even, I suppose, Debbie when she had hooked me dad.

At last, my new cruel power was to be tested over men.

Not Mrs Tall Paul, or Nina Fisher, or sad Debbie, but men.

The previous night I had left a sealed letter for PorkChop to pass on to Phil when he went for a drink in the bar. PorkChop had been threatened with a throat slashing should he choose to disobey. It was a love letter. Or what you might call a love letter if you knew zero about true love. It was flattery, pleading and lies. I begged for Phil's help, asked him to meet me, and though I didn't mention my plan, I detailed his manly and poetic virtues. He fell for it and returned, via PorkChop, a betting slip with the words: 'Oh yes, Mona. Yes!' written on the back. I in turn sent my maid, PorkChop, down with another sealed letter telling him to meet me outside the abandoned rivet factory at 12.30 a.m.

Now I would entertain Phil in such a manner that he could not help but gasp at my new charisma. And then not refuse to drive me to Goldwell. My plot was wonderful.

Phil had a copy of the evening paper held open in front of his face, which he lowered when he heard me running over the rubble.

I went straight for the door and a warm blast of smoke and sweat rolled out. There were enough cig packets, receipts, papers and sweet wrappers lying around to open a newsagent's. I yearned to be enclosed in the fug but what also hit me was that he was damn unsightly and was going to seed. I had no love fo him. He was wearing a very dadish acrylic jumper, eggshell blue with a row of diamonds overlapping across the chest. In fact, all his clothes had a cheapness about them, from the shiny grey trousers to the slip-on shoes with cracks in the vinyl where the toes curled up. I hoped no one saw me with him. Then I wondered if he'd had to dress especially like he *wasn't* out on a date, just to escape his wife and kid.

He had brought me a bowl of ice cream.

'Get in, gorgeous,' he said, speaking like he had a sore throat. 'I got you this out freezer before I left. To cool you down and cheer you up.'

'Gee, thanks, Phil. I feel five years old.'

He had brought me two scoops of pale pink ice cream in a green bowl, and had speared in a kite-like wafer and a silver spoon.

'And I've got yer another pressie. But you'll 'ave to wait for that.' Then he stubbed the cig out so nervously the ash crumbled over me bare legs and he had to say sorry. He stroked his hand over me leg and, like a sudden chill, his hands on me skin went straight to the bone. As we went by our pub, me gobbling the ice cream madly, he held the copy of the paper up by the side of his face like a getaway celebrity.

I looked back and saw the light going on in the bar, the curtains flicking back.

It was thrilling to think everyone was so fascinated by me that they watched constantly to see what I would do next. It was like being a member of the House of Windsor. How different to the old me when no one cared or noticed. How long ago those days when I had to ride the slipstream of my sad sister's life.

I loved the drama of it all, but I did not love him.

I loved only Tam. Yes, yes and I would for ever! Until the heat flash and beyond.

A crazed fly made passes at me lips and I tried to swat and not look bothered at the same time. It'd be one of the same flies which followed the Hoggins vans in a blue swarm, attracted by some rottenness.

'Are you for the miners?' he said.

'I would be but I'm no good at marches. I get lonely in crowds,' I sniffed.

'Well, we'll just have to have a revolution of two, young lady.' And he grinned like a murderer.

I truly hoped he was a murderer. I thought he was sometimes, and at other times I was sure he was innocent. At moments I truly wanted him to kill me so that they would be forever sorry.

I looked out the window at the far-off lights which were like low stars. I felt dizzy with the receding rush of me old life.

'Look on the back seat, Mona.'

I looked round and could see a high parcel wrapped in brown paper.

'What is it?'

'Aha, you'll 'ave to wait and see. Let's just say it's a token of my passion.'

I squirmed. I wondered what Phil could know about passion.

Tam and I could show him passion.

I had forgotten about the fat old auntie and now truly believed Tam was desperate and waiting for me. It broke my heart to think of her in that house without me.

'I had a long rainbow scarf. But I was married in 1968. I was eighteen. I was militant in my head. I take risks, that's my personal protest,' Phil was saying, like I'd asked him a question.

He'd been moaning on about how he'd been trapped into

marriage, how he'd been going to live in London when he found out his girlfriend, now his ugly wife, was pregnant. His life was the classic tragedy of missed opportunity and thwarted talent.

My capacity for emotion, hot tears and wet longing meant I felt utterly superior to every man I knew.

I weep therefore I am *better*.

How could men ever match women for romance?

His love was soggy and needy, like a patch of brown damp on a bedroom wall.

Mine was a waterfall, cascading down into a mountain stream.

He turned the cool air up higher and a litter of frail yellow betting slips flipped around me ankles.

'I try and do things in my work that are unconventional. As a protest against the petty-minded,' he said very seriously. 'Art rather than politics, you could call it.'

'Like taking wedding photos, for example,' I sneered.

'No, not that stuff, my other photography. My artistic work. It challenges the status quo,' he said without a trace of humour.

'Phil, no one under thirty says *status quo*.'

'You know what I mean, Mona. Art.'

'Porn,' I said, turning to look at him. I was braver with him now.

'Some would call it that,' he said gently. He smiled and stroked my face. 'I think of it more as liberating photographic art.'

'How radical.'

'Are you a radical, Mona? Would you like me to show you how to *be* a radical?'

His superior blokeness was not threatening. It was funny.

My hair will grow, cobwebs will overtake this lonely abode, bluebirds will sing to me sad songs.

I suggested Phil take a right at the junction. The direction to Goldwell.

The strange wrapped-up present toppled over heavily on the back seat.

Bees will make a honeycomb of my heart, and our love will turn into a fairy tale.

He pulled into a parking spot, one that I figured he already knew and had been looking for, one that was half hidden by trees. He looked at me in the darkness, like there were betting tips etched into me skin. He said he loved me. No, surely not. Then, yes, he said it again. I wanted to snigger.

I was delighted!

I was terrified.

I thought of Tam hungry and alone in the crumbling house, nightingales settling on her fingertips.

'Look, Mona, this is for you,' he said, interrupting my dreams. He lifted the present from the back seat. He was grinning. 'I wanted you to remember this summer. To always 'ave summat to remind you of our love.'

When I saw it I yelped.

It was an enormous, monstrous, gold-framed, boldly technicolour, topless photograph of me.

'D'you like it?'

It was not art. It was not even skilfully executed. But it was striking. The lighting was fluorescent so every bodily blemish looked like bruising. Me eyes were half open so I looked drugged and very weird. Me shoulders were rounded and me arms hung down ape-like, so it looked as if I was hung up at the back with a hook. I seemed to have no make-up on, only a mask of grim shadows. But worst of all were my nipples: touched up, they looked like two red bullet holes in my flat chest.

'You look sexy,' he grinned.

'I look like an out-of-work prostitute,' I said flatly.

He smiled. 'Well, I really like it. You can put it in your bedroom.'

I turned away, I couldn't bear to see it. And for a while we sat there in the dark in silence.

This was not the allure I had imagined.

'If you lie back there and look up you can see the *stars*,' he goes, sweeping his hand in front of him, like stars were a completely new concept he had just introduced me to. 'They're good this time of the year. Look.'

'Wow, Phil!' I mocked, though he didn't notice.

Get thee to a nunnery and meet people!

The roof of the car was white vinyl freckled with brown spots. Again, he said he loved me. Each time it startled me. Like there was someone else in the car, a different lover crouched unseen in the back seat. When I took me top off, me skin was stained blue because of the night, like I'd come up from under ice. I decided not to bother making any jokes about me tits. Again, he said he loved me. When I flipped over, the car seat itched at me skin. There was a rotten cig hole burnt into the headrest and I poked at the tawny foam and then looked away as he took off his jacket then put a hand down between me legs and under the seat and slid the seat back.

Then he was climbing over the gearstick and the handbrake, wedging himself between the seat and the dashboard. He said: 'Don't worry. When we're together for ever we can relax in a double bed. Imagine that.'

Before long I would be safe with Tam in Goldwell. I just had to do this thing.

His breathing was heavy, more like snorting, and I could hear him rolling his sleeves up and sniffing. Then just when I thought he was about to start fingering me arse again, he twisted heavily and stuck a hand awkwardly in his front pocket and took out some money and said: 'This is for you, Mona. For being such a good model and helping me out. I should've brought some oil.' And he started to snag his dry hands over me skin.

He had put the money in me hand and I held it tight 'til it got damp. I thought of Mr Fakenham and Nina Fisher and the girl from Little Helpers and how sex with the man who pays your wages is a common thing.

His hands were big and could encircle me ribcage, almost crushing the breath out of me. Me nose was pressed deep in the seat now and I could smell the greasiness of hair sprays and gels and perfume which had become dirtied into a rank reek. I was certainly not the first girl to take up this position. Though I comforted mesen that I was surely the first lunatic criminal.

He should've been scared to be with *me*.

If I put me tongue out the nylon tasted of deodorant.

'Turn over,' he said after only a few moments of massaging me back. I did, keeping me thighs clamped together and me fist round the money. His face felt flabby against me stomach. He said again how soon we would be together. For ever. The night seemed very still, as though even the birds were embarrassed into a whisper.

If a murderer were to stumble upon us now.

If I looked back I could see the grotesque photo scowling on the back seat.

He began the sex.

It was different than with a younger bloke, or a girl, certainly, like a different way of putting up shelves. Phil had it all unpacked and now he was assembling it quickly knowing what went where and sure it was taking shape and would soon be finished.

He'd done young girls before.

Just as I was thinking this and as his breath was coming very quick in shallow grunts, another car pulled into the parking space at great speed.

'I'll leave 'er for you. Just us,' Phil grunted. 'Just us. Go away, us.'

I clung to him like driftwood. There were noises of voices and squealing. I hid me face in his damp middle-aged flesh. There was a slapping of feet and banging of doors.

I inhaled his summer musk like a sweat drug.

There was shouting and then looking into the car was Father, Debbie, PorkChop and two small boys.

cake

O ut on the landing I could hear me dad snoring, but there was no sound from the pigsty. I was bare and light; the silverfish wiggling on the bathroom lino creaked more floorboards than tiny me.

I pressed the handle and walked into his room. It was darkish but the moon sky was beginning to blush with dawn. It was swampy with bloke rot, a sour salted stink. I pressed me hand over me mouth, but still gagged.

I was naked because on our return to the pub, a few hours earlier, Debbie removed all my belongings. My bedroom was a cell. She was keeping everything – clothes, shoes, cosmetics, Ventolin, cigarettes, records, posters, hair slides, jewellery, deodorant and my little ballerina – in black bin liners in her room until I 'calmed down'. Even the most precious thing I possessed, the letter Tam had written, which was by now just a soft, tattered rag, had been ripped from me.

The only make-up I'd been able to find was a dusty, lidless Puce-in-Boots, long ago lost between the carpet and the skirting board. I had applied this to eyelids, cheeks and lips.

'PorkChop,' I whispered.

The carpet was stiff with stains and scratched my tender soles. There was a dark wardrobe, the door hung over with enormous fat-man shirts. Shirts so huge that with just a few tent poles you could holiday under them for the summer. There was a wooden chair groaning with clownish trousers. A dressing table displayed a city of gunged-up cosmetics, a plate with a crust of toast, a full ashtray, a twist of underpants. There were three posters above his bed: a red car, a footballer, a herd of rhinoceroses bathing in a pool.

'It's me. Mona,' I hissed.

He was lying on his back with his arms curled out on either side, like he'd just splatted there from a tall building. Quietly, I lifted back the blanket and slipped in beside him. The bed was saggy and warm. He was dreaming of smoking; a gentle sucking noise, then a tight pocket of breeze.

I moonbathed for a few minutes. I could hear his stomach gurgling like old plumbing. Then, when I was settled beside him, I pushed the sheets and blankets off so I could see the whole mass of him. I stroked his shoulder with my knuckles. Real gentle, just a fly's touch. Both our bodies were white and wrong, but his was huge and mine microscopic, like a Dover sole lying beside a maggot.

His legs were rounded, thick and sturdy, more like furniture than limbs, posts more suited to supporting a staircase than a person. They suggested no athletic possibilities; no dance, skip or sway potential.

On his bedside table, besides a pint glass of water and a crumpled lager can, was a spiral-bound notebook and a pen laid across handwriting, like a message to Father Christmas.

Then I saw his belly button. It was not neat and discreet like darling Tam's, or my own. It was horribly swollen, pushed upwards in a hard ring. On big tough oranges you see a similar thing like they've clung with muscular force to the stem. I licked my finger and stroked it. I thought of my magical fingertips and how I'd let my fruity skills go to waste and must instead work hard to get back to my former level of skill and expertise.

He mewed drunkishly.

Then: 'It's funny how women are said to be curvaceous,' I hissed, kneading my fist into the swag of lard round his hip. 'When really you're the curvy one not me.'

The panic of flesh creaked the old bed, the sheets flew up like ghosts; there were urgh, urgh, urgh noises, and PorkChop tried to scramble out of the bed but I held firm, like a mad little dog, one hand on to his arm, the other gripped round his knee.

'What d'you want? Don't 'urt me. I'm sorry. I didn't tell 'em. Dad saw you in Phil's car. He followed yer. I didn't say owt.'

He could have punched me or snapped me wrist but for some reason he did not. He fought me like he was my size.

'Relax. I have seen naked men before, PorkChop.'

He scrambled for a dirty yellow towel from the side of his bed and clutched it around him.

'Fuck.'

'Though admittedly none so fleshily endowed.'

'I didn't say owt. It was yer dad who saw the car.'

'Forget it. It's history.'

'Will yer please go now?'

'I rather like it here. In this stinky little man nest.'

'I'll call yer dad.'

'I don't think so. Because I just might say you've been making me come in 'ere with you. That that's why I've been going so crazy and . . .'

The hours with Phil had been an embarrassing turkey. I would not fail my new self again. I had to evolve to the state where *whatever* I said was taken seriously by men.

'Why've you got all that stuff on yer face?'

'And however mad I've gone, I am still his darling daughter. And you, well, you are just some lump left over from a woman he used to go out with. Nothing more.'

'It looks like blood.'

'It's make-up.'

'Well it looks like your 'ead's been eaten by a dog,' he smiled. I scowled.

'Puce-in-Boots, it's all I have left,' I said sadly. 'What's that?' I pointed at the spiral notebook on his bedside table.

'Just summat.'

'Oooh, Elton. Give it 'ere.'

I ripped the notebook away from where he'd clutched it to his chest.

'Oh, don't read it out. Don't,' he said and sank his head into his hands.

'"Love's Motor Car" by PorkChop,' I read. 'Here goes. Ready?'

Then I cleared my throat and sniffed:

> 'Love is travelling in an automobile
> Being driven by an imbecile
> Cosy as a night in an abattoir
> La-la
> Pure as week-old caviar
> La-la
> Safe as an exploding cigar
> La-la
> Calm as a drugged-up superstar.
> La-la-la-la-la
> This journey in love's motor car
> Is fun if it don't kill yer.'

I left a long pause. Then: 'Oh, PorkChop!'

'Mona, I hate you.'

'Oh dear, oh dear, oh dear. Don't give up the day job, Porker. Oh, sorry, you don't have a day job.'

'You inspired that song, Mona. I wrote it tonight, seeing you and Phil in 'is car.'

'I don't love *him*!'

We argued about this for a while.

'I don't ever intend to aim for love that's cosy, pure, safe and calm, so you've got that wrong. In fact, I know now that I want love that's dangerous, dirty, risky and wild.'

'Is that why you love that crazy lass?'

I hadn't expected this but I must not deny her. PorkChop'd

once told me there were only four topics for song lyrics. One: I love you. Two: I don't love you. Three: you're going away. Four: you're coming back. My song must always be the first.

'Yes. I do love her.'

We were side by side in the pinking dawn, strangely married against the headboard, him clutching his yellow towel, me raw. We were both looking towards the window, at the pane of coming Sunday.

I had to not get dozy: to stay dynamic and forceful.

I had to demand to be taken seriously.

'Well, d'you wanna have sex with me?' I said wearily, as though tapping my red stilettos against the seat of my limousine.

'Er, no, not really.'

'Some girls might take that as an insult, PorkChop.'

'Well, it int meant to be.'

'I thought you could have sex with me and then in return you could do me a favour.'

'I'd rather just do you the favour.'

'Don't you find me attractive?'

'Er, no, not really. Sorry.'

We sat there in silence for a while longer. He had dropped his shoulder and lowered his head, shyly curling himself into a dough ball. His bulk was comforting. The pricking shards of sleeplessness made me sharp and brittle and I would've liked him to circle me in his arms, to smooth me out, to pull me to his fleshy mattress.

'I'm sure someone will find you attractive, one day,' he said uncertainly.

It was time for me to go.

'PorkChop, the favour is this. You're going to tell everyone I've gone to see Cleo for a few days. You're going to say this is a good idea to help me to get over everything. You're going to say you spoke to your mam and she's agreed.'

It was not quite as good as the fat old auntie scam, but nearly.

'Why?'

'I can't be here. I feel so . . . I miss her. Me dad only has eyes for that witch now Cleo's gone. Everyone's gone.'

'I know. That Debbie's dreadful. I can't believe she's stolen all yer stuff.'

'And it's three weeks now since Lindy's wedding. If I stay 'ere much longer I'll just be like a weed, tangling round her flowering life for ever.'

He looked at me sadly and said: 'Mona, you look real skinny. D'you want some food? 'ere, 'ave some cake.'

And he reached down and lifted out from under the bed a battered cardboard carton. He thumbed open the box and slid out a lump of ginger cake.

'It's still moist,' he said, squeezing it between his thumb and forefinger.

'Do you think this is what it's like at boarding school?' I said between gobbles. 'I mean, midnight feasts every night.'

'Perhaps. You should ask yer posh mate.'

'She's called Tamsin and she never mentioned midnight feasts. I don't think boarding school was much fun for her.'

'Sounds a right weirdo.'

'Her sister died. It's made her a bit strange.'

'Died? What of?'

'Starvation.'

'Yer what?'

'I don't expect you to understand that, PorkChop. It's not something likely to become a problem for a person with a pile of cakes under their bed, is it?'

We argued for a while longer and then I said I had to leave.

'You can't get out the landing door. Yer dad's not taking any more chances. 'e's got the key under 'is pillow. If there were a fire we'd all fry.'

'I know. That's why I'm here, stupid. That's why you're gonna tie these sheets into a rope and I'm gonna jump off the balcony.'

He smiled, impressed.

'Here, put on this T-shirt and these shorts,' he said and began to lift some mucky old rags out from under his bed. 'You can't run through Whitehorse nude. Tie a knot in 'em. And these gloves for going down the rope. And this 'at in case anyone recognises you.'

'Are you taking the piss?'

He smiled and got out of the bed. Shyly, carefully screening himself behind the yellow towel, he put on his big trousers.

'May I suggest, PorkChop dear, that you take advantage of Debbie's stunning laundry service? All yer clothes stink.'

PorkChop made the knots secure. He tested the strength by spreading his arms wide and straining 'til his face went purple.

'This really is like being in a character in a girls' comic,' I laughed, thrilled. I was nearly free! 'Tiptoeing from room to room. Midnight feasts. Daredevil escapes.'

PorkChop shook his head in marvel at me and eased the window up carefully. He tied the snake of sheeting on to the railings. I thought how truly useful men were, how, if marketed correctly, every home would want one.

Then he watched as I put on the enormous shorts and T-shirt.

'By the way, PorkChop. If for any reason you forget to keep this secret, you might be surprised to discover everyone in our pub clutching a copy of "Love's Motor Car" and la-la-la-ing as one. I've a right good memory for catchy tunes.'

'Oh, Mona,' he said sadly, shaking his fat head.

He helped me out the window and on to the balcony. Black Beck glittered beneath. He came out behind me and with both hands he clutched the sheet. He placed his sturdy undanceable legs wide and firm. I felt safe, with him on the end of my rope.

And then I dangled over, off, down and out into the free dawn air.

Get thee to a nunnery and love again!

eggs

When I arrived back it was 7.15 a.m. and she was cooking her Sunday breakfast. Hiding mesen behind a tree I watched her in the kitchen.

She was wearing a checked apron and her crazy hair was concealed beneath a neat headscarf. I feared, of course, after a week without me she'd found sanity. I went round to the back of the house where the door, regardless of security concerns, was flung open. The radio was on, playing pop music. For a few more minutes I stood hidden watching her. I could smell normal breakfast food. Something nice like bacon and eggs.

Then, stalking slowly, I entered through the back door, and skulked down the hallway towards the kitchen, keeping mesen hidden. Then creepily, in a spooky, deep, masculine voice, I said: 'Hi, honey, I'm home.'

She turned in panic, picking up a carving knife from the chopping board. There was some yelping, scattering, then general chaos, panic and joy as I revealed my face and then threw mesen against her.

I cared not if I died right them.

'I have drunk only one glass of hot salted water every day since you left,' she said, weeping and holding me, stroking my hair, licking my face. 'To remind me of our tears.'

Though this was the most romantic sentence ever, the sort of breathless declaration a prince would make in a story, I noticed that her face seemed strangely divided; her eyes expressing an emotion wildly opposite to that on her mouth. She smiled and her eyes looked shocked. She was no longer wearing the yellow gloves. And despite what she'd said about hot water I could definitely smell delicious bacon grease.

Then she said angrily: 'Why did it take you so long to come back? And what the hell are you wearing? God, you stink like a tramp.'

'They had me trapped,' I lied. 'They had bars over the windows and bolts on all the doors.'

'How dare they imprison my darling!'

'And then they stole all me clothes. This is all I could find.'

'Oh, you poor honey.'

'Everyone I have looked at since we have been apart has only reminded me how inferior the world is to you, honey,' I told her.

After that she bleached whatever she'd been frying, brought me a pile of Sadie's clothes, and began to make a celebratory bake of custard creams mixed with baked beans. She made a regular amount though we just ate a half-spoonful each. The rest she bleached.

'So what's been happening, honey?' she said, lighting a cigar for me and settling down at the kitchen table.

We discussed the cruelty of my family for a while. Then she said: 'Oh, I called Father at his office.'

'Oh.'

'The stupid man didn't suspect anything. He's not with that woman any more though. Apparently, he's moved into a hotel.'

'Why? What did he say?'

'He told me to work hard and not get too distracted by pleasures.'

'How dare he?'

'I know. I mean, hell, this is the man who gets an erection every time his sexretary brings him a cup of tea!'

'Oh, darling! I'm so glad to be back with you. Everyone else is so weak and tolerant.'

'He did sound tragic though,' she said. 'He droned on about all the *happy family times* we used to have.'

'How fucking dreadful. What a hypocrite!'

'I said, *Hey, Pop, why not write a book about it!*' Then she walked over and closed the windows and the back door. Then she said solemnly: 'Mona, we might have to take measures to avoid Father.'

'Hmm, he won't stay in the hotel for ever.'

'He's thinking of coming home, I'm sure. It's probably only a question of him clearing it with Mummy.'

'Oh, Lord, save us from weeping fathers,' I exclaimed laughing. 'But we're back together, that's all that matters.' And I reached for her hand, but she pulled it away and paced around the kitchen for a few moments anxiously.

'So how did you cope with that great lard lump? He hurt me, you know. He really damaged me when he flung me down on the tiles. We could prosecute for that.'

'Oh. OK,' I said cautiously. I didn't dare tell her that it was PorkChop who had helped me escape.

'I didn't like him, Mona,' she said darkly. 'Really I didn't. All that fat disgusted me. I hated him. How did he get like that? How dare he break into my house? I could call the police. If my father were to find out . . .'

'I know,' I muttered.

'Oh, Mona, darling, I do so want to be with you. But I fear Father might be coming back.'

I realised later that though she'd told me about her father she'd not said anything about what she'd been up to. When I pressed her she said she'd cried and slept, so she could dream of my safe return. She had done no house painting. She had discovered it was hard work and was losing interest.

'Painting's work that suits a man more than a woman,' she declared.

The idea of men seemed weird; after only an hour with Tam I could barely remember their purpose.

'I've been so lonely, so lonely,' she said.

'Me too, I've been so lonely too.'

Loneliness was even more special now that we both had someone to share it with again.

Little red cartoon hearts exploded with a ping above our heads.

We drifted through to the sitting room and sprawled on the sofas. Tam poured a few breakfast cocktails, and we watched little birds swooping beyond the French windows. We kissed and cried. My hand was limp on her belly which was dipped inward like a hammock hung from her hip bones. Our limbs were latticed into one another like the topping on a tart. We moaned and sobbed and praised one another as morning sunlight and green flooded the room. I took hold of a half-inch of belly flab and said: 'Hell, Tamsin, I should be in a clinic!'

'We'll have you back in shape in no time.'

I looked out at the shining summer beauty of the garden and said: 'I think we should paint the windows, Tam, seriously. With white paint. Not only because of the heat flash, but for our privacy. In case your father comes back, or pervy old Tall Paul comes snooping.'

'Or Nina Fisher with her bloody bleeding ear,' Tam said laughing. She stood up from the settee and began to hobble around the room clutching her ear, her eyes gaped in pain, in the exact manner of independent Nina Fisher all those weeks ago.

'Brilliant, darling!' I said clapping, and taking a gulp of my cocktail. 'That's it exactly!'

'Yes, we will paint the windows. I've no white but I have some of the pink paint left. I'll go out on the ladder and do it tomorrow.'

'It'll be much safer.'

'And you know what, I think we should move further upstairs. Look how vulnerable we were when your elephantine brother attacked us.'

'Stepbrother.'

'Let's move right out of sight. Right up to the top of the house. From where we can survey the landscape for Father's return. We mustn't let anyone get an idea we are here. We can trust only one another now, darling.'

'Oh yes, darling.'

I noticed that she had a fresh red strip of burn across her shoulders.

Like she had been sunbathing.

The next night, Monday, Tam did as she promised, she climbed the ladder and over three exhausting hours sloshed pink emulsion over nearly all the windows of the house. The ones she couldn't reach I did, by leaning out of the window and flinging a painty rag against the glass. Some would be more effective than others, for some were more accurately painted; a few on the upper floor had just a sunburst of dribbling pink in the centre of the glass.

We felt much safer. We were father-proofed.

When you hear the attack warning, you and your girlfriend must take cover at once.

Dear Tam was my only family now and evermore would be.

On Tuesday we did as Tam suggested and moved up to the junk room in the attic. The room was dark and musty. It had been used for storing props from Mrs Fakenham's early am-dram productions. There was a gold-sprayed cardboard throne in one corner, a moth-eaten settee piled with grim-looking books in another and a rail of tatty fancy-dress costumes. Crumpled in one corner was a plastic suit of armour. There were flags, candlesticks, handkerchiefs and bunches of plastic flowers.

The dust made me constantly wheezy.

We kept the heavy curtains closed by day and just had candles at night. We cried a lot and then took a wet joy in comforting one another. We did not answer the door or the phone. We did not take deep baths. We both had a severe heat rash and spent a lot of time itching. It got in the way of the sex which we were keen for.

There was no disco playing now. No 'Wild Thing'. No guitar. Occasionally, we heard the distant sound of voices in the court-yard, and once or twice knocking on the doors and windows, but we stayed hidden upstairs where our TV friends muttered and the candles flickered.

'I'd like to be an actress,' I said, stroking me hand over a leather tunic.

'You *are* an actress, Mona,' she said nastily.

'What d'you mean?'

'I mean, no one could be as entertaining and weird as you and be normal.'

I ignored this and carried on.

'It must be like being a kid again, being an actress. Imagine just playing around, dressing up, having fun. Getting all that attention.'

'Yelling and crying and begging and whispering. Declaring love like drugged-up idiots. Just like us this summer.'

'That's not true. No. We've not been acting.'

'If you say so, Mona,' she said, bored.

I was upset and shocked but perhaps she was just miserable. She was certainly quieter and gloomier since my return. A couple of times in the middle of the night/day I woke to find her sitting up in bed, stroking her hollow belly and staring wide-eyed at the emulsion on the window. If you looked at the paint patches without blinking you could make out strange pink shapes framed by the blue sky: animals, faces.

It was Wednesday, I had been back just three days, though it felt like a month and we had just finished eating a loaf of dry toast and watching a made-for-TV film, when we decided what to do next.

Every day/night in our small upstairs room by the blue light of TV we watched 1970s dramas, the ones considered so bad they could only play them through the night. We watched TV because we didn't really have anything to say to one another.

In between us the table was stacked with empty bottles, cups of wine with floating flies and uneatable scraps of the strange food. Tam had found a pack of After Eight mints in the cellar, gone soft like damp cardboard, the chocolate speckled with grey marks. Dipped in the only booze we now had left, green-tomato wine, they'd made gloopy gluey balls in our mouths and sent us giddy.

Even though the booze tasted like summat a desperate dog would refuse to drink, it seemed to have cheered her.

I was sitting on the gold-sprayed cardboard throne watching her and wondering.

'Look at her!' Tam yelled at the TV, taking a mouthful of the foul wine straight from the bottle and wiping the back of her hand over her mouth in the old imitation of the saloon-bar liquor drinker. 'At last a pretty one! Her bum's firm yet approachable. She's so effortlessly toned. Thin without being bony. Slim but curvy. A perfect woman.'

'And look at the way she smokes her white fags. Like they're magic wands,' I said. I leapt out of my throne and slugged down the booze the way she did, 'til we were both drinking like cowboys. I bounced up on the settee.

Until I met Tamsin it used to upset me seeing beautiful women on TV or in magazines. Their bodies, breasts and hair made me headachy and sick, but now, with Tam, despite me obesity, for the first time in me life, I no longer felt that way. I was sure we were living in another place where the world couldn't touch us.

A place where the female species were so obviously superior to men, that all women regardless of looks or personality were of a higher order.

Even fat, ugly women were superior to thin, handsome men. Imagine!

'Breasts that enormous should really make her topple over when she walks,' Tam sneered cruelly, curling her lip in the face of a great Californian beauty. I touched the cup of the push-up satin bra Tam had lent me. The dead sister's bra. Breasts that had gone floppy like suede pockets, pumped fat with glucose by angry doctors.

'That's why she goes everywhere in Jock's car,' I said. 'That's why the Chevrolet is such a key issue in their marriage.'

'Though, of course if she ever did topple over she'd surely land on her eyelashes.'

How we laughed!

We liked movies starring superior women with slender hips, whose curls bounced in time with their breasts when they trotted down garden paths to their Cadillacs. We particularly favoured alcoholics, abused wives, underhand business deals and way-ward daughters. We liked fashionable hot pants, husbands and houses. And we liked the women to prepare just the occasional glass of pink, freshly squeezed fruit juice in clean, sunny kitchens. We did not like the women to eat at all – unless they were going out to dinner, for an argument. Then they could have a few mouthfuls before pushing the plate away angrily. Though they could drink cocktails on or off the rocks, cold beers and stiff Martinis, alone or in company. We liked highly pressured jobs in slick offices high above busy cities.

'I lub you,' I sobbed. 'You are just as beautiful as those women.'

'I lub you too,' she sobbed, slumping on top of me on the settee. The green-tomato wine had made her breath slimy like old men's tongues, and stained her teeth a ghoulish lime. 'We'll do something exciting too, darling. Soon.'

While we were watching the TV that night I thought how Julie Flowerdew was now a half-remembered made-for-TV drama. An unsuccessful show taken off our screens a few episodes early.

I had not forgotten her. I would not. Though I remembered her now as a walking teenage corpse rather than as a real girl. In my mind she was acquiring the same fictional quality as the

Fakenham family. Often, while it was beyond the dead of night and we were watching TV, I'd think of her walking to school with her unfashionable skirt, her trumpet case bumping into hedges as she shuffled along the pavement. She was grey and her hair dusty and her fingernails blue. Was it a trumpet or a trombone? Her woolly tights wrinkled at the ankle. The way her cobwebby hair was still that mocking touch greasy.

We never watched the news so even if she had been found, dead or alive, I would've never known.

'That anyone should want to hurt such beauties,' Tam sighed, reading my mind.

She turned off the TV with her toe.

Without the TV on we were just two girls alone with our loneliness and yeasty sweat and green-tomato breath in a dark musty room surrounded by old theatre props.

A whiff of sick and diarrhoea was stinkable in the toilet and corridor below.

'We should really try and find Julie,' I said languidly. 'When I see those powerful women on TV I always think of her. She has no one looking out for her.'

I had only recently told Tam about Julie. I'd told it late at night when the movies had finished, and I told it like a ghost story. I had told of the soggy red books, her tiny little house, her scrawny ragbag mam, the bag of unwanted clothes, how she had perhaps sunk down to the mud at the bottom of Black Beck, how she had perhaps swum with the eels. Then I invented details of her character; her weakness, loneliness, how she was bullied and disliked. Just the kind of person Tam could not feel threatened by. I had to tell about Julie to keep Tam interested in me. We were running out of unusual situations.

'What clothes did she wear?'

'Oh, real sappy stuff. Cheap.'

'Oh. Still, she shouldn't've been killed for *that*.'

'Oh no.'

'I do admit I rather envy poor girls. With all that hopelessness the only way is up. Whereas for us rich girls the only way is usually down. I mean, you and Julie can only do better than your family, whereas for me it's not so easy. You're lucky really.'

So, we called our second taxi and prepared, for the first time since I had returned to her four days earlier, to leave the house.

'Do you want to see where they might've found the body?' I said.

The sky was suitably deep purple, the flyover hunched like an animal in the distance. A little boat with faded paint, and the wood warped and misshapen, rocked uneasily against the concrete bank. All the windows down this road were open but no TVs on, too late and hot for TV. I wished we had some violin music with us, some way of us staying true to the dead Julie, something to keep us powerful and unaffected by outside sounds. The night was better with music; it allowed you to believe things it was normally hard to accept.

'This is where I think they would've dumped the body,' I said.

'If there is a body,' she said.

'Must be. People don't just disappear.'

'They run away. They die. They divorce. They go to live with their sexretaries. They're murdered. They get too *fat* to leave the house. But they don't just vanish, you're right, Mona.'

'Correct, honeybunch,' I said smiling.

A few drunks passed on their way home from parties. A taxi went by. All the hedges were dead, the grass was tan, flower heads gone insecty on brown stalks. With our shoes off we crept along that murderous route, not talking, me in charge because I knew where we were going and Tam having to follow for the first time. We were alert and lively, because of the night being our day, 2.08 a.m. being our early afternoon and because of the wonderful sugar rush of eggy bread with golden syrup, like on our favourite TV movies.

'There could be where she's hidden. Come here,' I said and reached for her hand.

My own palm was sweaty, my armpits smelly. My period was making me stink like a one-woman rawhide factory. In fact, I hadn't had a period for a few months. And this one was scaring me. The weird blood seemed like a symptom of anxiety, like the asthma.

I hated the girl-person body juices – tears, menstrual blood, vaginal secretions, saliva, sweat – with a greater ferocity than ever.

'Oh,' she said, no doubt disappointed there was no actual face bloating on the black water.

'She's gone now, *obviously*. But this is where she could've been drowned.'

'How did she rate in the charm stakes?'

'OK. Not pretty.'

'Fat or thin?'

'Fat*ish*. She stole all these red schoolbooks to line her bunker with.'

'Did she have a boyfriend?'

'Don't think so. Though she went with blokes. She was a drinker. This is hers,' I said and pulled from my pocket a black plastic bin liner.

I unwrapped it slowly and carefully. The bag, which had lain concealed in the tartan suitcase for two weeks, rustled in the quiet night. Then I handed her the blue T-shirt from the bag of jumble Julie's mam had given for Cleo.

'I got this from her mam. She gave it away by accident.'

'You mean she was throwing it out. The bitch.'

'Oh, God! Yes, Tam, perhaps she was.'

'What a bloody bitch,' Tam said and brushed the blue cotton against her own smooth cheek. 'I'm so glad you saved it, honey.'

Tam's face was grey and her pointy cheekbones and seared hair gave her a hungry, wolfish look in this night light. Someone should make a documentary about us: appeal for people to send food parcels and cash.

'Actually, I know that Julie Flowerdew once did some modelling. For this bloke I know.' Even as I was saying it I thought I might tell her about me and Phil, but the look on her face suggested it was not wise.

'Oh no! What a little slag.'

'Yeh,' I muttered. 'He's called Phil. He drinks in our pub.'

'Urgh, disgusting. How could she? Modelling for some seedy old boozer.'

'Yeh, you're so right. Whatta slag!'

The river was down low, the drought sucking the water away and leaving the waves to lap weakly against the bank.

'Don't be scared, Mona,' she said and touched my face with both her hands. Earlier she had applied my eye make-up. I loved the way her cool knuckle nudged against me cheekbone. Because of no mirrors I didn't know what I looked like any more, only what she looked like. This felt like my earliest memories of being with Lindy. 'Why are you so scared? When my sister was in the hospital they did that to her too; took pictures. It was a kind of skeleton modelling.'

It was a while since she'd mentioned the dead sister. We no longer talked about Sadie.

Then, while I was waiting to answer, she threw a brick with great force and it splashed into the middle of the water.

'Missed,' she said and aimed another brick at the frail little boat. 'I can understand. Perhaps she had a wonderful body.' She picked up another brick and threw it. I knew she was infuriated by the idea of another girl being a model. 'We all have to make money somehow,' she said, though this was not true, because she did not need to make money. 'And if she had a fat-free carcass and thrilling tits then why not use them. Lots of girls would love to be models, but don't get the chance. I could never be one, for example, on account of the *blubber*.'

'You don't have blubber,' I said quietly.

'I do,' she snapped and turned to wander off along the bank.

'You're just like bloody Sadie you are, Mona. Always making out you're thinner and more attractive.'

She was disappearing into the darkness.

'Do you want to see more scenes related to the crime?' I shouted out after her.

'Take me on a complete murder tour,' she called back, skipping off ahead so I could barely see her.

It struck me that it was much harder to love someone when you were together than when you were apart.

We went to the gully to look at the spot where they had found the red dripping books. Then up to the top of the flyover to look down into the water. I picked up a stick and pointed it at particular buildings on the skyline.

'Tall Paul is the type of man who'd commit a crime like this,' Tam said seriously like she was making a point at the posh girls' school.

'Indeed,' I replied, nodding my head like a true TV investigator.

'Or your revolting brother.'

'Hmm, very true. They're both not stable. Neither can restrain their fantasies.'

'And both are so unattractive to women that they probably harbour deep resentment.'

'Good point.'

'Probably that man she did the modelling for as well.'

'Phil! Yes! Definitely Phil. I've thought of him already. He's the most likely.'

When we got outside Julie's house we stopped and stared, as though at a painting or a school poem with many different meanings. We studied her house. It was the last stop on the murder tour.

There was someone up. I sensed it, from the way me stomach chilled. The front paved garden was bleached, dry and white as bone.

Tam looked at me as if she was waiting to see what I would

do next, and because she expected something I crossed the road and she stayed where she was, pretending not to feel it, picking black balls of tarmac from the bottom of her feet, very quietly humming some old love-makey disco tune.

Behind her the corrugated iron of the rivet factory stretched and twanged.

I thought of Phil and how much easier it was to be with dumb men than smart women. Having a boyfriend was a complete *holiday* compared with having a girlfriend.

Then I turned to her and held up me hands. The fingers were stretched wide and me arms were up above me head so I looked like someone surrendering. She looked at me hands and nodded. Then I turned and knocked hard on the door.

My knock echoed in the dark house. I checked on me digital display watch and saw that it was 3.56 a.m. We had been wandering around in the dark for nearly two hours. Tam was about ten feet behind me, mostly hidden in shadows.

Then there was a clattering on the stairs.

The person was running and the door opened quickly, eagerly, and it was her mam, and me doing the same wide-eyed shuffle and smiling and saying how sorry I was, so sorry, and her mam there, looking beyond me, out over my shoulder, all tired and ghosty with troubled dreams.

She smelt not of soap and bleach, but unclean, of cigarettes and sour shattered sleep. Yet I was so glad to see a mother. I wanted to fall in a heap at her feet. She smelt of food too. A burgerish tinge to her hair, so I wanted to hit her, a fast punch of fist bone against face bone.

But behind me she sees this girl back in the shadows, with the moon on her frizzed-up hair. And then the exhausted mam was making a little yelping sound like an animal trodden underfoot.

I could not bear the pain on the mother's face. I liked mothers, I couldn't help it.

'It's OK,' I said, touching her arm. 'We've come to help. We've come to tell you who took Julie.'

honey

'**M**ona, I have to tell you some news.'

Tam was applying a sheen of gold lipstick, then fluttering the blusher brush over her cheeks, her elbow held at a high angle like she was playing the violin, as she stared crazily into the centre of the room. It was Thursday afternoon, the day following the night we'd been to see Mrs Flowerdew, and we were upstairs in our smelly little room. It was sunny outside but the room was gloomy and stank like a hamster's cage. I'd had nothing to eat or drink and was starving and thirsty.

'What did Sadie look like to you? I mean, how does Sadie appear in your memories?' I asked, changing the topic. She didn't answer. On the floor amid a litter of gunged-up disposable razors was a little silver bowl we were using as an ashtray. I wound me finger through the ash and dabbed it over me eyelids.

She had lost interest in talking about Sadie. There was no way she was going to wear a ridiculous lacy Sadie outfit for our mission. She was going very seriously for a full disco look and had put on tight jeans, and a breast-hugging T-shirt in a glittering fabric. She'd been out of the house this morning very early, while I was sleeping, and had had a haircut. Where she'd got the money from was a mystery. She'd had a smart, short style, which made her look as wholesome as a children's TV presenter, the same healthy mix of fun and sex.

'Whaddaya fink?' she asked, twirling in front of me.

'Oh, I'm certain all the policemen'll wanna rape you.'

'Oh, I do hope so.'

'Remember to ask if he's got a mate who'll rape me.'

'I have something to tell you,' she said, changing her expression.

I looked away. The room was a health hazard; a total pit. It reminded me of how Lindy used to yell at PorkChop: *Hey, piglet, muck out yer sty!*

'Mona, I *have* to tell you some news.'

I looked at the dust on the bedside cabinet; the first covering of muck had come suddenly like volcanic ash, but the next layer of more serious dirt was building up slowly. The Fakenhams were right, one needed staff. Two girls alone could not be expected to control the grime and body stink in an entire *house*.

'Mona! Listen to me.'

It was ridiculous, really you needed to dust *every day*, sometimes *twice* a day, if your life was getting particularly dirty.

'Dirt's like food, sex and money, no matter how hard you try you can't escape it,' I said.

'And men,' she added. 'You can't escape them either.'

'Oh, no, you *can*. You *can* escape men. That's the whole point. That's what "get thee to a nunnery" means, that you can escape the humiliation. If you're brave.'

'What are you talking about? Now, listen to what I have to tell you,' she said sternly, continuing to lap at her eyelashes with the mascara brush. 'OK. Mona, darling, we're going to have a baby.'

She blinked rapidly then applied more Summer Azure.

She squirted a cloud of perfume around hersen.

I reached into her smart make-up bag and found a stick of Totally Mauvellous and began to apply it over the ash.

'I'm excited about going to the police,' I giggled. My old attraction to officers of the law had waned only slightly since meeting Tam. At the thought of tanned, muscly sergeants and inspectors, me hormones still pogoed.

'Are you happy for me, darling?'

She was laughing and waving at me from the bow of a ship heading off into the sunset. I felt like Canada, some massive place people pretended to like but were bored by and desperate to leave.

'Mona, are you listening?'

'Wonderful, darling!' I smirked. Surely she was joking. 'But you should be careful. I mean of VD and crabs. The lads round here are more polluted than sewer rats. They think Sexual Diseases is the name of a horny magazine.'

She just looked at me crossly. 'It wasn't a lad round here, stupid. I do have some standards.'

Tam had sat down on the gold throne and was looking at me very seriously. She reached over and picked an inch-long cigar stub out the ashtray and, nearly singeing her eyelashes in the process, lit it. Then she hung her head back and began blowing smoke rings. This was summat we practised when extremely bored. After a few moments she exhaled one perfect trembling round. It rose up and over her head in a wide halo.

'Who'd'you think you are? The bloody Virgin Mary?' I snapped.

'That's a good name for a church cocktail, Mona: *Would you like your Bloody Virgin Mary shaken or stirred, vicar?*' she said, eyes up watching her halo stretch and evaporate.

'What happened, Tam, do tell,' I said, trying a boarding school approach. 'I'm simply dying of curiosity, darling.'

'You'll live,' she goes, getting down from the throne and marching to her jewellery box where she pinched on some pearly earrings.

For the first time I gave her my special look of scornful sorrow, shaking my head very slowly from side to side. But she just sighed and said: 'I keep thinking of this little seed, already with a brain, and arms.' And she sighed again, smugly like she should be given a trophy just for getting up the duff.

She was fertile. She could breed herself a best friend. My own belly was puffy and swollen; it was as silky, tight, fat and empty as a toad's throat. Inside me there was nothing but bubbles and air, and soon I'd be floating an inch off the ground.

Tam was getting back up on the throne, then blowing another smoke ring towards me. She wanted to lasso me and noose me in.

'I knew this lass at our school who had to go away to a unit. They wouldn't let her drink or smoke anything in there,' I said. I spied a drip of tomato ketchup on the side of a dirty plate and hooked a dot on to me finger and blended it into me cheek. 'She said it was worse than being at home with her parents.'

'Mona, darling, I think I'm a bit different to the *lasses* at your school, don't you?' she said witheringly.

I pictured a baby that was a mix of me and her: it had brutal make-up and gnashed its vixen jaws. Lactating, ovulating, menstruating, what good could come of it?

'So,' I said in the saddest, most pitying voice I could manage. Like I felt very sorry for her and her ruined life. 'Are you getting married then?'

'Mona!' she exclaimed, laughing so her whole throne wobbled. 'You really are such a hoot. No, of course not, you idiot. I haven't given up all hope yet, you know!'

Then I was struck by a terrible certainty that Tam was going to do something unusual and exciting with the established notions of motherhood. She'd be the sort of mam who called her kid after a Tibetan goddess and got it photographed by the papers wearing leopardskin. I had a sudden, awful feeling this would change her life, independently, for the better.

'I mean, it really is miraculous.'

'Yes,' I goes, 'you're up there with Jesus, Moses and all the other hip dudes now.'

'I'll need to ensure I keep hold of my independence, of course,' she mused. 'I mean, I'll still need a social life.'

'Social *worker* more like,' I muttered.

I did not dare ask who had made her pregnant, though I

imagined it to be a lad with a Ford Capri and a winning mix of brutality and hopelessness.

'It makes Derby Day even more important, doesn't it?' she said, exhaling another tiny halo. 'And when you're ready we'll tell everyone. Your family and my family.'

I tried to imagine telling Father I was having a baby with another lass: *Well, you've ruined your entire life, I don't know if that bothers you. Well, does it?* I rather missed my father, if truth be told. And Debbie's cooking, ironing and cleaning. And I'd started thinking of me home in the way I used to dream of other people's rosy living rooms: as a safe, warm and cosy place.

'So now we have to strike a blow for all women, in the future as well as the past,' she said, stubbing out the cigar and then making her mouth into a tight, pre-lipstick oval and applying more gold.

But there was no future. Not for planet earth, or for Tam, or for me.

'I'm thirsty,' I whimpered.

'OK, here,' she said. She marched over to the other side of the rank room, picked up a dirty glass and her bottle of bleach, and then angrily glugged out a glassful.

'There,' she said furiously, handing it to me. 'Drink that.'

'Oh, thank you, dear. You'll make such a good mother.'

We were silent for some time.

'So you're certain?' she asked eventually, licking her lips and tossing her head back so her new hair fluttered. I looked at her bemused. Her belly didn't look any different. 'About that man Phil, silly.'

''Fraid so. I've told you. He took pictures of Julie.' My voice was flat.

'It might be better if you could offer some more evidence, stupid. I mean, something concrete. Like maybe you should say you found that blue T-shirt, the one her mother gave away, in his coat pocket or something. At the moment the story's a bit shaky.'

'Yes. Good idea. I'll say I found it at his photography studio. I've been there once.'

'Good,' she said firmly, snapping shut her make-up bag. 'I've laid you out some more clothes, Mona. Chop-chop. You can't do this wearing scruffy clothes. Mrs Flowerdew will be so relieved, poor woman. To be a mother. To be a mother and lose your child,' she sighed, shaking her head and going quietly out the door and down the steep attic stairs.

I went downstairs ten minutes later and found she was sitting on the baby grand piano swinging her legs and waiting for me. She had her left hand twisting in a jar of honey and slowly she licked her fingers adoringly.

'Do you want to see something really frightening?' she said, sucking the honey from her thumb.

'I think I've 'ad enough shocks for one day.'

'Just one more.'

Since we had pinked out the windows the hallway cast a strange purple light. She was holding what I thought was a silver picture frame. She had it pressed flat against her chest, like a religious book. I could tell she was hiding a giggle.

'Get ready, Mona, for the shock of your life.'

She was a mother now, anything could happen.

'Here, you want to see what Sadie *really* looked like?' she said, lifting the frame from her chest and handing it towards me. 'Here.'

The next moments happened very quickly. I could imagine her heartbeat all around the house, as though I too, just like the baby, was deep inside her. The face in the frame looked tired and haggard. It was no surprise really. The eyes were a stagnant pool, the girl's skin tight and reddened, perhaps with the pressure of skull bone which pressed up in a pronounced nose, chin and cheekbones.

The 'small almond' gone rotten and poisonous. Still, there was something disturbingly chic about the angular bones and the obvious distress. You could see why at some time in the distant past men would have glanced twice, maybe even crossed the street for a closer look, but definitely no longer.

It was me.

Tra-la!

Looking at the face was making me feel faint, it was strange as realising the hands of a clock were moving backwards. It was worse than Phil's photo of me. I pressed me fingertips against me skin to feel the bumps, ridges, eyebrows of the sorry face. Tam burst out a giggle when I did this.

'Hell, when you catch a glimpse of yersen in a mirror and want to hide behind the settee in terror, then you know summat's gotta change, hey?' I said in the loser tone she most loved.

'Things are about to change, stupid,' she said sternly and hopped down from the piano and marched out the front door.

Mrs Flowerdew stayed in the foyer with three friends. She had a heavy coat on and a hat, though it was June. When she sat down, her head cupped in her hands, her spine arched over, I thought of me mam. Then of Nina Fisher and her bovine struggling. It was women ill and weak that I didn't like. Mrs Flowerdew was red-faced, clutching white tissues, her voice frail as faint pencil markings. Her hair looked ratty brown like the hair on cancer patients or corpses.

'So when did you find this information?' the policeman asked.

Unfortunately, the officer was not young, tanned or fit. He was old, pink, sagged and reminiscent of that most unsexy of things: an elderly maths teacher.

'She saw some pictures of Julie Flowerdew in his studio,' Tam said. She had her hand laid very gently across her stomach, giving her a polite and vulnerable edge. So far she had done all the talking, saying I was too upset to speak, though she hadn't even asked me if I wanted to. It was amazing how her lies sprang up strong as weeds.

The policeman seemed fascinated by her full, soon to be milky, breasts and pretty new hairstyle, both of which gave our story much greater credibility than it would've done had I been relating it on my own.

Men were not very alert to oddity in women. Though I looked like the crash victims seen on posters in the foyer, no one took me aside and stared closely at me.

It was late Thursday afternoon, nearly a month since Lindy's wedding. In houses throughout Whitehorse mothers were washing up, ironing. I could go now, leave her here pregnant and alone. I could return to my life of little houses, teapots and TV.

'What sort of pictures?'

'Some without clothes, officer,' Tam said shyly. What she was saying was true, though for some reason she had a way of making even the honest things seem like lies.

'Topless pictures?'

'Yes. I'm afraid so.'

'And when were these pictures taken?'

'Before she died.'

'We don't know she's died, Tamsin,' the policeman said kindly.

This came as a shock to me and I stopped picking at me nails and looked up. He had a wedding ring dug into the pink fat of his finger. He was right, of course, we did not know she had died, though in me mind she was as dead as Sadie Fakenham. Mrs Flowerdew thought so too. When she shut her eyes she saw freshly dug graves and empty coffins; in her sleep she saw her daughter as a tiny biro drawing laid out on a white cotton pillow. Surely.

'Sorry. It's just such a terrible thought that I can't help . . .' And here she put her head down and gasped. The policeman had to stop writing and put his hand on her bare arm, surely taking the opportunity to have a good ogle down her T-shirt.

Emotions thumped at me in black and white. I felt ignored and jealous. No, it couldn't truly be called a feeling. I had stopped feeling, I just got pains at different times.

'You mean before she was missing, Tamsin?'

'Yes, officer. That's right.'

'And what other information do you have for us?'

'No other information, officer. I hope we are not wasting your time. We were very nervous about coming but in the end it seemed the most sisterly thing to do.'

She managed to make even the word 'sisterly' sound inno-cent, though to me it was as loaded as 'terrorist' or 'thief' or 'killer'.

He smiled, then wrote down the name of Tam's school, and asked us to excuse him for a moment.

How had Tam got to have sex with a boy? And when? This was the question the old officer should've asked. Did she walk into a pub, smiling, alone and just get chatting at the bar? Or did she hang around the dark streets of the village looking deranged and darkly sexual?

There was abortion, of course, but I don't remember this being mentioned. I thought of an abortion doctor hooking the little baby slug out of the womb. The way you'd hook a rubbery cockle out of a white styrofoam pot with a plastic spear, and how there is a little scraping of the spear against the pot, then that quick burst of vinegar as it bounces between your teeth. That's all.

The station was busy and understaffed because most of the police were away on picket duty. No one had offered us a cup of coffee though we had been waiting for several hours. Still, despite the disappointing potato faces of the officers, I was very happy there, and I could tell Tam was too. The station was clean and orderly. We liked the bustle and the marching around and I thought how one day I might like a career in the force. I liked the way they'd bothered with me, folded up me dress when I'd taken it off, and stroked me aching back after the photographs. I thought how I would've liked to be a nurse married to a policeman. I particularly liked the use made of hands in these professions; used to help, comfort and care, and to restrain. The way they worked with fingerprints. And the way these unique fingertips never put on weight no matter how much you ate.

'I love it! They should think of offering weekend breaks in here for the lonely and dispossessed,' I whispered to Tam ironically. Tam looked at me coldly. She seemed, for the first time, worried and anxious.

'Shut it, Mona. Don't you think we're in enough trouble as it is?'

Then the officer returned with a woman. Tam continued to talk. She was very impressive, looking down at her feet then up at the bare ceiling and speaking in a low girlish voice, very educated, very posh.

'Mr Rush threatened my friend on several occasions, didn't he, Mona?'

'Er, yes.'

She looked like she lied professionally. I realised her face, when it was lying, was no different at all from at any other time.

By 9.35 p.m. the policeman had fallen in love with her and if she'd told him Julie was swallowed by a large haddock, Jonah style, he would've ordered ten thousand divers to search the North Sea.

I looked up then with the dirtiest most flirtatious look. Like I had just risen from a sewer: *please, we are only girls, believe us at your peril.*

Then I took a blast on the Ventolin the policewoman had given me, and looked at him very directly, as raw and honest as I could manage, laying all the lies before him. All he had to do was to sniff, lace his fingers over the cold grey table, take a look out at the night sky and then shake his head, *no*, and that would've been it.

But the policeman didn't do any of these things. He just smiled, liking the idea of us mucky schoolgirls, and at last we were given a plate of biscuits, the malty type with cute pictures of stick people playing sports, and sweet weak tea.

Just as I was about to binge on the biscuits, Tam smiled kindly at the policewoman and pushed the plate away. She said she thought we were both too upset to eat. She touched the collar on my lacy dress and told the policewoman I was taking the whole thing very badly and had lost all appetite. Tam looked over me real tenderly, then she patted me arm, like some wildlife campaigner who's been asked to bring along an example of the kind of dumb animal she wants to protect.

Actually, I did feel very ill, an aching in every bone and a watery weakness in my blood. I wondered if this was what cancer was like. I wondered if I too had a cancer. Tam had her baby, and I had my cancer. It would stand to reason.

Finally, we handed over as our evidence the blue T-shirt Mrs Flowerdew had given me the first time I collected jumble from her house. Tam told how this had been found at the Cinema Studio. The policeman put it in a clear bag. My mouth was cold and salty, my tongue like a winter road freshly gritted against ice.

Eventually, my time came to be the main attraction as I told the plain truth about the heavy petting and the pervy night drive. Tam, assuming that this was all delicious lies, brewed out of the cauldron of my imagination, looked on in wonder. I had never seen her so impressed.

Though the policeman didn't smile at me or stroke my arm like he had with Tam, his pen moved very fast, pecking over the page.

lamb

Above us, as though drawn by a child, the great orange sun hole radiated shards of brilliant light. Caravans, whites, greys, creams, hulked in concrete driveways like heat-stroked whales. The front lawns were open patches, pale green head-scarves laid politely before each house. The flowers in the brown borders were stiff nylon. Three kids, jolly and skippy, bounced around. Two white dogs yapped at their heels, so fizzed up and sugary it seemed they too quaffed lemonade.

This was a newish estate, twenty minutes from our pub on the north side of Whitehorse. It was built out of Lego, each house the same as the next, each red brick regular. All the mummies had been moulded and melded in a factory and they clocked you through glass eyes. Even the birds were paid extra to chirp especially tunefully.

As I walked up towards his house I sniffed on a strange scent. Lupin Close was far enough away from Hoggins not to get the full blood, gut stench, but still near enough for a faint splutter of chemicals to mix with the dahlias so the place seemed drenched in cheap air-freshener. From some-where the sound of a chainsaw massacring an entire family droned just like a lawnmower rattling up and down, up and down.

The only people who could possibly be excited about this place were our mam (who thought of a house on this estate as life's top prize) and murderous ice-cream van owners who fancied stirring little girls into their mint chocolate chip.

It was possible the police would have already arrested, charged and imprisoned him on suspicion of murder. Surely, if our girl fury was worth anything, they would have had him in for questioning. I was ready to see his ugly wife weeping in the street surrounded by astonished housewives. Cameras following him from the doorstep to a waiting black-windowed van. His *pooetry* being discovered in the attic, reams of odes to me and my beauty, and published in the evening paper; him being hailed as a poetic genius, me as a tragic muse.

I would be news!

Then I saw he was running through the sunlight towards me. He looked so pale like he'd been dipped in a bucket of dust: love; I recognised the symptoms. He'd had a minced lamb dinner and I could smell the sweet flesh on his lips as he came and clutched my hand and began marching me back down Lupin Close. A girl on her bike stopped and watched us.

'I had the picture of you up in my loft,' he panted.

'How flattering.'

'They found it. Police.'

'Oh, you idiot.'

'Women have to refuse to feel the fear men want them to feel,' Tam had warned as I left the house this morning. 'They have to throw that fear back in their faces like a strong, clean punch.'

This from the girl who at this moment had her feet up on the calfskin settee reading the *Mothercare* catalogue.

'It was. The. Only place. I could. Go up there with. A torch and look at you.'

'So what happened?'

'*I have just been visited by the golden angel Gabriel and Lo! I am with child,*' he might as well have said given the look of complete bafflement which was stitched over his face. In fact, he said: 'I've to go back in for questioning tomorrow.'

When we got to the bottom of Lupin Close, he said: 'Mona,

you look terrible. Are you OK?' I gazed around. The cul-de-sac was on a slight hill so there was more sky than strictly necessary. I shook me head and said: 'Jesus, Phil, how did you ever end up living here?'

'It's quiet, no one bothers you, it's safe, relatively affordable.'

'So is Whitehorse graveyard.'

'Oh, Mona,' he said, and I noticed that one of his eyeballs was watery and streaked pink, like it had fine threads of ham woven through it.

'Toughen up, Romeo,' I smirked. I patted his stiff hair. 'Hell, we could be heading for a world hair gel shortage given the amount you've slapped on.'

'What are we going to do, Mona?'

'I need money. A thousand pounds.'

'Hey, there's no need for that. I love you.'

Ha! he thought I wanted his love, when all I really wanted was his money. Dear me, all the time you see men making this mistake. He blabbed on about how he loved me but he didn't understand it. He said he had depression, that things were not going well with the business, that he had a family to support and a mortgage to pay. He said: *For God's sake, Mona, it's the eighties!* as though this would come as important news to me.

'Oh, wise man, please teach me about the world,' I mocked.

'I'd like to give you the money but . . .'

'No buts, Romeo. I'll pay you back tomorrow. It's a loan. You're the Loan Arranger. Geddit?'

'I can't, Mona.'

'No one will ever know. Then I'll go to the police, give you an alibi, say I did the photos willingly, to launch my,' I looked down and sighed, 'my modelling career.'

'But . . .'

'Phil, no,' I said turning him round and leading him back up Lupin Close again. 'Listen. Just think of it as a temporary token of your affection.'

The girl on the bike was circling near us now. A couple of

mummies, grimly zinging with minty toothpaste smiles, were gathering in their goddamn wide, wide windows.

Tam was the one who had suggested blackmail, though she'd not called it this: 'It's not blackmail, it's asking for money from some murderer who should pay for his crimes,' she'd yelled. 'Are you thick, Mona? We are having a *baby*!'

We were nearly back up at the top of the close, near to his house. Behind us mummies were leaking out on to the streets, circling like sharks for the blood of Phil's humiliation. His pink eyes were fixed in this hyper-real look of terror.

'They came here. Not with the lights flashing. Though they might as well have done. With everyone looking an' all. You believe me, Mona, that I didn't do a thing?'

'Oh, course, Phil.'

He mumbled on for a while about how appalling everything was.

I stroked the bald spot which shone like a pink puddle in the middle of his hard hair.

'Let's go to the bank,' I said. 'We only need a thousand pounds for tomorrow. Then we'll talk about an alibi.' He looked at me as though I'd expressed a particularly girly and ill-informed opinion: contempt and ridicule. I slapped him.

There was a great burst of electricity, as the plastic mummies exploded in clapping. The fear had been thrown back in his face like a punch and I felt the victory rhythm pumping through my veins.

'Wait there. I'll just go in and get my wallet and car keys.'

'Can you get me a bottle of drink from your cabinet? Vodka, gin, or summat?'

He came out with a bottle of gin. By the time we got in the car he was so breathless he could barely drive, and I had to change gears for him and keep slapping his face to stop him from letting his head loll on to the steering wheel. I thought men were meant to be good at driving but he had all the skill of a nervy grandma. Masculinity, hell, it was like faithful fathers, friendship and happy families, one great big fucking myth.

His sweaty hands made wet marks on the steering wheel.

Still, it all had a delightful cartoon edge to it; the way I held the bottle in one hand and hit him with the other, slurp, slap, slap, as we curled down Lupin Close, so the kids had to scream and scatter, the bubbly pups yelp for their lives, and the mummies dash into the road howling. The way I wore Sadie's lacy Laura Ashley and him the brown crumpled anorak. The way we passed the gin between us and yelled when it hit the back of our throats.

And it was true to say, as I was much later reminded by the police, we were laughing all the way to the bank.

I had planned to put half the money on a greyhound at Perry Bar, Birmingham, but remembering that we needed to be braver, at the last minute I decided to put it all on a dog at an Irish track.

We had to do the Derby Day bet soon.

Then we could run away together and live, for planet earth's last few weeks, on our winnings. I would wash nappies and tend goats and Tam would breastfeed and hunt wild boar.

In Vienna or France or Hartlepool.

We would have love! Love and laughter before the heat flash.

We would be pied pipers, basket weavers, rat-catchers, handbag designers.

I walked very fast with a straight back and rigid arms, and this must have looked suspicious in the melting heat because people on pavements stopped and stared. It was so hot door handles were almost too burning to touch and the orange-yellow blinds were down on shop windows to prevent sun bleaching. I liked the thought of the metal cooking me flesh.

I pictured a human barbecue, which is exactly what the nuclear explosion would be like.

I was so right! How could I not pick the winner?

It was a lass at the till, one sandwich short of a picnic, with her hair in a pineapple and her nails painted silver, steely claws. No one should've known me there but some of the blokes were looking at me strangely. Licking their lips. Clicking their sour, greeny tongues quickly.

Queuing, I looked out of the door which was held open with an iron weight: a market town with farmers in caps and mothers in summer skirts they'd run up on the machine themselves; off they went to the doctors with the kiddies, or to the greengrocer with a basket, or the post office pulling a tartan trolley. Folk were still collecting for the miners. Dreary Labour Party women were pressing stickers on T-shirts and handbags, and men were rattling tins.

One day they might all realise they were not ordinary at all. That real life was just an enclosure you could live in, like a sheep pen; where you retreated when you were exhausted by romance.

I knew now there was another world you could live in, one where your imagination dictated what happened day to day.

One where the heat flash would be a liberation.

Collecting tins made me think of the weeping sores of charity. Neediness, like a big sob snivelling down the street.

Pineapple girl didn't want to serve me at first and ran her tongue over her upper gum and eyed me up and down. Maybe she thought how hot it was, unnatural, something strange going on, perhaps I was a vision, a hangover dream. Perhaps she wondered if far away a war had started and soon we were to deep-fry.

And then I showed her, and when she saw the wad of notes packed tight in me hand, she was drumming on the counter in keenness and she took it most willingly. She had the money hunger all right, though, for now, she was only a bloody counter girl.

Tam had said soon we would assert ourselves by the display

of our new wealth. Money achieved through our personal cunning and skill. Soon they would see that were a force to be reckoned with.

Dan the Man. 4–1. The 5.40 p.m. at Shelbourne Park. This sexed-up commentary like a breath. I could see it in me head. He got away well, hungry, took the first bend in the lead, teeth set in a snarl, mine too, my lips sealed into an arse with wanting, his eye on the hare which was actually a fluorescent rubber glove, his jacket flying, my stomach willed into a grip of iron that pushed up through me, and which would, I'd have thought, burst right out of me now he was in the lead, but, but then, somehow I didn't know how, there were butterflies in me now and me legs gone cold; on the second Dan the Man was scrabbled out, I didn't know how, I could feel me skin clammy cold, by the four dog, that pot-bellied little bastard that looked at first like he'd just had a three-course meal, rigged, the whole thing was rigged it must be because, no, and there was an explosion of dust and he was reeling, Dan was sent flying, confused and amazed and eventually second last.

The girl watched me and I would've truly liked her to come and put her arms around me, curl my head into her shoulder, but she was not the type, she might have the money madness but she was not the type for comfort.

I'd not even ten pence to play the fruity.

Because I was slumped down on the floor the men were looking at me, some bending grey heads together and laughing about me. I heard someone say about calling the police. I heard someone ask if they should call an ambulance. I lifted me sad eyes up, and I shook me head.

Instead, I put my lips round the Ventolin and sucked and sucked at the plastic funnel, 'til there was hardly anything left to squeeze.

soup

'So, how was Cleo?' Lindy snapped when I wandered into our living room at 6.08 p.m. that day. 'Strange that she invited *you* to stay, when *I* haven't heard from her at all.'

'Fine.'

There were three empty soup bowls on the table, an orange Saturn of scum round each rim.

'What you doing here, Lindy?'

'I did used to live here, you know,' she said, not looking at me, but concentrating hard on the TV.

Dad was there too.

'It's good to have you back, love,' he said and blinked several times, which meant he was feeling deep emotion. Him and PorkChop were watching the six o'clock news. Someone had obviously advised them to be very ordinary around me.

I looked at the empty bowls. I felt dizzied with hunger but tomato soup was worse than twenty B & H for giving you a sore throat. And really soup was just liquidised food, though they tried to pass it off as a slimming drink.

I would not be fooled.

I looked around and for a moment thought I saw Tamsin there, her blonde hair spilling over the back of our settee, sipping brandy and chatting to Dad about communism.

'The man's a monomaniac,' goes Dad.

'A what?' goes PorkChop.

'A nutter.'

Lindy had her arms folded rigid over her chest, as though only they restrained this flesh volcano in the chair. She was wearing a home-made blue polyester maternity dress, with a pinafore bodice which covered a white blouse, her hair was smoothed back into a neat clip, on her feet she wore a pair of flat, comfortable shoes. She was smoothing her ringed fingers over a pile of soft white wool, like Princess Anne just come home from knitting class.

I didn't want to ask Lindy if Tam could have her baby clothes after she'd finished with them. It all seemed rather ridiculous, as most things with Tam did when I was not with her.

There was the hot force of everyone deliberately ignoring me and pretending to be engrossed in the TV.

'He's one sandwich short of a picnic. He's a fruitcake. Bananas!'

'You 'ungry, Dad?' Lindy said sharply. Dad looked at her puzzled, then after a dumb while got the joke. He's no Einstein, though I was very pleased to see him.

'He's a lunatic – just look in his beady eyes. Look! Look at 'im, kids.'

He'd never called us 'kids' before. It was like he'd suddenly decided that because we were all back together, from now on we'd be all checked shirts, big grins, apple cheeks, tumbling around on haystacks.

I turned away from the TV and said again to Lindy: 'So what *are* you doing here?'

'I'm not on probation, you know!' Lindy shouted. 'I can go where I please. It's none of your business.'

I turned to PorkChop and said: 'What's she doing here?'

'She's picking up some stuff Cleo's knitted for new baby,' PorkChop said, still watching the TV. Then he winked at me and said: 'Cleo said she'd forgotten to give 'em to you so she just posted 'em on.'

'Oh yes,' I smiled. 'It's kind of her to do knitting when she's so busy with *other things*.'

Dad glanced at me angrily and I twinkled him a sweet smile.

'It was kind of her to have *you* to stay when she's so busy with *other things*,' Lindy snapped.

'I'm off down to the bar,' I said, wearily. I was much older now than I was a month ago, and she no longer terrified me. I wanted to see the only thing that I truly loved and that truly loved me: my fruit machine.

'Oh, no, you are not,' Lindy roared, twisting round and up like a cyclone rising out the armchair. 'I wanna know what's been going on here. I've been hearing all sorts of stuff.'

Dad and PorkChop pretended this had not happened.

They were watching Scargill on the news.

'Me mam thinks he's got principles!' PorkChop mumbled.

'Principles! Hey, kids, what d'you make of that? Someone'll get killed. Or murdered. But I don't suppose that bothers any of you. Well? Does it or doesn't it?'

A few weeks ago I would've said something about cruelty to police horses on picket lines, but nowadays I no longer cared.

Then PorkChop uttered the thought that had occurred to everyone over the last few weeks: 'D'you reckon me mam fancies him?'

We all considered it. Dad too, because suddenly he said: 'Right, I know work's unfashionable nowadays and we should all be out there fighting for the workers' revolution, but I'm going to open the bar.' But he didn't move. He looked at the TV very intently, a shadow of anger setting on his face. 'The men in white coats should come for him if you ask me.'

'I think she did fancy him,' PorkChop mused. I wondered if Scargill and me dad had anything in common. They didn't look alike; Dad was thinner, shorter, darker, but both had some craziness perhaps Cleo liked in a man.

Dad turned to go. As he closed the door it was like he'd thrown a firework behind him into the room: 'I've been so worried about *you*,' Lindy shouted, chomping out the last word angrily.

'Not everything in *my* life is about how it makes *you* feel,' I muttered, slumping down in the armchair and gazing on the TV.

'I've been getting advice from everyone,' she said, ignoring me. 'Do you want your new niece to grow up with an alcoholic loon for an auntie?' Then she stormed out and immediately PorkChop leapt up and slid a fag from her packet.

'Jesus, what's wrong with 'er?' I sighed.

'I didn't tell no one,' PorkChop said proudly. 'Everyone thinks you've been six days with Cleo. Though it was 'elped by the fact Debbie said she'd leave if Dad tried to get you back.'

'Thanks. I didn't tell anyone about "Love's Motor Car" either.'

'Thanks. Don't worry about 'er, Mona. She just wants you to be a good auntie for the new baby.'

'Hmm. Well, actually with a midget Christian for a father and a polyester housewife for a mother, a criminal lunatic auntie might provide a welcome balance.'

'I think she's been in your room, getting everything back in place. I heard her telling Dad that he shouldn't 'ave let Debbie move your things. All morning she's been getting everything ready in case you came 'ome.'

'Well, why's she acting like a . . . a . . . like a mother?'

'It's all just 'ormones.'

'Well, she's not the only one with 'ormones.'

'What do you know about 'ormones, Porker?' Lindy said, marching back into the room. 'And buy your own fags.' And, snorting down her nose like a bullock, she ripped the fag out his gob and ground it into the ashtray.

It was rather comforting to think that no matter how housewifely Lindy tried to be she would always seem like someone on the brink of being arrested.

'I lived alone with me mam for ten years, I know all about 'ormones.'

We watched Arthur Scargill for a few more minutes in hot silence. He was speaking loudly and waving his hands. I liked this forcing people to take notice of you but Lindy was right too, in a way; I was bored with causing all the problems. If it was true, it was very kind of Lindy to get my room back together. Perhaps I would say goodbye to Tam and invest in some polyester.

Lindy was standing in the middle of the room, deliberately blocking out the TV. This was the sort of provocation that got you thumped in our house.

Then, for added effect, she picked up one of the soup bowls and dropped it on the carpet and, surprisingly, it cracked with a shattering ring. Orange droplets of soup bounced up.

Hormones.

'I want to know if you're seeing Phil Rush still,' Lindy demanded, pointing her finger in my face. 'I can't believe he had you in the car with him that night. I've heard all about it. Tell me it's not true. The seedy bastard. Using my little sister like some common tart in the bar. Well, are you or are you not seeing him?'

I shook my head. I thought of poor old Dan the Man, scrambling round that corner.

'And tell that lass to leave you alone now. You've had your adventures. It reflects on me, you know.'

'Oh. I am sorry!'

'I've a job and a family and everyone knows about you and what you've been doing.'

PorkChop at first pretended to be suppressing giggles but he was scared, gnawing on a plastic bottle top.

'Well, let's hope God doesn't strike you down with a thunder-bolt just for being my sister.'

'It's not God I'm worried about, it's the people at Frink's, and Shred's boss at council.' She made a sob-like sound. 'I've been married a month on Saturday and it's meant to be my anniversary. You're ruining everything.'

She was right; this was the problem with sisters. We were cooked up together like lumps of gristle in a foul stew; one rotten chunk could not help poisoning all.

'I'm so sorry for ruining your first month of marriage. I mean, it's probably just because I'm jealous of your great happiness and your husband and babies and job.'

She narrowed her eyes, not sure if I was joking. My irony was becoming so perfectly honed that it unnerved people without them knowing why.

'Well, anyway, just remember, whatever you do reflects on me. So think before you go mental next time.'

'Oh, OK,' I muttered into the cushion. 'Every time I think of doing anything, ever, for the rest of my entire life, I'll consider how you'd feel about it.'

'We're gonna be getting a Chinky takeaway on Saturday to celebrate the month anniversary. We're having some people round from the church. You can come if you want.'

'OK, wonderful. Thanks.'

Then Debbie Courtney came into the room to get a box of tissues. She saw me and gasped. All three of us folded our arms, and pulled our lips like a drawstring to seal our mouths into a tight pucker.

'Oh, God! What on earth's going on? What's *she* doing 'ere?'

And we all looked around confused, like the table lamp had started chatting.

Beneath Debbie's white bar blouse, where her bra strap cut into her flesh, you could see tough rolls of fat, trembling in a kind of flab fury.

'La la-la, la-la la la la,' Lindy began to sing, then picked up Debbie's magazine from the floor and began to thumb through.

'I said,' Debbie shrieked, 'what's *she* doing 'ere?'

'Who's She, the cat's mother?' Lindy said, not looking up from the magazine. 'Oh, Mona, look, dear, there's some very good fashions in here for the older woman with the fuller figure. Perhaps we should tell our grandma.'

'I don't want 'er 'ere causing more trouble,' Debbie said, snatching the magazine from Lindy and making her face in a ratty little pinch. Lindy leapt up from the sofa like someone had stuck a cow prod in her bum.

'Don't talk to 'er like that!'

'She's crazy. She's out of 'er mind.'

'No she's not, she's totally normal. She's my sister and I'll decide if she's normal or not.'

'Normal? Is sobbing and shagging any old bloke that comes into the bar normal?'

'If I say that's normal it's normal.'

I put my hand up and said quietly: 'Excuse me, I've only ever shagged two old blokes from our bar in me entire life.'

PorkChop was smoking hard and watching us all like we were playing ping-pong with a hand grenade.

'Well, it's not normal in my book.'

'I imagine your book would be rather a slim and cheap little book, Debbie, darling,' I added in a Fakenhamish way.

'Mona, shut it,' Lindy said. 'Let me 'andle this.'

I was safe now. Curled up in an armchair. The TV on. A cigarette. My big sister defending me. It was all wonderful again and the last few hours with Phil had never happened.

'You're just as bad as she is. You're two peas in a putrid pod,' Debbie hissed, glaring between me and my warrior sister.

Oh, life was wonderful!

Nothing bad and irreversible had happened.

'And I suppose you think normal is charming an old defence-less pub landlord, abandoning your husband and moving your snotty kids into someone else's home.'

'Charlie and I are in love.'

'Please excuse me a moment while I wipe away a tear,' Lindy said, and reached and took a tissue from the box Debbie was holding.

'Watch it, madam. Neither of you will come to this 'ouse if I don't want it.'

'You do know she wouldn't be this way if you 'adn't come 'ere. She was fine before you came 'ere. We were all fine.'

This went on for some time.

Then sunlight made a quick electrical flicker, and a block of shade darkened over the room. I thought for a moment Debbie and Lindy were about to have a fight. PorkChop did too because he moved to the edge of his armchair and began to watch more keenly. Slowly, Lindy took off her watch and, without losing eye contact with Debbie, she began to roll up the sleeves on her blouse.

'I'm off to get yer dad to sort this out,' Debbie said, beginning to cry and flying out of the room.

'Why don't yer fight yer own battles,' Lindy called after her triumphantly.

PorkChop and I burst into a round of clapping.

Lindy wiped her hands over the front of her maternity dress.

The TV showed an angry knot of women shouting at police. We all looked closely, but there was no sign of Cleo.

'That cow should have a government health warning,' I said, grinning.

'I know,' Lindy smiled, and offered me a fag. 'Look, whatever happens to you, Mona, at least it won't be as bad as waking up one morning to know you are, and always will be, Debbie Courtney.'

'Oh no. Nothing could be that bad.'

'Here,' Lindy said quietly. 'I got you a copy of this.' And she reached down to her handbag and got out the photo of me mam I had seen at her house. She'd had it framed. I laid it on me lap and me mam smiled up at me. The skin at the corner of each eye radiated like a lady's open fan.

'Can you see her?' PorkChop said urgently, leaning close up to the TV, searching for his mother. 'Can you?'

Lindy and I sighed and ignored him.

'Mona, please go and tell that lass that tomorrow you're coming back 'ere. Tell 'er we're going to get you all sorted out.'

'Leave it, Lindy,' I muttered.

'I've got Dad to put all yer stuff back in yer room. We'll put it all behind us now. I mean, it's not as though anything really bad's 'appened. Put it all behind you.'

'Don't, Lindy.'

'Mona, I'm serious.'

'God, hell, Lindy, let me sort my own life out,' I yelled.

I ran out of the room sobbing, and into my bedroom where the door was unlocked, and the windows were open, and someone had changed the sheets and folded the blanket back, and all my things were polished and neatly displayed. I flung mesen into the bed, still holding the photo of me mam. I put me hot cheeks against the thrilling cool of the pillow, let the sunlight stroke me, TV sounds dance around me, the drift of Lindy's fag smoke tickle me, traffic rumble through me and the water in Black Beck close over me. If only I was not part of anything else. If only it were just Tamsin spewing up and eating mush in Goldwell, and lying to police, and plotting and breeding. If only I'd not just lost a thousand pounds. If only I were not in more trouble than Arthur Scargill. If only what Lindy thought were true, that nothing had happened and I was here, just sixteen and ordinary, safe with my fat stepbrother and my mad sister and the fights and the dust and the sparkling summer of my crazy family.

gin

When I returned to the Fakenham house the next morning a sprinkler was rotating slowly on the front lawn, sending wide whips of water over the khaki grass. This was banned, but they didn't care.

I stood and watched the pinking house: a car screeched by, a child was screaming and far off a burglar alarm was dinging like an endless school buzzer. The real world was seeping in and I scowled with loneliness. Mr Fakenham's silver car was twinkling in the drive, a star of sun glinting on one corner. A horse box rattled by. It was Saturday and Goldwell was humming with rich business. Every so often the green hose, which wove round to the front of the house from the outhouses at the back, shivered like a vein. I had been wandering the streets, plucking the courage to come here, since 6 a.m. I was sober and solitary as a newborn baby.

Our windows were still emulsioned, though the paint looked sad and tatty. Like the house had been abandoned; like fantastic girls had never lived there.

Then I got down on me knees on the dirty ground, closed me eyes, breathed and tried to pray, though I could not keep me mind off the house. Phil had asked me to meet him in the car park of our pub this morning. I had agreed, partly out of pity but mostly out of guilt.

Now I wanted to kiss Tamsin Fakenham goodbye.

The high front door was open and I walked through the cool corridors. A radio was on and the show was a phone-in, the cheery chatting of two voices arguing jovially. Elsewhere, people were really like this; happy and ordinary. The cruel smell of scouring powder was urgently everywhere. I hiccuped an alcohol-less burp.

Poison Ivy was in the kitchen cleaning. Time felt blank and thick like fondant icing and me tiny plasticky body was sunk in it. Ivy had bleached all the surfaces, swept the floor and polished the taps to a shining silver, though it was not yet 10.30 a.m. She was filling the cupboards with food from supermarket carrier bags which covered the kitchen table. All sorts of crinkling cuisine in packets, plus fresh vegetables and fruit. There was chocolate, biscuits, after dinner mints, cake, ice cream. She ignored me.

I strayed through the rooms looking at the fresh carpets and polished wood. I looked in at the downstairs bathroom where the bath had been cleaned and fresh towels folded on the rail. A vase of flowers. Two large mirrors had appeared. In the hallway I saw Tall Paul's face close up to the window. He was circling a cloth furiously, scrubbing away the emulsion. His tall body filled the high bare glass. He pretended not to see me and twisted his face in the pressure of wiping away the paint. His servility made me want to punch a fist through the glass.

People wanted to be treated like servants. They liked to be bullied.

I began to touch things: a vase, a piano, a statue with a naked breast, an ashtray, an umbrella stand, the stiff raised pattern of the wallpaper, goodbye, goodbye, goodbye, goodbye, goodbye, goodbye, goodbye.

Next I went into the living room where the furniture had been piled into the centre of the room and the carpet was covered in a white cleaning foam which sucked at wine and other bad girl-person stains. The family photo in bright colour was still on the wall and they were still smiling.

The happy nuclear family.

Then I saw that Mr Fakenham was in the corner speaking into the telephone, wearing a suit and tie. He was looking out over the garden. His elbow was bent and his flat palm rested on his forehead like a grey fin sticking from the side of his head. He turned and waved his hand at me, either meaning *Hello* or *Go Away* or *Wait There*.

His face looked watery and sore.

Then I heard Tamsin calling quietly from far away. A sort of madness beckoning. I walked out of the living room. Her footsteps were quick and she seemed so small against the great architecture of the staircase: those brown oil paintings, that polished curl of white banister, the wide tongue of red carpet. Her skin watermarked with pink streaks. She was leaning to the right to balance the weight of the large blue suitcase she was carrying. Another matching suitcase was already at the bottom of the stairs. She had on a tight, modern mid-length minidress which stretched taut across her flat belly.

'I have everything in these two cases. Clothes and food,' she hissed when she was down the stairs and standing close to me. 'I've packed shoes for you too. Day and evening wear. Enough for a few days. It might be cold.' She was breathless and reeked of hot girl fury.

'We'll not want for anything, dearest. We'll exist simply but richly,' she whispered. I wondered in which cave she thought we were going to live, but before I could say anything she kissed me on the lips. It was the kind of kiss a parrot might give you; a hard peck.

For a moment we both twisted and turned in the hallway. The radio was still on. Mr Fakenham was still speaking irritably into the phone. The windows knocked, a devilish drum roll, when Tall Paul pushed with his chamois leather.

I knew for me own safety I should shake her hand and walk away. But I did not do this, maybe because I wanted to end our friendship with more normality than we had lived it. I wanted to say goodbye, in private, properly.

'Have you got the money?' she whispered and I nodded. Though, of course, this was a lie, I had lost every penny. 'Well, we have to go *now*. Everyone's back. If we don't go now they'll make me *stay*.'

'Okey-dokey, honeybun,' I said, staring at her flat belly. I realised I did not know how to say no or goodbye to her. It was like trying to stop a train when you were only a passenger.

'But we will need some *more* money, won't we? There won't be enough to go away and to live for a while.'

'We could go back to the pub and get some from PorkChop,' I said nervously.

We seemed very small and insignificant. Though I was standing next to her, I felt like I was viewing the two of us through the wrong end of binoculars.

'Yes! Yes, what a good idea, darling,' she giggled. 'I'd like to see in your pub. We'll sit at the bar and have big manly pints. Though promise me I won't have to see that horrible fat man again.'

'Tamsin, Mona, please wait.' Mr Fakenham was before us. Tam held on to the handle of the suitcase with one hand, and then grabbed my hand with the other so my fingers were entwined with hers. The father's breathing was irregular, making his words taut and anxious. His face was full of a horrible, soggy emotion.

Tamsin's fingerskin felt damp and cold.

'I'd like you to wait here, Mona. I think Tamsin has some explaining to do.'

With a father to oppose us we were united once more.

I continued to twist and turn, me feet making tiny dancing steps on the wood. Why had Mr Fakenham reacted so calmly to the ruination of his expensive, executive home? Why had he not even mentioned the maiming of his girlfriend? Because he too was disorientated and reeling from an overdose of bad love. That morning he was as dizzy and damaged as someone who had just thrown themselves off a fairground carousel while the crazy ride was at full throttle. His soiled home, his angry servants, his empty cellar, his stained carpets and stolen cigars, the bunker in the cupboard under the stairs, his nutty daughter and her loony mate, well, hell, these were the very *least* of his problems.

I could hear more footsteps now, and a body coming down the stairs behind me. The window on the stairs was wide open and for a few seconds I heard the frenzied chirping of birds. Dear Cleo once told me that if she woke too early in the morning she lay and listened to birds. She recommended this. I turned round to look at the window, to check for birds. Then I saw her. It was rather beautiful, ghostly and filmish. Posh girls can be this way: they do not have to try too hard.

I knew immediately and then felt only the simple sadness of betrayal. And shock, which is not the same as surprise. I was not surprised. Perhaps I had suspected this for some time. Anyway, betrayal was a familiar feeling, I'd had it many times and you just had to regroup very quickly, marshalling your loneliness and all your individual resources. You had to relax and listen to the birds.

Then do something so purposeful and fierce that it cauterised the pain.

'Hi,' Sadie said, coming over and stretching out a tanned arm and a slim hand. 'Here I am. I hear that you've been told I'm *dead*. Which is nothing but an outrageous exaggeration. Well, pleased to meet you.' Of course Sadie used irony too. She seemed older. Like a woman. Kindly. An achiever.

A bit like pretty Nina Fisher.

Of course Sadie had forgotten ever meeting me.

I fumbled for the Ventolin and sucked but it was still all gone.

Sadie was talking to me and her words rustled through the cool silence of the room: *Here I am*, the sound of many secrets being unwrapped. And then we were there in that clear moment and I felt naked, thin and hungry, and she shapely, flawless, ash blonde, beautiful. I wanted a drink.

'It's good to meet you,' Sadie said encouragingly, like she was speaking to a shy child. 'Oh, hang on, have we met before?'

'We're going,' said Tam. Tears were on her cheeks. She clutched at my hand. Her eyes were red with sleeplessness. She was breathing through her nose like an angry toddler.

'Thanks so very much for staying here with Tammy. She pretends to be so brave, but I'm sure she'd have hated being here on her own. After everything that's happened. I'm sure Mum's told you about everything.' Her voice had receded to a whisper by the end of this sentence. I nodded. Though I should've explained that I was not the type people explained things to.

'Did the two of you manage to get plenty of revision done?'

I saw it clearly then. There had been no fat auntie, no clever friend in the country scam. The Fakenhams knew I'd been there all along, they just didn't care.

'Yes thanks,' I muttered.

'She needed a friend,' Sadie said, shaking her head slightly and making her mouth into a grimace. 'A girlfriend. Didn't you, eh, Tammy? You poor thing.'

Sadie spoke of her sister with the same false sorrow that Lindy no doubt spoke about me to the Christians.

'Girls,' said Mr Fakenham. Fathers often said this as a call to order, but today Mr Fakenham made it sound like a cry of puzzlement.

'Piss off,' Tamsin whispered.

'Poor Tammy had been having a simply awful time at school. So thanks for cheering her up,' Sadie smiled. Her eyes were sliding over me, soaking up all my imperfections. 'I mean, it does seem very harsh that Tammy was the one to get suspended. I'm sure it can't be true that she was the cause of everything and the others were just innocent victims.'

227

'That's enough, Sadie,' Mr Fakenham said flatly.

Sadie reached out and patted Tamsin on the arm. It was the first time I'd seen Tamsin patronised, and it reduced her 'til she was almost like any other lass.

'And I'm glad to see she's putting on some weight. At last,' Sadie smiled.

'Yes,' said Mr Fakenham, who was looking down at his feet with his hands clasped behind his back. His chin was trembling. 'But, well, I mean,' he muttered, and here he made another of the tiny animal moans, 'this has all been very silly. I'm glad it's all been explained. Really, I mean, as though we didn't have enough very real problems. It's going to take a lot of work to get this house shipshape.'

He stroked his hand over his forehead again, and I could see a dark patch of sweat under his left armpit. He didn't care about his home or his weird daughters, he cared that his last chance at youthful love, with the lovely Nina Fisher, had, over one hot summer, gone inexplicably wrong.

Sadie was teasing Tamsin; telling her her skirt was too short, and she shouldn't go on public transport dressed like a hooker. I longed for the cosy blood gut stink of me own home. The screwball Fakenhams did indeed make my family look like the Waltons.

'But I really wish you hadn't worn my clothes, Mona. That was very naughty. Daddy, all my stuff needs dry-cleaning now. I'm rather angry about it.'

'Sorry,' I muttered.

The four of us stood there in silence for a moment until we heard the gentle breezy sound like a tiny tap dripping. No one wanted to be the first to look up, but when I did I saw Mr Fakenham was crying. He remained very rigid and he still had a smile on his face so it looked like a mannequin in a gentleman's outfitters had started sobbing.

'I need her,' he gasped. 'I am . . . without her. I can't seem to . . . myself . . . without her.'

'Daddy, don't! Stop it! Don't!'

'Tammy, sssh! Dad, stop it please. Not in front of Tammy's friend.'

'I am sorry, I am. Oh, girls, I'm so very, very sorry.'

'Jesus, Daddy! Grow up!' Tam yelled.

We all looked down at the floor again. We stayed that way for a long time and it felt like we were praying in church. Eventually, Mr Fakenham sniffed and blew his nose, and when I looked up, in a sudden breeze Sadie and Tam's hair lifted and tangled, and for a moment made one strand of hair. They both smiled at me.

'Sorry, girls,' Mr Fakenham sniffed. 'And I should say I've just been speaking to your mother. I hope, God willing, that she'll be home with us tomorrow.'

'Daddy,' said Sadie, 'shut up.'

'Sorry,' said Tamsin, smiling a cute and guilty smile. 'About Father.'

'And?' said Sadie, prodding Tam hard on the arm.

'And for lying to you about Sadie.'

'I should think so,' said Mr Fakenham, still dabbing at his snout with the handkerchief, but now cheery catalogue dad once more. 'What a cruel trick to play on Mona. After everything she has done for you. And Willow. I don't know.'

'I'm the one who deserves an apology, don't you think, Mona? I mean, I'm the one whose young life has been so cruelly snatched away. What do you think, Mona?'

The Fakenham family laughed.

I laughed too.

Later I wondered if Tam would've warped without Sadie, but I knew that without Sadie there would've been no Tam, not as I knew her anyway.

To be free for an entire summer was indeed a blissful thought.

'Tammy can certainly be a bit unfathomable. You will have to excuse her,' said Mr Fakenham, smiling at his daughter. 'I really don't know.'

'Don't start, Daddy,' Tam muttered.

It was exactly a month since the wedding, since Mr Fakenham had trotted up to me and asked me to be a friend to the girl-person.

Mr Fakenham ruffled Tam's hair and smiled the guilty dad smile. Of course he thought that whatever had gone wrong with Tamsin was his own fault.

'Yes, it's a shame,' Sadie continued, looking down at her neat feet. 'I'd've been pretty worried if you hadn't been with her. Looking after Willow *and* Tammy! Gosh.'

'So you girls will have one last chat then we'll dash off to the station, yes?' Mr Fakenham said, backing away into the sitting room. His tears were coming again.

'I think it's very good of the school to have Tammy back to sit her exams, don't you, Daddy?' Sadie sighed. 'I mean, after everything that happened.'

'Sadie, stop it now,' Mr Fakenham said, trying to be stern. 'Paul and Ivy should have the place shipshape by the time we get back. Tamsin, leave that suitcase there and I'll put it in the car, darling. You only have five minutes.'

'Good to meet you, Mona,' said Sadie, as she moved back up the stairs.

'Let's go,' whispered Tam, pushing her damp fingers through mine.

'Let's get some wicked liqueur first, honey,' I said, and lifted a bottle from the new drinks tray which rested on the sideboard in the hall.

Swallows darted through the air sharp as harpoons. We were up to our thighs in green barley which pricked and cut our calves. I was wetly breathless. The suitcases made yelping bruises on our ankles and our elbows were flamed with aching. We stumbled on, taking it in turns of a few yards to carry the bottle of booze. We were a good six feet apart. I could not look at her, so fuelled was I by rage.

'So he's back,' she shouted to me. 'But in body only. I keep thinking that he might shoot himself or something dramatic.'

'Just so he feels something,' I said quietly.

'What?' she shouted, quickening to try and catch me. 'I can't hear you.'

'He might want to shoot himself so that at least he feels pain. It's better than numbness.'

We carried on for a long way without speaking. Behind us barley had been trodden into a wavy path. The floury dust of pollen our hurrying kicked up made our faces itchy and sore. Then: 'I got a thousand pounds off Phil. I tried for two thousand but he didn't have it,' I shouted back to her. 'Turns out he lives in a pretty little Barbie house in a sunny cul-de-sac and has no money.'

'Yuck.'

'I know. But a thousand pounds is better than nowt.' I found I could now lie as expertly as Tamsin. This summer had been useful after all.

'Hell, Mona, is that all? Porn's big business. That can't be all he's worth.'

'That's all he could get out at one go. When we see him we can ask for more. Today's another day. I'm meeting him in half an hour outside the pub. We'll get more. He'll give it. He's mad with love. He don't know what he's doing.'

'You vixen! Yes, let's ask for lots, lots more,' she said like we were talking about sweeties and lemonade.

'He wants to meet me, but the police might have him now. Arrested. They'd already had him in for questioning.'

'Well, Mona, jolly well done. Now it's only a matter of time. I imagine when everything's proven we'll get quite a bit of praise. I imagine we will be in the paper.'

'Yes, then everyone will know about us.'

'My father keeps saying that he can't tell which of his feelings are true and which are just pain. Sadie thinks he's about to have some sort of breakdown.'

'Hmm. It's such a sham that love brings honesty and truth, isn't it? I mean, you hope that it's true but usually it just brings hurt and lies.'

'Don't be awful to me, Mona.'

'What I mean, Tam dear, is that I think really we're all just alone and have to fight for ourselves, don't you think?'

We struggled on. We were going over the fields so Mr Fakenham would not see us when he came looking. We were now into a pretty meadow splattered with buttercups, daisies and furry balls of dandelions. Crusty brown pools of cowpats dotted the tough grass. Thistles scratched our legs.

'She's a bitch. Could you see? I mean, I know what I did was wrong. But, you know, well, I was sure you'd not be interested in me ordinarily. I'm so sorry I did that lie on you, really I am. I really am so, so, so, so sorry.'

I stopped. I was looking at the sky, the stream, the soil. I drank the gin and gasped like a fire-eater. I looked closely at leaves and flowers. I was taking in all the details of planet earth that I could manage.

She caught up with me and dropped the case at my side. She was crying in a whining, annoyed way.

'The thing was, I think I was jealous. I remember the first time I saw you, last year when you came to look after Willow. You looked so sad and special, to me it was very attractive. I wanted to be friends with you even then. You see, you had a dead mother, I knew that before you told me and, well, I thought you'd think my life very middle class and ordinary. There's nothing more boring than coming from a rich middle-class family, is there? I mean, it's the worst. The most embarrassing anyway. I mean, going off to boarding school and stuff. No real people ever want to be friends with you. I wanted to empathise with you but I couldn't because everything in my life was OK. I had ponies and music lessons and holidays. I'll probably go to some God-awful honey-coloured university, then marry some tall strong-jawed man in a stiff suit and tie, and you, well . . . Do you understand?'

I would not let her see my rage. I would remember every detail of what life on earth had been like.

'Mona, talk to me. Do you? Do you understand? I wanted you to *like* me. That's why I made up the story about Sadie being, well, er . . .'

'Dead.'

'As a dodo.'

I wanted to run from her but I wanted also to be close to her so I could hurt her harder than she'd hurt me. Revenge.

'It's OK,' I smiled. 'My sister's a bitch too. What a cow. I know what you mean.'

'It is sort of funny, isn't it?'

'It's evil and wicked and cruel, but yes, it is *funny*.'

'Of course, I told her zilch about our baby. Though she'd love to have known. Can you imagine what Father will say when he hears?'

I walked on. My chest was aching with breathlessness.

'I'll ask Lindy about some baby clothes. If she can lend us some,' I called out.

It was all back on again. There was no way out.

Ahead of us, patched over a hill, was a square of yellow rapeseed. A church steeple. A farm. We passed a stream, glinting between an arch of gnarled bushes. When we saw a tractor we put our heads down. We checked regularly on our watches.

'Though of course he deserves to feel upset, and hurt, and worried, and have to think about me for a change rather than himself. I mean, at the moment he doesn't even seem to notice that Sadie and I are there at all.'

'You have to make people feel your presence. Don't you remember telling me that?'

'Yes, that's right.'

The heat made a gully of sweat over my breastbone. I swigged on the bottle. I decided I had to take me T-shirt off. My tits had not changed since the beginning of the summer, though everything else had; they were still just two big buttons sewn on to my chest, and if anyone had seen me with Tam they'd have thought me her little brother.

I was bare-chested and I carried a stick.

I had booze dribbling down over me chin, like spit or tears.

'You can't be angry with me, Mona, because it will be bad for our baby. Please forgive me.'

'I do, Tam,' I shouted back to her. 'I do.'

'The baby is a blessing, isn't it?'

We were going to the car park of the Adam and Eve. It was like a magnet pulling me. I wanted to see Phil. I wanted to see he was all right, and I wanted more money, then I wanted to go home to my pub and father, where the lies were confused and unintentional.

As we neared the pub there was the familiar rumble of English dinnertime voices, loud and jumbled and so warped by the sun that you could believe these English mothers were speaking Brazilian. I was in front, her a few paces behind. The bottle was finished and my breathing was dry and jagged because of the asthma. We carried on through the streets, me topless, her panting, the sweat swimming over her meaty flesh.

'I lub you,' she sobbed.

'I lub you too, dear,' I said coldly.

Children chalking on the pavement lifted their heads to watch us. A small boy twisting dizzily on a rope steadied himself against a tree to stare.

When we got outside the pub I noticed how the water in Black Beck was so low that a rusty pram chassis was exposed. The rust was giving off a reddish bleed. The smell from the rawhide factory was twisting through the whole of the town, like we all had our noses pressed up against one enormous animal skin. And it seemed to be getting stronger. Everything in the Black Beck reminded me of death: the bloated crisp packets, the plastic tubing, the frayed pony nut sacks.

Now I did not want to see any police.

Far down the towpath three men were straining back diagonally pulling on a rope from a barge. Overhead a couple of seagulls were yip yip yipping.

It was then I thought I saw the front edge of Phil's car peeping out of the gap between the animal feed factory and the tyre warehouse. This was to one side of the pub car park.

'Look, it's Phil's car,' I said quietly. I had stopped walking.

'Oh. Will he give us some money?'

'Perhaps,' I said. 'At least he'll buy us a drink.'

'You do forgive me, don't you, darling? You do love me, don't you?'

Calmly, I looked away, focused on the dip of a gull. Tam had put the suitcase down on the hot tarmac and was staring at the car. Bright pink spots of heat rash were appearing on me pale forearms and I itched at them making dotted red lines like bloody stitching in me skin.

I put me suitcase down next to hers.

Across the road a cyclist gripped his brakes and gaped at my half-nakedness.

It is said Phil the Flash was first seen by a woman pushing a pram, his face bubbled against the side door. She thought he was sleeping. She assumed he had had too much to drink so he had decided to sleep in his car. This had happened many times before to drunk and desperate men so it was a reasonable assumption. We all knew what men did. How removed from the everyday world they were. How they did exactly as they liked regardless of what was expected of them.

I did not see his face bubbling the first time because I only got as far as the steamed-up glass and the solid outline against the window before I walked away again. I looked at Tam, stared at her. I thought of Lindy and how I would kiss her lightly on the cheek, when everything was over. I remembered the time I was sure she'd died and how I managed to conceal my distress.

'Oh dear,' Tam said when she saw what I saw.

Some time later, when it had been revealed to us that he had gassed himself in the car, I imagined his baldish head pressed against the glass, pink and mottled, like the rounded corner on a block of corned beef. At other times I imagined the dead head wide and fleshy and bluey-grey, as hard-boiled as a bad egg. And if you'd sunk a knife and fork through they'd have kept pressing until the blade and prongs came out the other side. This is what I thought every night for a long time after anyway. I could smell deadly fumes every time I lit a fag or turned on the gas. I could not go easily to petrol stations. I wondered if the warmth of his head had seeped out on to the windscreen, like food heating up a plate. I imagined his fingers snowy as candle wax, crossed in the lap of his brown anorak.

'We must go. Go. Let's go down there. There is a place. Bulrushes. Reeds. There is a cottage. Unused. I don't think anyone lives there.'

'Yes,' Tam said.

There was no irony. She was hurrying to keep up with me. We had left the suitcases on the tarmac near Phil's car. She pressed her hand against her belly as she trotted along beside me.

'Boats,' she said.

'Let's run,' I said.

It was nothing to do with Tam. She had never met him. She did not even know him. She did not even know I'd ever been to model for him, or driven with him in the car. It was me. Everything was just me.

We galloped. Then stopped. I was sick. It was so fierce I got an explosion of headache. She watched me and whimpered. We ran. We had nowhere to go so we ran. Tam held on to her belly, like it was a pocket full of money. We stopped. I sat down on the wall that bordered the water. We had nothing with us but our terrible bodies. I could not breathe. Tam was behind me turning. I could hear voices in the car park shouting.

'Come on, darling. Let me help you,' Tam said, like a kind mother. She hesitated to touch me, then forced herself and pulled at my arm and I stood up. 'There's nothing to worry about. Let's go to the end for a walk. And then we'll go into the pub. Then we'll go away, darling. It's not your fault.'

'The flyover, let's sit under there in the shade,' I said. 'Let's sit under there and think what to do.'

I thought for a moment that maybe the world was tilting, spinning and we were still. After a while she said: 'Do you think my father will be all right? I mean, in a way I hope that he doesn't . . .'

'Who cares?' I said.

I could see it in the distance. The flyover. As a child I would sit under there after family rows, or maybe just go there and search for condoms. I liked the word: flyover. It was hopeful. It seemed a long time since Lindy and I had left in the horse and carriage, and Cleo had hooked up the basque from the back and Phil had taken the photos, though it was exactly a month ago today.

Tonight Lindy was having the celebration takeaway.

We sat on a concrete ridge and looked at the cubic graffiti, the carefully sprayed names of motorbikes and heavy metal bands. It was shadowy, cool and reeking. Pissy and stale like a slice of city. Tam was opposite me, beneath a sprayed word which said 'Kawasaki'. In other circumstances she would have looked cool and stylish. 'Suzuki' to her left – like the boy who'd sprayed them had a string of Japanese girlfriends. I thought of the fleshy fat pads beneath his armpits, and the cushion around his waist. This man was thirty-four. He was going to be a poet. His body now cold and slightly sticky to touch. I had touched dead people before, there was no *pooetry* in it. Most of the graffiti was about love. Who loves who and how much and for how long: *4 eva, loads, hiya sexy, heaps and heaps, never dyingly*.

I held Tam's hand. We were both crying. Our joined fist was slimy with snot, spit and tears.

Then she let go of my hand and edged along the ledge away from me.

Her head was down but her eyes flicked me a narrow sideways look.

'Mona?' she said politely. 'I mean, seeing as I never really knew him, or met him, well, it's not really anything to do with me, is it? It's not my fault at all, is it?'

fish

'You came to the police,' I snivelled, reaching out my hand and trying to grasp her.

'Well, not really. Only because you told me about him and Julie.'

'Yes, but you said about us finding the T-shirt.'

'You suggested it.'

'No, you suggested it.'

'You said those lies to the police about all that modelling.'

'You told me to go and get money from him.'

'No I didn't, Mona.'

'Well, you did the worst thing. You had me believe your sister was dead. That was all to do with you. It was nothing to do with me!'

'Oh yes it was! In fact, it was entirely your bloody fault.'

'My fault!'

'Totally. You believed. You were stupid enough to go along with it. Anyone else would've known I was just joking. But you actually *liked* the idea of my family as eccentric, rich and doomed.'

'But . . .'

'When really,' she continued, pointing at me and sneering wickedly, 'really, I see now that I am just as ordinary as you.'

'No, Tam, you and me are not ordinary.'

'Yes, yes we are,' she cried. 'We are, we are, we are.'

The sun was blazing. It was steaming away our tears and drying the snot slime into a pale crust. Tam walked. She was angry, holding her fag close to her knuckles and smoking in great bites. I sat sunk in the concrete. I didn't know my town any more. I felt that lost weariness like when you arrive jet-lagged at your holiday resort.

'I thought you'd have guessed earlier that I was making it up,' she said furiously, then putting her lower lip over her upper and pouting in an imitation of regret.

'I mean, it hardly needs a detective genius to know it was not plausible, Mona.'

I looked up at her and because of the strong sun, I had to shield my eyes with my hand. 'It was a very clever trick. Perfectly executed. You're bright, Tam. In fact, you are so bright you are like a great sun,' I said, and she giggled nervously. 'And I'm just a pale, weak moon. I just reflect the light you give.' She didn't say anything. I stood up and both of us paced around for a few moments. I was not frightened of her. 'Maybe I can only be noticed when you're not around. Like the moon.' She tried to touch me and I jerked away. I wanted to be near the walls where it smelt most foul.

'I notice you,' she said. 'Don't shout at me.'

'In all relationships perhaps there's a shiner and a reflector, eh? A sun and a moon. Two suns and it just won't work, will it, eh?'

Shadows fell in angular slabs and I lurked between them.

'He's dead,' I said, not turning to look at her. I was about to be sick again.

'How dare he! The bastard. And now he'll never be caught. And poor little Julie will never have her revenge. The cruel spineless nasty little bald man.' She was a few feet away from me and shouting.

'Look,' I said. 'It's PorkChop. My stepbrother.'

'Oh my God! No! He's so disgusting.'

I was glad to see him. He was out in the sunlight running

towards us. He'd been watching as people spilled out of the pub to look at Phil's car. A police car had just arrived. PorkChop's running was like another person's falling. With each footstep it looked like he was about to collapse on to the pavement. But it was a great relief to have another person arrive to divert us from our inaction.

Both of us bristled with anticipation.

'Mona, Phil's dead, maybe,' he yelled from a distance. He looked pleased to see me. 'I 'ave to go tell 'is wife.'

Then, as he got closer, he saw Tamsin and noticed I was topless and he looked confused. He looked away then stared intently at my chest.

'Eff off,' I said, folding me arms over me titless chest and snapping me head to the side like I had been very seriously insulted. I could feel me ribs, the knots of me elbows, the bony knobbles of wrists. Me movements were fast and jerky. Tam was bobbing like she had music in her head. Then Tamsin stepped towards him and said: 'Have you any idea what that man did to a girl?'

A car rattled above us a great speed and fumes spilled down to us.

'I 'ave to go tell 'is wife. Fetch 'er.'

'Well, tell her that her husband is a murderer while you're at it.'

'PorkChop, he took Julie. He killed her. That's why the police have been after him,' I said quietly, but moving me feet in fast little steps. I did not look up. Now I had me head in me hands, then I was slapping at me cheek to calm mesen.

'What? Never. He's OK. He didn't.'

Tamsin stepped forward and pushed him. 'Don't disagree with Mona, she knows more about it than you, don't you think?'

'Put some clothes on, Mona,' PorkChop said quietly.

'Don't you tell Mona what to do, you fat . . . fat BAS-TARD.'

'Stop screaming.'

'Don't leave me, Mona. Oh, darling, I lub you.'

'I lub you too.'

'Fuck me!' Porkchop muttered.

'Wash your foul mouth out, fat arse. Mona, I do feel so sorry for you having this elephant for a brother.'

'He's not my brother.'

'Yes he is.'

'No he's not.'

'He is. Though he's at least five times as big as you. Just look at the great mass of him.'

'Leave him! Don't push 'im. Leave him.'

'Fuck off, lessy. Lesbian. Get your 'ands off.'

'PorkChop, don't touch 'er! Don't.'

'Stop fucking screaming.'

'Leave her! She's having a baby. Don't touch 'er. Don't touch our baby.'

'Yer mucky . . . Fuck.'

'Don't. Don't. Don't.'

'No.'

'Stop. Don't. Stop.'

And yet by doing something together our love was complete again.

'He's so disgusting. All this flab is an insult to the human race, isn't it, Mona?'

'Yes,' I muttered.

'And you hurt me, you revolting man. You threw me down. If my father hears about that!'

And they began to fight, gently at first. I was sitting down but now I stood up and pushed at him with Tamsin. I had a very bad headache. It was hard to push a fat man, he kept springing back at you like a meat yo-yo. His arms were windmilling. His eyes were narrowed and his fat fingers before him scrabbling, like he was fighting his way through a swarm of bees.

Tam was tugging at him hard and sinking her nails into his

wrists. He deliberately tried not to hurt us. He fought us in a girly way. She was better with her nails than he was. I grabbed at his flesh too and could get a disgusting fist full without touching any bone. I scratched him, and watched as a furrow of skin ruched up, then, almost beautifully, blood blossomed.

He lost his footing and fell off the edge of the concrete and was on his side in the water. It happened quick, it was my fault. Tam followed him in and at first I was sure we were going to help him. He thought so too because when my hand dipped under the water he clutched for it, like I was saving him. I was aware of a bird, a thrush I think, that had landed on a lamppost on the opposite side of Black Beck, and that it was watching us, its tail flickering.

Quickly, Tam's short skirt was sodden and clinging tight round her thighs. She lifted it up, like a little girl, and tucked it in the legs of her knickers. She was pushing both of her hands in his pink face, like she was throwing a football. The way she'd held Nina Fisher's face in her hands. She was muttering about how awful it was for me to have a fat brother. She turned to me, panting, and smiled, then raised her fist in victory like she'd just won a race.

I followed her deeper into the coolish water which was a relief. I let my hot itchy arms sink under. I wanted to wash the wax of death off me in the cool summer water. Feet in mud soft as cold floury pillows; tiny wiggly creatures flipping between me toes. I felt sure that an eel, or a rat's tail or a water snake was trapped beneath me feet and I hopped to try and free it. I bobbed down so me bare chest thrilled against the water. I thought of Phil, and Tamsin's baby, and then we were unbirthing PorkChop, pushing him down into the black water. He would stand and yell and we would pull him under again. My skirt was all twisted so I could not move freely.

Cars, lorries, motorbikes thundered over above us. It seemed a busy day.

Our fingers brushed together under the water. All of our

243

fingers, PorkChop's, Tam's and my own, like we were twirling, underwater country dancing. Or sealing a secret pact. Then Tam was whooping over and over like the Americans you see on TV. I was so glad the rage between Tam and me was over. Anger between women was too hot and frightening, too terrible to be believed. I hung on to her arm to steady mesen as I pushed and pushed him under with the flat palm of me thin little hand.

Cleo had given birth to this massive man, *give, give, give*, how she had pushed life into him, and now we were pushing it out.

It was fun.

'I've got him, darling.'

'Well done, darling.'

'I'm holding him.'

'He's really struggling,' she panted.

We were two little girls taming a wild pony.

We were up to our waists now. My hair was rat-tailed with mucky water, with sand and soil, and the splashing was so great my eyes could not see. My eyeballs rolled upwards in their sockets and I looked up at the grey roof at the fungused cracks where slab joined slab, at the wide frills of damp, the bloomed stains of oil and petrol. We were still in the shade of a wide shadow that extended over the water.

Beyond the shade the Saturday sunlight screeched down at us.

Tam yelped and picked up from under the water a brick she'd hurt her foot on.

Tam was pushing his head under when she hit him in the face with the brick. It was surprisingly hard, almost impossible, to knock the life from a fat, young man, but gradually he began to resist less. I picked up a stone too, a heavy glistening grey lump like a solid piece of ancient muscle. I thought of Cleo coming home to nurse him back to a dry health. I thought of her sitting on his bed with a towel, patting his back and letting him spew all the green river water out into a blue bucket. There was blood. But he was not dying and for a long time his face kept coming up out of the water, spluttering and white, then whiter and less spluttering, then quiet and grey. And each time he rose he clutched for me.

'Go on Mona.'

'It's OK.'

'Go on, go on.'

'Oh.'

'Yes, that's it.'

When killing you have to pant and gasp and moan and urge, urge, urge it on to the end. It's like manly sex.

His tired hands went round my arms softly, again and again, gradually weaker and more slipping, but still each time like he was expecting help. Still, after everything, right to the very end he was expecting me, his weird, starving stepsister, to save him.

And as I pushed him down memories rose in me. It was like falling to sleep. Sunlight on a pavement puddle, a soft ballet ribbon curled, a spider plant on a window ledge.

And then, there, there in the water, in the moments of silence when he was under the water and didn't come up, I saw my mother.

She lifts me out of the water. She is tall and strong and can easily carry a wet child. She carries me out from under the dark of the flyover, beyond the shadows and lays me on a slab of hot sun. I open my eyes and sizzle. She looks into my face and smiles, smiles then begins to make curling little touches with her fingertips over my stony brow. She smoothes my bones over, like softening cold butter. She has long pale hair which hangs down her back and falls over her shoulders so it silks against my thin skin. She rarely wears make-up, she does not need to. When she gets to my ribs she strums them over with her index finger, and begins to sing a song, without even opening her mouth. She leans over me as she sings so I can feel her rounded belly against my dead hand. Then when the song ends and I am dry she leans against me so I can feel all the soft plumpness of her.

*   *   *

Later, how much later I do not know, we went to fetch the suitcases and watched as the police wound a ribbon of red tape around the car park. The blood gut whiff was so strong it felt as if we were bathing in it.

We were not covered in blood. We must have washed the blood off our bodies in the water, and for this reason I dared not turn round for I feared the Black Beck red. All the rivers in my town running ruby. Taps gushing scarlet.

A Saturday afternoon crowd had gathered. Mainly women and children, some workmen, drunkish blokes from our bar. An ambulance had arrived but Phil had not been removed from the car. Some of the women were crying, others were thrilling with a babble of whispers. Children were jostling to get a better look. No one seemed concerned by our wet and battered bodies. We collected the cases and walked away down an alley where we stripped.

'Are you OK now? You fainted. I saved you,' Tam said, but I didn't reply. I remember looking at her naked body in the bleak alley of thistles and tall hollyhocks, as though for the first time. In air, under sky, her bubblegum burst had popped and her nakedness seemed grey and chewed.

We put on fresh clothes from the suitcases. I wished it was night. Though I did not know the hour I was very aware of the rhythm of ticking, like a great clock was pulsing around us. At the end of the alley a dense briared bank stretched up. We towelled our hair. We were not talking, but taking more care with our appearance than we had in some time.

After the war I knew it would have to be this way too: unsentimental. You had to take any dead bodies out of the bunkers and pile them up in a communal place. You had to be cool and practical, perhaps sacrificing contagious members of your family for the good of your group. You had to deal calmly and efficiently with blisters, sores, diarrhoea, vomiting, ulcers, hair loss and cancers.

Tam crouched in the alley and applied her lipstick, making extravagant mouth gestures. I watched a bruise blackening on my arm. We applied the make-up like a balaclava. Tam dug the black pencil into her brow like she was scrubbing an error out. We made thick arcs of green eyeshadow above each eye. She squeezed carefully at a tube of antiseptic and wiped the white cream over the cuts and scratches on her arms and legs. I took great care with the mascara, combing each lash into a separate strand.

Tam spat on the ground urgently, gob after gob, like she'd swallowed some poison. I ignored her and just made sure my foundation was perfectly blended and lined my lips with a darker red. We creamed in purpley blusher in wide stripes down our cheeks. Tam began to wipe the inside of her mouth with a wad of cotton wool. She did this for a long time, like she was dabbing at some stubborn foulness.

'Do I look nice?' she asked. I said nothing and she asked me again. 'Oh yes, they'll all want to rape you,' I said, not looking at her.

We stepped out of the alley looking gaudy and mean. Her make-up was a mirror of my make-up. My mouth felt very dry, like I too had eaten a gobful of cotton wool. We wobbled slightly on our high shoes. Our reflection in the black window of a factory looked like dogs walking on their hind legs for the first time.

We saw the ambulance take Phil's body away.

'Let's go in and win some money,' is the only thing I remember saying after.

'Here comes trouble!' Ken said when we walked into the bar and they all nodded at me and smiled. The room was hot and quiet, though somewhere I heard a low hissing, like we'd stepped into the gas oven. Tam stood behind me quietly. She had a fresh scratch behind her ear, and it was dribbling a pearl of blood.

'It's the beautiful bridesmaid,' said Bob, smiling and winking. 'You look superb. Wow!'

That is when I saw the digital display temperature, a witchingly hot 87 degrees. Later, it would storm.

I turned on my fruity and played. But she just kept looking at the lights and the flashing and the noise and after a time the pub was gradually covered with diamonds of orange evening light and at last, when the pretty young blond policemen came in, everyone looked at us, in horror, and we seemed to sparkle in the dark.

ACKNOWLEDGEMENTS

I would like to thank the following people: Eric Dupin, Anna Garry, Clay Lister, Verity Watts and Miranda Yates; my teachers Marge Clouts and Andrew Motion; my editors Alexandra Pringle and Marian McCarthy; my agent Deborah Rogers, and, of course, Andy Williams, who helped every step of the way.

A NOTE ON THE AUTHOR

Helen Cross was born in 1967 and brought up in East Yorkshire. She was educated at Goldsmiths College, University of London, and the University of East Anglia. She currently lives in Birmingham.